# Fiend's Gold

## A Bill Reyner Mystery Adventure

Wentworth M. Johnson

A Record of this Publication is available
from the British Library

ISBN 978-0-9561032-9-1

First Published in 2001 by
E-booksonline (UK) Ltd

Second Edition - 2009
Local Legend Publishing
Park Issa
St Martin's Road
Gobowen, Shropshire
SY11 3NP, UK
www.local-legend.co.uk

Cover Design by Titanium Design
www.titaniumdesign.co.uk

Cover illustration courtesy of
HAAP Media LLC – All rights reserved

This book is dedicated to
Christine Ann Johnson

# *Table of Contents*

# About the Author

## Wentworth M. Johnson

Born in the town of March, Cambridgeshire, England, in 1939, Wentworth M. Johnson is now a naturalized Canadian. He served for twelve years with the Royal Air Force and saw action fighting pirates in the South China Sea. He was also the very last RAF man in RAF Kahawa, Kenya, when he handed the station over to the Kenyan Air Force. Subsequently, he worked as a studio technician at a local TV station in Hamilton and then worked as a broadcast technology buyer before retiring in 2000. English history, from Julius Caesar to modern times has long been a passion, and writing has been a hobby since school days.

# *Chapter 1*

## *June*

The great lakes are like inland seas of fresh water. Lake Huron rests 100 kilometres north-north-west of Toronto and 200 kilometres west of Canada's capital city of Ottawa. Georgian Bay, an easterly extension of Huron, is almost a lake in its own right, bordered on one side by the Bruce Peninsula and the Manitoulin Islands and wild land, giant parks, forests and smaller lakes on the eastern shore.

Making its last run of the day from South Baymouth on the Manitoulin Islands to Tobermory at the head of the Bruce Peninsula, the ferry sliced almost silently through the shimmering water. Bathed in silvery moonlight, Lake Huron sparkled like a billion jewels. Waves rippling off of the bow and the rumble of the ship's powerful engines gently broke the silence in an otherwise quiet night.

'Radar shows a small craft approaching off the port bow, sir,' the watchman reported.

The skipper peered out through the window, shading the green radar reflection from the glass with his right hand. 'Don't see any running lights. How far?'

'About three clicks, sir.'

'It poses no problem, but keep an eye on her.'

'Aye-aye, sir.'

The sky lit up as a fireball rose lazily into the hot night air. Resembling a clap of thunder, the boom from the explosion followed only moments later. Captain Davis peered out of the window at a burning cloud enfolding itself with blackness and smoke.

'What d'you make of that, number one?'

'Another careless tourist, I shouldn't wonder, sir. Should we heave-to for survivors?'

'See what other vessels are around first.'

'Aye-aye, sir.'

The first officer gave the order and the radio operator made a call. He found that a coastguard vessel was nearby. Without any delay, the ferry continued on its journey to Tobermory, with most passengers knowing nothing of the unusual event. Whatever the incident may have been, it was all over.

Now, you might wonder what fireballs and ferry ships have to do with anything. Well, allow me to elucidate. You see, 1997 had been a bad year for me and 1999 seemed to be following the same downhill slope. It had been a particularly difficult time, partly as a result of me failing every course. Nobody has ever done as badly as yours truly, at least not at McMaster University in Hamilton. Well, there were good reasons, you could say. So there I was, "sent down" after two years' hard work. For the unenlightened, sent down means fired, got the boot, sacked or otherwise no longer required. There was obviously no future for such a lowly being as myself. God, the world looked black, really black.

The gang threw a sort of party for me. First, we had a meal at the refectory. Yuck, no big success there. Then we all went over to John's Tavern. There was me, a handsome, debonair 20-year-old failure, Dee, Pete, Henny and Alic. We called her Alic, as in a man's name, but she's no guy. Her real name was Alicia. We were known as the five musketeers until my brain crashed.

Food didn't interest me, but drowning my sorrows in booze sounded good. You have to realize it was a very sad occasion, being my last day at McMaster University. For them it meant school's out, but for me it's the end. Well, I still had my job at the doughnut store, but that's not a wage a man can live on.

Dee pushed another pint of cheep beer in front of me. 'Come, me ol' mate, drink up, eh! What yah say?' He had that typical all Canadian way of speech.

I smiled and said, 'Sure, why the hell not?'

Dee was a neat kinda guy, even if he did look a bit like an undertaker. His real name's Dizzy. Would you believe, Dizzy Spells? I guess his mom had a thing about movie stars, naming him after Dizzy Gillespie, or maybe she just had a keen sense of humour. No one could be more kind-hearted or generous than Dizzy and if you had a motor that wouldn't go, well ... man, he could work magic. I swear he could get a car to go even if it was out of fuel.

'I've got a great idea,' Pete announced, standing up and using his beer bottle more like a baton.

I sucked at the ale and then wiped the froth moustache off my face with the back of my hand. 'Yeah, go on, tell us, Pete. What's this great brainwave?'

He smiled a sort of sly grin. 'Let's get school done with and have a frat meeting. We'll all get together, say, er ... how about the first Saturday after term end?'

'Sure,' we all agreed.

It was a real drag going back to my apartment in Westdale, a sort of village in the west end of Hamilton. It wouldn't take a genius to guess that the old landlady would kick me out once she knew I was no longer a student. Sure thing; because school was out, she said my stay would be limited to a month and then I would have to go. You know, being poor is the shits, as in no car, no money and no one who cares.

At least the doughnut job was only evenings, so that gave me time during daylight hours to find a position more reasonable and suited to my talents. Did you know that there are no jobs for duffers and dropouts? Hamilton is one of the biggest cities in Canada. I mean, it has got industry up to your eyeballs, but no jobs. They even call it Steeltown.

It's amazing how time passes. Before you can wink, it's the first Saturday after term end and time for the frat meeting. I didn't want to go. I knew they would all have jobs, cars and money, while dickhead here had none of the above. My money supply was getting short and feeding oneself in non-subsidized nosheries costs the earth, leaving absolutely no spare change for frivolities.

I tried to put on a good show. You know, a big smile, a swagger and back slapping, 'how are yous?' sort of thing. Don't think I fooled anybody, though. I mean, a round of drinks just for the four of us at John's Tavern costs twenty bucks; Dee paid for the first round. Everybody turned up except Alic. I figured she'd be out with her boyfriend or a facsimile thereof.

'So, where yah working?' Pete asked.

He looked quite dapper, even in this heat he wore a tie and looked like some kind of yuppie. Bolt upright and clean-shaven, he would pass for a councillor or a junior executive.

'I'm, er ... well.'

'Still pushing dog-nuts, eh?'

'Yeah. I guess I'm sort of between jobs. What about you?'

'There ain't much in the arts. However, I got a neat position at the Hamilton Art Gallery: usher. You wanna job?'

I looked at him and tried hard not to show any enthusiasm. 'Yeah, I guess so. You know of one?'

11

Pete smiled and thumped me painfully on the biceps. 'Not at the gallery, dickhead.'

'Stop being a pea-brain,' Dee snapped. 'Give the poor bastard a break.'

Pete punched me playfully again. 'Alright, sucker. My uncle's got a gas station in Stoney Creek. Pays $8.50 an hour; fifty hours a week. Interested?'

'Doing what?'

'Pumping gas, dummy.' He put on a hoity-toity voice, pretending to be English. 'You know, old boy, filling people's petrol tanks.'

I had to think about it. Stoney Creek is 10 kilometres across town. I tried to look non-committal and said, 'I don't have a car, how'll I get there?'

'Walk,' Pete said with a big grin. Then, with a serious expression, he said, 'Well, do you want the bloody job or not, my hesitant friend?'

I nodded in agreement. 'I don't have a choice.' I figured I'd ride the buses until I moved and the smart thing would be to move to Stoney Creek.

'Having got that shit out the way,' Dee said, 'who's buying the next round?'

'I will,' Henny volunteered.

Henny was always a quiet sort of follower, never the leader. He came from rich parents, so it didn't matter how many times he failed at the big "U", they'd pay to keep him in school till he either passed or passed away. His real name was Gavin Henderson, but he hated being called Gavin. He was a lanky dork and usually the type to be teacher's pet. You could say he was a do-gooder or just a creep.

Pete's eyes sparkled and smiled when he said, 'I always thought you'd make a good grease monkey. So, are you taking the job or not?'

'Sure. When do I start?' I managed to say with obvious reluctance.

He wrote the address and phone number on one of his business cards and handed it over to me. 'Be there at nine, Monday morning, and the job's yours.'

Though grateful to him, it felt important not to show it, so I put on an air of non-committal. It doesn't pay to be too eager or people'll think you're soft.

'Don't worry,' Dee said. 'We'll all stick together. One for all and all for one, eh?'

'I've got a real brill scheme,' Pete said with a wide grin. 'How about one last meeting? Say, er ... how about the first Monday in August?'

Shaking my head sadly, I replied, 'I'll be working by then, I hope.'

'No, you twit. The first Monday in August is a holiday Monday. A national day off work. We'll meet here and drink our last farewells before we all enter the big, angry world.'

'What the hell's the point?' Henny said softly. 'We're grown men, not kids. Life's pulling us apart. School's the only thing we have in common. When we leave, we're different people in different worlds.'

'That's exactly it,' Pete snapped. 'We'll defy the system, a fraternity for life. Can't you see the irony in it? The five musketeers, the five banditos.'

There was a resounding, 'No.' It didn't matter, friends are friends. When Mom and Dad died, they left me all the debts, bills and people with their hands out. After the funeral, selling the house and settling the debts, I had just enough to get through school. That's before they put the tuition fees up, before inflation and before I learned to control spending. In fact, before I grew up. There was always old Granny Hubert, but only as a last resort.

It's funny somehow. As I looked at the guys I had this feeling inside, well, you know… like after Mom's funeral. A sort of hollow yearning, a wanting for something that's just not there. Sometimes, when I look at the gang it makes me want to weep. I don't know why, but it just feels depressing, a sad occasion. You could say it's the loneliness, maybe. The gang are there in front of me, they are visible, but it's as if I can't touch them. They seemed to be a group of imaginary clowns in the circus of life, only there because of my imagination. That's enough of that melancholy crap. We were no longer kids and for me, school had finished forever.

Suddenly, I said aloud, 'I don't know what the shit I'm gonna do with the rest of my life.'

It must have been the drink that made me say it or maybe Tourette's syndrome. Either way, the voice came from me and I guess it's what I needed to say, though it didn't make me feel any better. It reached my ears as though coming from someone else.

'That's it,' Pete said with enthusiasm. 'Let's go into business together. There's something for all of us. What d'yah say?'

'What the hell would we do?' I asked in full seriousness.

Pete had obviously got the itch, something had struck him. With a big grin from ear to ear, he said, 'I'm not sure yet, but the idea's gelling. We've got to find something that has engines for Dee, some form of art for me. What's your thing, Henny?'

He shrugged his shoulders. 'I don't know. How about something with accounting? I enjoy counting money and stuff like that. What about Alic?'

13

'She likes men,' Pete said. 'So we'll have to add something where a lot of men are concerned.'

'I've got it,' Dee said jumping up. 'We'll run a tour bus. I'll fix the motor. Bill can pump the gasoline, Henny'll count the cash and Pete can artistically drive it. Oh yeah, and Alic can amuse the customers by doing a striptease or something. Now, how's that sound?'

'Alright,' I said, raising my voice. 'Tell yah what we'll do.' I looked at their grinning faces. They were like a bunch of expectant kids, each with a large glass of beer in their hands. 'Alright. We'll all do a lot of thinking and we'll meet here, let's say noon first Monday in August.'

'What'll we think about?' Dee asked with a puzzled expression on his simple face.

'We'll think about the business. We'll start a business. I'm out of school. I can put in full time. The rest of yah'll do whatever you can. How's that sound?'

'Never mind the business,' Dee joked. 'Let's get thoroughly pissed. It's a pity Alic couldn't make it. Man, I enjoy watching her wobble. She's got the most fascinating front end.'

I scowled at him. 'You nutcase. Are we agreed?'

'Sure.'

'Then let's do some serious drinking. Pissed city here we come.'

Chipper as a squirrel in a bag of peanuts, I was at Pete's uncle's place dead on the dot of nine. The sign read: Gordon's Gas Bar. It's a large establishment with a cafe, right on the 20 Highway. I walked into the office, where a big man with hair just like Pete's was giving some poor kid shit for just being a kid. He looked over in my direction, with no smile, no display of friendship and hardly any form of recognition at all.

'You the asshole Pete sent?' he growled through his teeth.

I nodded in the affirmative.

'Alright you got the job. You know how to pump gasoline?'

I nodded once more in the affirmative.

'Cat got your tongue, boy?'

'No, sir.'

'That's better. Around here we communicate verbally, no bloody signalling. You get that, boy?'

'Yes, sir.'

'Alright, ten hours a day, five days a week, $425 gross weekly. You got that, boy?'

'Yes, sir.'

14

'Good. Piss off a customer and you walk. You got me?'

'Yes, sir.'

'Start tomorrow and you'll work Saturday this week. Clock-on time eight sharp. That's a.m. You eat running; bring your own or buy from the cafe. Are we still in tune, boy?'

'Yes, sir.'

'Never have more than fifty bucks in cash. Bung it in the holder.'

I felt about 2 centimetres tall and I could feel my knees shaking. This guy could eat a fire-breathing dragon and use the tail to pick his teeth.

'What's a holder, sir?'

'The safe, you idiot. It's that concrete block in the corner over there. See, it's got a slot in the top. Bung everything over fifty bucks in there. I'm the only one with a key.'

I nodded in the affirmative.

'Well, do you understand, boy?' he said, raising his voice to a crackling growl.

'Yes, sir. Yes, I understand.'

'Fill this out.' He pulled some sort of employment agreement from the desk drawer and thrust it in front of me. I began to read it, not wanting to sign anything without understanding it.

'I gotta go pump,' he said and marched out of the office.

Man, I felt stupid. I thought slavery had been abolished, yet this guy thought he was God. I read the paper, filled out the details and signed it. Then I sat and awaited his return. I couldn't help but notice how self-reliant he was and how really sure of himself he was. I guess you'd call it intimidating. If only I could be like that.

He marched in and snatched up the paper. After humming and hawing a couple of times, he said, 'William Reyner, eh? What do they call you? Bill?'

'Yes, sir.'

For the first time, he smiled a friendly smile. 'Okay, Bill, see you tomorrow.'

'Yes, sir.' I lit out and felt like whooping, but managed to control myself in a dignified fashion.

Mrs Nethercot my landlady was in the hall waiting for me to return. You'd think she could find something better to do. 'I don't want you about the house all day now the university is out,' she said in her annoying tone of voice.

God, I wonder what happened to her husband. She probably had him stuffed and mounted. I'll bet he stands in that dark living room, with a shocked look permanently waxed on his face. She wasn't really a dragon; least ways, not the kind St George killed. She was built like a cylinder, black dress and hair in curlers. She had a face that would grace Frankenstein's monster.

'I'm working in Stoney Creek for the summer, Mrs Nethercot. I just got me a good job.'

'Good. Remember, no girls and keep away long enough for me to do the housework. I don't want you under my feet. In fact, I would like you out of here altogether.'

'Yes, Mrs Nethercot.'

What a life and it was going to get worse. Getting up at dawn was a new experience and taking the bus to Stoney Creek meant a transfer. I sure as hell didn't want to be late on my first day; $425 was infinitely more than I got flogging doughnuts. Of course, I quit that job. Couldn't sell coffee and treats by night and work all day.

A day pumping gas is not a pastime for wimps. Running up and down, sometimes three or even four pumps going at a time. God, some of those customers ... I'd like to stick that nozzle somewhere other than in their tank and watch their eyes flood. One guy took 68 litres and then he got all pissed off, cos there was a slight drip when I pulled the hose out. With him, that made two drips. I tell you, if I wasn't being paid I'd have given him a knuckle sandwich.

Mrs Nethercot jumped on my case as soon as I got back to the pad.

'You're filthy. I don't like filth like that in my clean house. See to it you don't brush against any of my walls. The last thing I need is garage grease all over my clean house. Is that clear?'

'Yes, Mrs Nethercot.'

'Why can't you wear overalls and take them off outside? Don't bring that filth anywhere near my carpets and curtains.'

'I will, when I get enough money to buy some. I'll be real careful, Mrs Nethercot.'

'I'll put your rent up if I see any trace of dirt or grease on any of my walls, floors or drapes.'

I walked into my room. Jesus! You know, after a hard day's graft you just don't need that kind of shit. I ripped off my sweat-soaked shirt and threw myself onto the bed for a welcome rest. Lying there staring at the ceiling I just wanted to weep. Life is the shits, sometimes. I wish I was still a kid or Mom and Dad were there to greet me home from work.

Mom was a lovely woman, kind, gentle and understanding. Dad was an okay guy, too. Sort of quiet, but still a hell of a nice guy. It was 1997,

16

just a couple of years ago, when they both died. The insurance and the sale of the house just about covered the debts and the funeral. If it hadn't been for Granny Hubert, I don't know what would have happened to me.

I sat up and tried to shake off the bad thoughts. Tomorrow would be another grind. Holy mackerel. I gotta get me a real job. What in the hell do I want out of life, anyway?

# *Chapter 2*

## *Zelda*

I tell yah, slavery must have been easy compared to being a pump jockey. Mrs Nethercot had become a continuous pain in my rear end. What with her constantly moaning about dirt and locking me out of the house, I could easily strangle her. Man, I'd had it up to my ears with that woman. This next Sunday was going to be my day of rest come hell or high water. Just to sleep-in would be a godsend. To relax and have no worries – man, that's a laugh.

It's surprising how many cracks you can find in a ceiling when you've got nothing better to do. Just lying there listening to the traffic was sweet joy and it added to the excitement of counting the cracks. No school, no work and nothing to do except count cracks in that ugly ceiling. It's kind of funny how your mind wanders. Thoughts of that rainy day at Mom and Dad's funeral filtered into my head. I never asked to be an orphan. I should have been in the car with them. It would have saved a whole load of pain.

Suddenly, there was a "bang, bang" on my door. The shock almost made me jump out of my skin.

'I'm asleep, go away.'

'Don't you talk to me like that, young man,' Mrs Nethercot snapped. 'You have a visitor. You'd better come to the door quickly or there'll be trouble.'

God! the last thing I needed was a visitor. 'Alright, alright. I'm coming. Keep your shirt on.'

I wrapped a bed sheet around my otherwise naked body and walked to the door. It's difficult to say who was the most surprised, Gran or me.

'Well, William, it's half past noon and you're not even dressed. Have you no shame?'

'Sorry, Gran. Come in. I've been working hard and I'm just trying to catch up on a little sleep. It's harder to sleep around here than it is in the market and besides that, it's hot.'

Gran's a funny little woman, a mite on the heavy side and quite a bossy old gal. She eyed the devastated apartment with all my clothes scattered around. I guess if I'd smoked, the ashtrays would have been full, too. You could see the annoyance building up in her eyes and almost feel the temperature rising.

'What kind of filth do you live in?' she barked at me.

'Sorry, Gran, I've bin busy.'

She knocked a pile of old socks off the only chair. 'I promised your mother I'd look after you. It seems to me I should begin right away. You definitely need looking after. What about school?'

'Ma's dead, Gran, when did you speak to her? What school?'

She shook her head in disgust. 'I received a letter.'

'From Mom?'

'No, silly boy. It said you've been discharged from the university and with bills outstanding. Why was I not informed?'

'Ah, well ... yes, Gran.'

'So what do you intend to do about it?'

'Do you mind if I get dressed first? I kind of feel at a disadvantage like this.'

'Go.'

Somehow, she always managed to make me feel like a scalded kid. Wouldn't matter what I did, it would still be wrong. In the bathroom, I dragged on a pair of slacks and a T-shirt – hardly Sunday best. When I emerged, she had begun to tidy up the room.

'Don't bother, Gran, I'll do it later.' I sat on the bed and tried to smile.

Gran sat on the chair again. Funny, the old girl was kind of nice-looking. Her hair was greying, but why not, she'd seen her sixty-second birthday, though she didn't look it.

'I came to see you,' she said in a mellow tone of voice. 'I have bad news, sad news.'

'Oh, what?'

She sighed deeply and then stared out the window as if looking for inspiration. 'Well, Uncle Edgar is dead.'

I shrugged my shoulders in dismay. 'Uncle Edgar. I don't recall any Uncle Edgar. So who's he?'

'He was your father's older brother. Surely you must remember him. He was in Australia for awhile.'

It seemed appropriate to shake my head sadly. I didn't remember the name. 'I'm sorry, but ... well, I didn't know him. I don't remember Mom or

20

Dad ever mentioning him. So what's so sad about losing someone I didn't know?'

'There were three siblings as I remember. The oldest child – I think her name was Jane. You remember; the one who ran off to Australia with some salesman or other. Well, Edgar was a couple of years younger than her and seven years older than your father.'

'If you say so, Gran. I still don't remember him.'

'Well, he obviously remembered you. Edgar Reyner was a playboy. He had a lot of money and as far as I know, he spent it on fast cars, fast women, drink and any other iniquity he could imagine.'

'So why's this sad news to me, Gran?'

She looked at me and smiled sweetly. 'My boy, you're the only survivor. My only child was your mother and you're an only child. There is no one else. You're the end of the line, the Reyner line, that is.'

'What about aunt … whatever her name was? You know; the one in Australia. Doesn't she count?'

'We haven't heard from her for over thirty years. I remember your father saying something about her dying in a motor-vehicle accident.'

'Okay. Well, so what?'

'We have to look after you. There are no other descendants. I propose you come and live with me in my Dundas home.'

I didn't want to upset the old girl, but I wanted to live in Stoney Creek.

'Gran, my work's the other end of town. It would be even harder to get to work if I lived in Dundas; it's the opposite end of the city from the Creek.'

'I have a car. Can you drive?'

'Yeah, sure.'

'Well, if you're a good boy, I see no reason why you couldn't have it and drive to work. Would that alleviate your problems a modicum?'

Now, the idea of owning wheels definitely appealed to me, but living with Gran didn't.

'Well thanks, Gran. I appreciate your offer. I guess I'll have to think about it.'

'Don't spend too much time thinking. I've given your notice in at this disgusting dump.'

'You did what?' I said, trying not to get excited.

'I don't like that Mrs Nether-whatever. The woman's morose and totally unsuitable as a landlady. When you come to live with me, you'll pay rent and abide by the rules.'

21

'But I have my own room here, Gran. I like it here,' I lied and winced as the words escaped my lips.

'You can have your own room at my house. Now, young William, I don't want any arguments. You're moving in with me. You'll have a car and home-cooked meals. Other than living in decent quarters, there'll be very little difference.'

'Yes, Gran, if you say so.'

'Now, I wish to address those debts you left at the university.'

'Do we have to?'

'Yes. I have settled them. You owe me big, young man. How are you going to repay me?'

I shrugged my shoulders. I couldn't think of anything sensible to say. 'I don't know, Gran. What d'you think would be best?'

'Your rent will be $100 per week; that includes meals. You do your own laundry. And I want another $100 per week repayment on your debts. Is that fair and equitable?'

I nodded in the affirmative and smiled weakly.

'Good,' she said. 'The car is yours. If you take me home you can have it today.'

That was an offer I couldn't refuse; $200 a week. That means, after taxes, I'd be up about sixty bucks a week. I wiped the sweat from my forehead. 'Do you have air?'

Gran glared at me. 'I'll give you air. You can perspire in my house just as freely as you can here. Do I have air, indeed.'

'Okay, Gran. I'll take you up on your offer. With luck, I'll be able to find a better job when I've got wheels.'

'It's a pity you're not still at school. Don't you have any ambition?'

I had to think about it. 'Yeah, sure.'

'Well, what?'

Licking the sweat from my top lip, I thought about it some more. She sure knew how to jerk my chain and make me sit up.

'I'd love to work on tricky things, like solving problems. I think I want to be a detective. Yeah, that would be real cool, me, a detective.'

She smiled and clutched her handbag to her chest then, shaking her head, she said, 'And what have you done about it?'

'Nothin'.'

'Exactly. Nothing. And please use the Queen's English in my presence. Now, we should put some thought into solving that problem. I suggest we consider schooling.'

22

I smiled at what I took to be her way of being funny. 'So did this uncle leave us anything, Gran?'

Slowly, her head swung from side to side. 'No,' she said softly. 'Uncle Edgar was a playboy; one of the high-roller set. I never actually met him, but your father often talked of him. He made his money in some dubious way, gambling I do believe. I understand he gambled on the stock market, horses, dogs and at casinos.'

'So was he a millionaire or something?'

'I doubt that he had two coins to rub together. The lawyer's letter I received merely informed me that Edgar had died and he needed your address.'

'What's he want my address for?'

'I don't know. The communication was curt and tacit.'

'Well … do you think he left me something?'

She smiled. 'Work for a living, dear. Don't build dreams of inheritances and things of that nature. *Great Expectations* was a novel, this is real life. Work reaps greater rewards than dreaming.'

'Well, you can't help hoping, can you, Gran?'

Gran stood up and said, 'I've given your notice to that Mrs Nether-whatsit. I told her you would be out within the week. Do you want to drive over and take a look at your new room now?'

'Room. You mean I already have one?'

'Yes, of course. You've always been welcome at my house. I told you that at the funeral.'

'What about my friends?'

'Do they stay in your room here?'

'No, of course not, Gran.'

'Then I see no complication. Do you want to take me up on my offer or not?'

'Sure, Gran.' I walked over to her and gave her a hug. I didn't want to admit it, but I guess she really saved my bacon. This dump and the resident dragon were fraying my nerves.

'Get dressed in some decent clothes and then you can drive me home.'

Grabbing a few things, I walked to the bathroom and cleaned myself up. I tell you, the heat was getting to me. It was the hottest summer of my life and I've seen twenty of 'em. Gran seemed calm and cool, dressed in her cotton-print dress. When I emerged clad a little more like a gentleman, she handed me the keys to the car with a big smile on her sweet old face.

'I don't understand why you're giving me your car, Gran.'

23

'You have far more use for it than I. It's part of the deal. You do understand, don't you?'

'Yes, Gran, sure.'

It wasn't a very new model, I guess almost ten years old. There were only 50,000 clicks on the dial – barely used. She always kept it in the garage, so there was more rust on last year's models than on her neat little motor. I bet there were no more than three grains of dust on the inside. I opened the door for her and then, chauffeur fashion, I ran round the other side and climbed in. Man, it felt good to have wheels again.

Dundas is a neat little town, sort of joined to Hamilton on the western side at the end of Lake Ontario. You can barely tell when you leave Hamilton and enter Dundas. Her house was what the realtors would call a century home at over 100 years old. A great big old Victorian brick place, with two stories and an attic. I parked out front on the street, to avoid backing out of the driveway. It was a nice-looking house, with big trees all around in its ample grounds.

She climbed out. 'Are you coming in to see your room?'

'No, that's okay, Gran. This is my only day off. I've got things to do. When do you want me to move in?'

She leaned in through the driver's window and kissed me. 'Now, you be a good boy; there aren't many of us left, you know. I'm almost always at home. Come when you feel easy, there's a good boy.'

'So when, Gran?'

'As soon as possible would be best. But I'll leave it up to you, dear.'

'What if I get grease on your walls?'

'Then you'll clean it off.'

I smiled, waved and drove off. A big, deep sigh was in order. At long last I could tell Mrs Nethercot to go stuff herself. Now, I had a job and a home. Kinda sad though, Granny Zelda Hubert my only living relative. Kind of makes you feel lonely – humble, even.

God, it was hot. Typical of old folk, no air conditioning either in the house or the car. The sweat fairly poured down my face and back like the spring melt. It was too damn hot to think clearly. Global warming and all that; still, it didn't matter – they reckoned the world was going to end at the turn of the new millennium. At least I'd be around to see it go.

Dragon breath was waiting for me at the front door. Either she had radar or a crystal ball. 'You can't park that thing there,' she said in a shrill voice.

'Yes, Mrs Nethercot. Where would you like me to park it?'

24

'Not there.'

Ignoring her instructions, I got out and slammed the door. It was a public street, with no signs to forbid parking. 'Won't be long,' I said in a sing-song voice.

'You ignorant little brat. I told you not to park there. You youngsters just don't listen.'

'I'll be leaving in a few minutes. It won't bother you.'

Paying no heed to the old bat, I walked into the house. Not owning a great deal of stuff, I figured it best to take a load over to Gran's.

'Who was that disagreeable old lady?' Nethercot asked, following me into the house.

'I'm too busy to talk, Mrs Nethercot. Please excuse me; I've got things to do.'

'If that pile of rust isn't moved, I'll call the police and have it towed. I have the right; I'm a homeowner and a taxpayer and you're only a tenant.'

'Oh, bugger off, you old fart,' I said under my breath, not having the courage to actually put her in her place.

As quickly as possible, I fled up to my room. Somehow, there was consolation there. The door kept the big old dragon at bay. I threw myself on the bed and pretended I couldn't hear Mrs Nethercot still grumbling on the other side of the door. God! Tomorrow is Monday and the whole bloody cycle begins again.

As I lay there sweating, imitating a porous water carrier and just looking at the familiar cracks in the ceiling, the thought struck me: how many poor bastards are trapped as I am? There had to be a way of getting off this track. Go to work, come home, go to bed, sleep, get up and go to work again. Oh, to be one of the idle rich.

My stomach began grumbling; it was worse than old Mrs Nethercot's incessant gabble. I couldn't ignore it for long. A quick look at my watch revealed the time. 'Holy Mackinaw.' It was past two. That settled it. Packing could wait till later. Not wanting to run into the old dragon again, I listened for a moment at the door – not a sound on the other side. Quick as a flash, I opened the door and fled down the hall and out of the front. The dragon lady headed me off halfway across the lawn.

'Your rent was due yesterday, where is it?'

'I'll pay when I get back.'

Somehow, I managed to dodge round her and jump into the car. With a sigh and a surge of gasoline, I roared off down the road. Just across the street from McMaster University was a takeout; as good a place as any. I figured I'd go there and stop the midsection grumbling. If only old Nethercot could be silenced so easily.

Gees, it didn't work out too well. I only had three fifty and fries cost two and a quarter and a drink was one ten. It's enough to frost you when one skimpy meal leads to bankruptcy. I sat in the car eating my repast and sweating cobs, watching the happy people walk by. My life was the shits. No girl, no real friends, a shitty job and now I've got to live with Granny Hubert, but I do have wheels.

It wouldn't have been so bad, but I still had to face the dragon of Westdale at least once more ... and me unarmed. Christians to the lions was easier; at least they died quickly. This was more like having your hands and feet tied and then being pecked to death by an old chicken, two if you count Granny Zelda Hubert.

Man, it sure was nice having wheels, though. I motored downtown and then to Pier 4 Park. I just wanted a little breather, a little space. It's very hard when you've only got yourself to talk to; looking in from the outside it seems so simple. 'So what do you want to do with your life?' says Gran Hubert. Gees, those words echoed round and round in my hollow head.

I want to be a detective. No, not just a detective, a PI. Yeah, that's it, William Reyner PI. Man! that sounds good. Say a Beretta in an underarm holster. 'Listen you, Nethercot; I've got your angles. Grab some sky.' Oh boy! Ah well! With a big sigh, I started the engine and slowly drove back to Westdale.

The radio played a sad tune, which fitted my mood. Jumping Gemini! The sadness suddenly turned to rage when I rounded the corner. Not on the lawn but right on the sidewalk stood all my gear. The whole lot, photo album, CD player and clothes. She'd tossed the whole kit and caboodle out. And where was the wicked witch of the west?

Jumping out of the car, I reasoned that she's not stupid and not gonna hang around after waving the red flag. Gritting my teeth, I consoled myself with the thought that at least now I didn't have to pay the back rent. 'Screw you,' I shouted in the direction of her house.

After loading the car with my meagre possessions, I turned to face the dragon lady's abode and gave old lady Nethercot the finger. I hope the old bat was peeping round the curtains. With luck, it would give her a fatal heart attack or an attack of anything she used as a heart.

26

# *Chapter 3*

# *The Communiqué*

Anger still pulsed through my veins as my new wheels stopped in Gran's driveway. My heart pounded from the encounter with the Westdale dragon. Man, it makes a person feel stupid. Just a couple of hours and here I was, lock, stock and barrel, begging for a bed. Gran didn't come out to greet me. I figured that maybe she was out shopping or otherwise engaged. With a deep sigh of relief, I grabbed an armful of my junk and headed for the front door. On reaching the door it opened.

'I thought you said you were too busy today,' Gran said softly, her old eyes twinkling with delight.

'Well, you know, like plans of mice and men an' all that, Gran.'

She replied with a big smile and when I entered the hall, a strong and inviting smell of hot, freshly baked cookies assailed my nose. Gran closed the door quietly behind me and said, 'I'm so happy you could make it today. Please, follow me and I'll take you to your room.'

The stairs were right there by the front door. Gran led the way up the soft carpeted steps. The place sort of reminded me of a museum. The wallpaper matched the carpet, sort of dark roses. The red colour matched the brilliantly polished walnut woodwork. My room was the first one at the top.

'I feel kinda stupid, Gran,' I said, trying to apologize.

She waved her hand at the door across the upstairs hall. 'The bathroom. I have my own, so you may spend all the time you wish in there. I would appreciate dry floors, though.' With a quick push, she opened the door to my room. 'This is your room, do as you will. Though again, I would appreciate some semblance of order.' She kissed me on the cheek and added, 'You're a good boy. We'll get along famously.' With that, she walked off and disappeared down the stairs.

Man, the room, wow! There were two sets of drawers, a tallboy, a walk-in closet, a dresser and two bedside tables. The bed was a monster; at least twice as big as the one I had at old Nethercot's. A big bay window

27

with a window seat overlooked the side garden. I figure the house was at least twice the size of Mom's. And everything seemed so clean and ... well, showroom-style.

I wanted to be independent, a man on my own, stupid me. I stood looking out of the window, mentally kicking myself for being a nitwit. She offered me help two years ago, when Mom and Dad died. Dumping an armful of junk on the bed, I set out to collect the rest from the car. On reaching the front door, Gran called me from another room at the end of the entrance hall.

'William, please step in here for a moment.'

With a sigh, I walked the carpeted hall to the kitchen. Again, I found a clean and well-appointed chamber. The smell of cooking was mouth-watering. A modern chrome and plastic dining set with six chairs stood near the back window. 'Yes, Gran?'

'Please sit, William.'

I sat on one of the chairs and she perched on the edge of another. Her eyes seemed sad. 'What is it, Gran?'

She took one of my hands gently in hers. 'William, I believe a relationship should begin the way it intends to continue.'

'Yeah?'

'The one thing I believe in is honesty. That is, honesty between us. I solemnly swear never to lie to you and you must reciprocate.'

I shrugged, feeling a little stupid. 'Sure, I swear.'

'We're the last of the line, William. I do wish you had come to me earlier. Still, never mind that now. This house is now your home. I want you to treat it as such. Please have respect and treat both me and this dwelling with courtesy and civility.' She pulled a key from her pinafore pocket and handed it to me. 'This is the key to my ... to our house. Come and go as you please.'

I nodded in the affirmative.

She stared directly into my eyes and said, 'I don't want you to waste your life. We will have to collude and devise a plan for your future. What do you want to do?'

Shrugging my shoulders, I looked round the room for inspiration. 'Dunno.'

'Surely, William, you have an ambition?'

Somehow, I couldn't say it. Man, it would make me look a right berk and she seemed such a sweet old lady. 'I don't know, maybe ... I don't know.'

'What did you take at Mac?'

'Well, law, and –'

She cut me short. 'Why law?'

With a big sigh, I raised my eyebrows and said, 'I want to be a detective, I guess.'

She smiled. 'There you are then, that didn't hurt a bit. Did it?'

'No, I guess not.'

Gran stood up, leaned over and kissed me. 'Silly boy. Honesty, remember; honesty is always the best policy, at least it is with me.'

'Yes, ma'am.'

'I'll make inquiries. There must be a course you can take somewhere. You finish your moving in. Supper will be at six.'

Man, what a funny old girl. Somehow, she could pluck your heart out painlessly. I guess I'd been a real fool. I should have moved in with her in the first place. Mom would have approved, but you gotta realize, there's a generation gap between me and Mom and a chasm between me and Gran.

Having gotten all my junk into my room, I bounced on the bed, flat on my back. Nice bed, soft and springy. Another thing I noticed, this house didn't have a furnace-like atmosphere. It was cool and less overwhelming than old Nethercot's. Great leaping lizards … and no cracks in the ceiling. That had to be an omen for the good.

The one worrying point – none of the interior doors had locks. Who the hell cares? You know, that was an amazing ceiling. A house that old and no cracks in the ceiling. I bet the mice even wear slippers. I was suddenly jolted back to reality with a knock on my door. 'Who is it?' I yelled.

'Who do you think, dear?' came a soft and gentle reply.

'Oh, Gran.' I jumped up and ran over to the door and opened it. 'Sorry, I wasn't thinking. I guess I was sort of daydreaming.'

She shook her head gently from side to side. 'Who is it? indeed! You don't have to lie on that bed all day. There's a TV in the living room and another in the playroom. I can't watch two at a time. I came to tell you that we have a perfectly nice sitting room. You can do your homework there.'

'When?'

Again, she shook her head. 'Anytime you wish, dear.'

'Oh, gees. Thanks, Gran.'

I took a gentle stroll around the house. Gran didn't follow, as she was doing something in the sitting room. It's ridiculous when I think of it. How could I have been such a fool? Gran had everything, and I do mean everything, and me a crummy pump jockey. It kinda makes you feel conspicuous, like a duck in a puppy farm.

29

Living in a house that had everything made work even harder. The soft luxury of living with Gran and then ten hours of sweat ... and I do mean sweat. The weather was the hottest I could remember. Monday was a killer, but I had a car to drive home in. Gran was an angel and supper was ready when I walked in the house after work.

On entering, the aroma of fresh baking filled my lungs, yet it was still cool and no air conditioning. After a quick clean-up and a change of clothes, I reported to the dining room. Gran was already seated. I looked at her and smiled weakly. 'Sorry, Gran.'

'What for, dear?'

'Well, I'm a little late.'

'It's your supper, William. If you prefer it cold then that's your choice. You have the freedom to do as you wish.'

'I am sorry, Gran.'

'Eat up and shut up.'

'Yes, Gran.'

The meal was great. Soup followed by steak and home fries, with some cake stuff that she called Yorkshire pudding. Then, would you believe, dessert. I ate my fill and kissed her, thanking her for the meal. 'I'll do the washing-up for you, Gran.'

'No you won't. The dishwasher will do it. Go do whatever it is young men do.'

'Gee, thanks, Gran.'

Talk about falling on your feet. The pure luxury of living with the old girl erased the sweat and tears of a day's labour. I think it was Thursday when things changed. Well, they didn't really change; it was more of a start to things happening. I went home as usual and rushed to clean up and put on some clean clothes. Supper was ready and Gran was seated. I sat and said, 'Hi, Gran, how was your day?'

She didn't smile; instead, she just handed me a letter. 'What's this?'

'Read it, dear.'

It was from Purvis and Pringle Law Partners. Carefully opening it, I pulled out the neatly typed letter.

'I don't understand it, Gran. What's it all about?'

She sighed. 'I have one as well, dear. Mine says I have to be in their law office at 9.00 a.m. next Tuesday, the twenty-second.'

'That's what mine says. What's it all about, Gran?'

She pouted her lips and her eyes twinkled. Then she said, 'Could be "great expectations", after all.'

'Really. You mean ... not Uncle Edgar?'

'It's the same law firm, dear.'

'What'll we do?'

'Did you read it?'

'Yes, Gran.'

'It says that my presence is imperative. Sounds very melodramatic. It doesn't say what the alternatives are.'

I had to think about it for a few moments. 'Do you think he's left us some money or property or something?'

'It says, 9.00 a.m. prompt. I'll phone tomorrow during business hours. This has to be a practical joke. Did you note the address?'

'Yeah, but I don't know where that is; up north, I guess.'

'I'll find out what I can. Don't worry about it, dear.'

'That's great, Gran. What do you know about Uncle Edgar? I mean ... well, like, who was he? What happened to him?'

She took a deep breath and looked at the ceiling for inspiration. It was several seconds before she replied.

'Well, he was about seven years older than your dad. Robert, your father, had very little to do with his brother. I think he disapproved of his lifestyle: gambling, fast cars and fast women. As far as I know, Edgar never broke the law and there was never any mention of fame or riches. I suppose he could have had a house or something.'

'So how much money do you think he had?'

'Millions, but he spent it all. I remember shortly before your parents died your father went to see Edgar. I don't know what it was all about. Robert was furious. I thought it had to be something to do with money. It seemed to me that Edgar was in some kind of trouble. Your dad wouldn't discuss it.'

'How much do you think he's left us, then?'

She shook her head again. 'Nothing. I would hazard a guess there are debts to be settled and we'll be responsible for them. If we are named in the will then we'll have to sort out whatever mess he left.'

'So are we going?'

Gran stroked her chin thoughtfully for a moment. 'I don't know – I really don't know. What are your thoughts on the matter, dear?'

I mean, wow! Fancy throwing the ball in my court. Edgar was totally unknown to me. I can't remember Dad ever mentioning him.

'I don't think they'd contact us for debts, would they?'

She shrugged. 'Who knows? If you want to go, well, then ... I'll go with you. I've been summoned, too.'

31

'That's great, Gran; we'll make it an adventure, a day out. How's that sound?'

'Alright. A day out up north.'

'There was a third one, a sister, wasn't there, Gran?'

'Yes. Aunt Jane. She married some beryl miner or something from Australia; or was he a salesman? Either way, she ran away against her parent's wishes. You know, Edgar had also been to Australia.'

'So what happened to her? Aunt Jane, that is.'

Gran shook her head slowly. 'I don't think anyone ever knew, except I do remember your father saying something to the effect that she had died. Though I can't imagine how he knew. Perhaps Edgar told him.'

'I thought they didn't speak?'

'Well, I've no idea. We'll get this episode out of the way and then concentrate on your new career. Alright?'

'Sure, Gran.'

It's a funny thing, my life had been sort of dull since my parents died, but at Gran's house things never stopped moving. That night, I didn't sleep too well at all. The thought that Uncle Edgar may have left me a fortune bugged me. When I did get to sleep I had nightmares. Demons came after me looking for gold. Gees, I'd wake up sweating like a pig and shaking like a leaf.

You know, it's kind of nice to have someone to talk to. At breakfast, Gran and I hashed it all out again. The drive to work was boring, the job was boring and, above all, the customers were boring. Several times, I made mistakes with the change. I couldn't concentrate, as thoughts of Uncle Edgar haunted my every conscious moment. I'm not one to worry, but this was different. The mysterious way we were summoned to this lawyer's place intrigued me. One of the maps in the office said that Parry Sound was 270 kilometres from Hamilton. That's a good drive; even at the legal speed limit that's about three hours.

At supper that night, Gran said we had two choices: either go the day before or start out at about five in the morning. Getting up early these days seems to be my thing; besides that, I didn't want to miss two days' work. There and back in a day would have to be the call. My days off were Thursday and Sunday.

On Friday, I managed to corner the boss in the office. For a few minutes at least, I had no customers. 'Excuse me, boss.'

'What?' he growled in his usual unpleasant way.

'I need Tuesday off.'

He blinked furiously for a few seconds, staring at me as though I'd suddenly turned purple. 'Are my ears playing tricks, boy?'

'No, boss. I need Tuesday off. It's very important.'

He slowly rose to his feet. Man, you'd think I'd just asked him for a ten grand sub. He pointed his finger at me and said in a growling tone, 'Listen, boy. We work our own shift. You work Tuesday or bugger off. Is that clear?'

'I have an appointment with a lawyer I have –'

He interrupted. 'No Tuesday, no job. *Comprendez?*'

That really pissed me off; I guess I lost my rag. 'You stupid, slave-driving shit-head,' I shouted. 'You can't fire me.'

'Oh no, and why's that, boy?'

''Cause I quit. You can stick this job where the sun don't shine. Find some other asshole to work your Tuesday.'

'You're fired, boy.'

'No, I quit, dummy.'

I walked out before I really got mad and thumped him, which I probably would have. Gran says I'm as big as I'm obtuse – whatever that means. Stupid slave-driver, what the hell does he take me for? Oh boy! Now I've got to face Gran. What's she gonna say when I tell her? I looked at my watch – it was only mid afternoon. Well, there's only one way to face the music and that's with honesty, right?

When I parked the car in the drive, Gran was working in the side garden. 'Hi,' I said, slamming the car door.

She stopped work and smiled. 'You're home early, dear.'

'Gran, I. Well … Gran …' I couldn't think how to put it. 'I've … that is …'

'For heaven's sake, William, spit it out. What are you trying to say?'

'I quit my job; well, actually, I guess I was fired.'

'Did you quit, William, or were you fired?'

'I quit.'

'Why?'

'The boss is an ass … I mean, he's an idiot.'

'So what was the reason you quit?'

'The man's a fool. I wanted Tuesday off. He wouldn't cooperate in any way. The man's an idiot. I would've worked another shift to make up.'

'All bosses are idiots; that's why they're bosses, dear. What about your salary?'

I pulled a silly face and shrugged my shoulders. 'I don't know, Gran. What do you think is best?'

33

'Let's go and have a cup of tea and consider our options,' she said with a sigh.

I couldn't believe how well she took the news. One would have thought she would rant and rave; after all, how would I pay the rent?

It was at least ten degrees cooler in the house than outdoors. 'Why is it so cool in here, Gran, you don't have air?'

'Trees, William, trees. Nature's own air conditioning.'

We walked into the kitchen and she put the kettle on. 'Tea will be served in a few moments.' She sat at the dining table opposite me. 'I'm glad you've quit that awful job, dear. It's not fitting labour for a smart boy of your calibre. I've contacted Mohawk College and we can get you in on a law course.'

'A law course?'

'Yes, it's the beginning of a career in detective work.'

'Detective work?' I echoed parrot fashion.

'Yes. How does "Grantham and Reyner Private Detectives" sound?'

'Who's Grantham?'

'Me, dear.'

'I thought your name was Hubert. Oh, I get it; it's your maiden name.'

'My maiden name is Harris.'

I had to think for a few moments. 'So, who's Grantham?'

She smiled sweetly and avoided an answer. 'The kettle's boiling. I'll make the tea.'

'What about Tuesday? When'll we leave?'

'Well, if you're not working, we could go Monday but, on the other hand, if you're not working, we can't afford the hotel. I think we'll leave the plans exactly the way they are, don't you think, dear?'

34

# Chapter 4

## Tuesday the Twenty-second

Working for Gran turned out to be almost as hard as pumping gas, but without the stink of petroleum. We went to Mohawk College and booked on a couple of courses, neither of which started till September. She also talked to her lawyer about a letter to Pete's uncle concerning my firing and wages due. I tell yah, she didn't hang around; thirty years as a librarian must have taught her something. One has to admire the old gal.

The big thing that worried me was money – I didn't have any. Without work, how long could the old gal support me? Somehow or other I had to find myself a viable job. Pity I quit at the doughnut store. Something was bound to turn up. Gran knew a lot of people. She was a real dynamo, a get-up-and-goer.

Suddenly, it seemed to be thundering. I opened my eyes and it was still dark. Gran was pounding on my door.

'What?' I yelled.

'Come along, William. It's time to get up. We have a long drive ahead of us.'

Reluctantly, my feet met the floor and my hand found the light switch. Click ... and a blinding glare filled the room. It's very hard to open your eyes when it's four in the morning. I looked at the clock again, this time doing a double take. The stupid thing must have stopped. Wiping the sleep from my eyes, I tried to focus on my watch. God, it really was four in the morning. Staggering like a drunk, my feet dragged me to the door. It took almost every ounce of effort to poke my head out.

'Do you know what time it is?' I yelled.

Her voice came from the kitchen. 'Shut up, William, and get dressed. We have a long drive ahead of us. Today is the day.'

With a sigh and my mouth tasting like last week's socks, I retreated to the bathroom. What the hey! Having been awakened, there was no harm getting dressed as well. Breakfast was on the plate when I eventually made my way to the kitchen. Gran was dressed up all neat in her Sunday best. The clock was still trying to insult my intelligence.

'It's only half past four, Gran. What's the rush? Parry Sound will still be there when we arrive.'

'I want you washed, dressed, fed and awake by five. We will be on our way at that time. Wakey-wakey, William.'

It was dark outside and this person has never in his life been up before the sun, at least not in the summertime. I ate, drank, stretched and somehow managed to be ready to go at about ten minutes to five. Gran was still fiddling with the refrigerator and a few plastic shopping bags.

'Go inspect the car, William. Check fuel, water and oil. We want to get there without a hitch.'

'Yes, Gran.'

There was no problem, we had plenty of everything, even the tyres were happy and ready to roll. She loaded several things in the trunk, which she insists is the boot, and then dead on the dot of five, she sat in the passenger seat.

'Well. Young man?'

'Well what, Gran?'

'Shall we sit here all day or do you think we could beat the rush-hour traffic in Toronto by commencing this journey?'

Starting the engine, I felt momentarily puzzled and couldn't think which way to go. 'Toronto?' I asked.

'Yes, dear; 401. We'll go 403 to QEW, then the 403 bypass to 401 and then the 400 north. Do any of these numbers mean anything to you, dear?'

'Sure,' I nodded and backed the car out onto the street.

Man, is Dundas ever quiet at 5.00 a.m. Not a soul around; not even any traffic on King Street. It was still sweltering hot. Surprisingly, there were several vehicles on the 403 highway and when we reached the Queen Elizabeth Way, there was far more traffic than I would have expected. You wonder where everyone came from or where they're going.

The number of vehicles on the 401 was staggering. I couldn't believe that all that traffic could be about at six in the morning. By the time we passed Highway 427, the speed was well below the limit.

'Gran, we're gonna be late with all this traffic.'

She chuckled a little. 'There'll be nothing beyond the 400, dear. Just have courage and drive carefully.'

Gran was right, as usual. I'm beginning to think the old girl has a crystal ball. At length, we reached a service centre not far beyond Toronto. Gran saw the sign.

'Pull in there,' she said. 'We need to stretch our legs.'

I knew what she meant and could certainly do with a coffee and something to nibble on. Gran went to the can while yours truly queued up for drinks. She returned and found a seat long before my queuing was complete.

'Man, this place is busy for this time of day.' I put the coffee and a bag of doughnuts on the table and sat down. 'How we doing for time, Gran?'

She smiled. 'We have plenty of time. Sit down, William, and relax. We don't want you becoming overtaxed.'

I sat and asked, 'Did you ever phone the law firm to find out what all this is about?'

'Yes.'

'Well, what did they say?'

'The secretary wouldn't discuss official business on the phone and the lawyers were too busy to attend to me.'

'Oh! So you didn't find anything out at all?'

Gran shook her head and smiled. 'Enjoy it, William. Today is the day. Whatever is in store for us will soon be revealed.'

After Toronto, the countryside becomes rolling hills, with trees and small forests as far as you can see. We made one more stop before Parry Sound. As we were entering lake country, we found a really nice lay-by picnic area near Horseshoe Lake with a heavily forested lake shore, a rocky beach and toilets. Considering I'd never heard of Parry Sound before, it was a much larger town than I had imagined; kinda impressive, too. Not really knowing where to go, I continued driving down Bower Street, which seemed to be the main drag. Eventually, we saw shops.

Time was getting on and by the time we stopped and climbed out of the car, the clock was approaching nine. The stores were closed and there wasn't a great choice in pedestrians.

'Excuse me,' I said to this woman hurrying by. 'I'm looking for McMurray Street.'

'Straight up, turn right on James. You can't miss it; right opposite the courthouse.'

'Thank you.' With a sigh and a slight feeling of trepidation, I climbed back in the car. 'Well, Gran. It's appropriate, we need the courthouse.'

The lady was right. Funny little town; it seemed more spaced out and less confusing than Hamilton. We drove slowly up James Street and easily found the courthouse, the only large building in the area. McMurray was opposite, a residential street.

'You got the number, Gran?'

'Yes, park the car by the courthouse and we'll walk to our destination.'

Man, it's like being a condemned man. We stood in front of the huge Victorian house. Unlike Gran's, it was very utilitarian. No garden, just concrete and tarmac. A brass plate with the name of the law firm screwed to the front wall confirmed we'd found the right place. No trees and a humongous air-conditioner heat-exchange unit sat out front almost on the driveway. With sweat pouring down my face I rang the doorbell.

Gran nudged me and said, 'Did you read the sign, dear?'

'No, what sign?'

'It says walk in.'

'Oh!'

Together, we entered. There was a small foyer, with dark brown polished hatstand and dismal brown wallpaper. A young woman, very smartly dressed in jacket and slacks, approached us from another doorway and smiled.

'Hi,' I said. 'I'm er –'

She interrupted me. 'Yes, sir, you're Mr William Reyner and Mrs Hubert.'

I nodded in agreement.

The woman opened a door to our right. 'Please enter and take a seat, sir, madam.'

The room had thick carpet and dark wallpaper. At the other end stood a huge chocolate brown desk. There was a bunch of seats and most of them occupied by people I didn't know. We sat on the first unoccupied chairs. No one paid any attention to us at all. No one was talking. It was rather like a funeral, except for the redhead. Man, you couldn't help but notice her. She sat to one side; long red hair, plain white sweatshirt and the biggest breasts you could imagine.

Gran noticed me staring and elbowed me in the ribs. After a couple of minutes, two very officious gentlemen entered, followed by two larger ones. The quartet walked to the desk. One sat and switched on a reading lamp, the other officious-looking man stood behind him and the two big guys stood one either side.

'Good morning,' said the seated gentleman in a slow drawl.

Everyone hummed, hawed and grunted. I heard one say, 'About time, too.'

'I'm Edwin Purvice and this,' he said, indicating the other pompous-looking character, 'is my law partner Alistair Pringle.'

Again, we all mumbled and grunted.

'This is an unusual occasion,' he said, clearing his throat. 'Mr Edgar Reyner was a very unusual man. All of you in some way or another are concerned with him. Would you continue, Alistair?'

The other guy cleared his throat and said, 'This is the reading of the last will and testament of Edgar Reyner. He set rules for this meeting and the dispersion of his fortune.' The man sounded very pompous. Clearing his throat again, he continued, 'The rules are these: only those present at the commencement of the meeting may receive the bequests and each must sign a release.'

'Release for what?' someone grouched.

'Please. All will be revealed. Mr Reyner was a very wealthy man and he left provision for only those invited to this assembly.' He looked at his watch. 'The deadline is nine fifteen. Those who are not present by then will forfeit all and any right to the reading. Miss Gorman will lock the door at precisely nine fifteen. As there are still several minutes to the deadline, are there any relevant questions?'

An older man near the front stood up. 'Why all the theatrics? It don't impress no one.'

'Please sit, Mr Wrangler. It may appear to be theatrics, but Mr Reyner placed these rules upon us and we have to oblige. On my right is Inspector Spadafora of the Ontario Provincial Police and on my left is Sergeant Devine, Royal Canadian Mounted Police. There was to be a representative of the US government but, unfortunately, she could not get here on time.' He looked at his watch. 'The time limit will be up in just a few minutes.'

'So why don't you get on with it. We've all got jobs to go to?' someone up front said.

'Mr Edgar Reyner may have been a mite eccentric, but he devised this meeting not knowing he was soon to die. You have all probably heard about his death in a boat explosion. Well, that accident has brought us all together in this room. Are you ready, Mr Purvice?'

'Yes,' the seated man replied.

'Good. The time limit has been reached. The front door is now locked and secured. The proceedings may begin.'

Purvice cleared his throat. 'Thank you. The rules are simple. Any bequest not settled here and now will be donated to charity. After each bequest is settled, the beneficiary must leave. Representatives of the law are here to witness all signings.'

The two policemen nodded in agreement.

Purvice continued, 'I call Sylvia Devine. Would you please step up here, Miss Devine?'

A slim, nicely built woman of about thirty stood, straightened her skirt and walked to the front by the desk. 'I'm here,' she said in a clear but subdued voice.

'Miss Devine. I have to read this short dissertation before the presentation.'

She nodded in agreement.

Purvice continued reading. 'For my friend Sylvia, who warmed me on a few nights when we were in London, I leave cash. The only thing she really understands. Sylvia, if you had stood by me, you'd be rich. I leave you one thousand dollars cash.' Purvice handed her an envelope. Please sign here, miss.'

She seemed more embarrassed than pleased. Grabbing the pen, she scribbled something, snatched up the envelope and whispered something to Purvice.

'No, miss, you must now leave. Would you officers please sign as witnesses?'

The other lawyer escorted her out, while the cops signed in turn. Purvice waited patiently until everyone was settled and then he began again. 'Mr Sid Pilkington of Pilkington's Garage, would you please step forwards?'

An older, balding grey-haired man stepped forwards. He was dressed in a respectful black suit. 'I didn't ask for no money,' he mumbled.

Purvice read from his papers. 'Though I can't call Sid a friend, he is the first and only honest motor mechanic I have ever met. For your honesty and courteous service that rainy day when you helped me out, I would like to leave you a cheque for five thousand dollars.'

Sid smiled and took the pen. 'Where do I sign, sir?'

'Well, if it goes up every time, Gran, I reckon we'll be rich,' I whispered.

'Quiet,' she growled.

Again, the lawyer waited for his dwindling audience to settle and his partner to return, before reading the next piece. 'Mr Orville Wrangler, would you please step up?'

The grumpy old fellow from earlier stood up and thrashed his leg with a dirty old baseball cap. 'What's bin left me, then?'

'Mr Wrangler. I thank you for being a patient and forgiving neighbour. I don't know why, but you held your tongue about the many indiscretions you spied. I also thank you for the story of Fiend's gold. For all your good deeds, I bequeath you six thousand dollars in bonds.'

'Yup, I was right, Gran, the price is going up every time.'

'Hush, boy.'

I looked around. The room was thinning out. There were only six of us left and we'd topped six grand. After the old man had gone, Purvice continued reading.

'For my publisher, who tried very hard to make me famous, I leave you my antique collection of Victorian classics. I know you eyed them every time you came to my house.' Purvice looked up. 'Is Mr Samuel Endsmith present?'

A tall, dark-haired older gentleman stood and walked to the table. He said nothing; just signed the document and then, placing his glasses in his pocket, walked with the other lawyer to the front door.

Purvice scanned the room. 'I see that Dorothy Googe is not present. Her twelve thousand dollars will be donated to charity. She was Mr Reyner's private nurse after his skiing accident in British Columbia some years ago. Next is Jane Denver.' He started reading again. 'To my dearest and sweetest Jane. However could I have operated such a large household without you at the head? For your many years of faithful service, please accept fifteen thousand dollars towards your retirement.'

An old woman walked to the table and signed. She was crying and holding a white handkerchief to her face.

'Gees, we're up to fifteen grand, Gran.'

'Be quiet, William.'

The room was deathly quiet as Purvice looked at his four remaining vultures. Picking up the documents he read again, 'I remember and regret a certain boat accident. I'm sorry, George Smithers. You lost your outboard and it was my fault. I was angry and stupid. I regret my actions and hope that this will buy you another motor. Please accept a cheque for twenty thousand dollars and don't think too badly of me.'

And that left three: me, Gran and the broad with the huge breasts and long hair. I really didn't care who was next, as we were already up to twenty grand. It wasn't just the heat that made the sweat pour down my face and back.

Purvice cleared his throat. 'For cunning and gold digging, in every sense of the word. I would like to make Adeline Reyley think about her future and our past. I leave to her my house on Gibson Street plus forty-five thousand dollars in cash. Take it, my dear Adeline, and leave us all in peace.'

The big-busted broad jumped up angrily and knocked her chair over. She marched to the table. For a second or two, I thought the cops would have to do something and then she signed and stormed out, without even saying a single word. Kind of weird, though; she was wearing sunglasses indoors. My heart was pounding; we'd reached house values. Man, what was I gonna get?

Mr Purvice looked around the room as if expecting more than just me and Gran to be there. 'Well, we have come to the end of this reading,' he said.

'What?' I yelled jumping to my feet. 'We were called here, too.'

'Yes, yes, Mr Reyner. I do mean that you are the last. Now, if you would please sit silently and allow me to read the final bequests.'

'Oh, sorry.' I sat and waited breathlessly, with visions of great riches being handed over.

He cleared his throat and straightened his papers. 'Mrs Hubert, though I never met you, it is as though I knew you well. Your son-in-law admired you greatly. When Bob died, I was going to come and see you. Alas, I never made it and neither did I get to the funeral of my dear brother. I hope it's not too late to make amends. Please accept fifty thousand dollars sympathy money. I have specifically asked that the proceedings be enacted in this fashion for reasons of my own. Bill, William Reyner, I want to leave you Fiend's Rock. Now known as Saucer's Island. However, I decided to make it a joint venture, half yours and half Mrs Hubert's. You both own the island and anything you find there.'

Purvice cleared his throat again and then continued. 'Listen to this,' he said.

> 'A wall of gold as deep as hell;
> Old Jeremiah Fiend's buried it well;
> Find the lamp where it burned at night;
> Then move a rock, the gold is out of sight.'

Mr Purvice paused and with the silk handkerchief from his breast pocket, he wiped the sweat from his brow in a dabbing fashion and then continued reading. 'The rest of my fortune, whatever it may be, is yours, William. I am sorry we just never got together; I would love to have known you. By the way, keep a lookout for blond gold-diggers; they could be the death of you.' Purvice closed the folder and looked at me expectantly.

'Now?' I asked.

'Now, Mr Reyner. Please come and sign the documents.'

I was so excited. Man! I could barely walk straight. I knocked over a chair and then fell headlong over another one. Man, did I ever feel stupid … and rich.

# *Chapter 5*

## *Saucer's Island*

When Gran eventually led me out of the lawyer's office, the heat seemed no longer to bother me. My mind was in the clouds, island hopping. I felt as a child feels going to the fair, yet Gran seemed calm and serene.

'Aren't you excited, Gran? You're rich – you're filthy, stinking rich.'

'Yes, dear.' She sighed deeply. 'I have worked as a librarian for over thirty years and have both a company pension and a widow's pension. Your grandfather left me well provided for. I have no need for extra money. What I have is quite sufficient for my needs.'

'But you can buy those things you always wanted, Gran. Anything you want.'

'I have everything I need, William.' She leaned forwards and gently kissed me on the cheek. 'So, are you hungry, dear?'

I looked at my watch. It was already twenty to twelve. We'd been in that lawyer's place forever. 'Yes, Gran. Let's hit the big time and then have a look at this Saucer Island.'

'That's Saucer's Island, dear.'

We walked back to the courthouse and collected the car. Sitting and buckling up, I looked at that dear old lady beside me. Man, had she ever changed my life.

'Which way, Gran?'

She shrugged. 'Your idea is as good as mine. Let's find somewhere to eat.'

'I saw water near the big trestle, we'll go that way.'

Virtually the way we came. We drove back down James Street and down the hill towards the harbour. The excitement seemed to bubble up inside me. I wanted to get out of the car and scream, telling the world we'd both hit the jackpot. Though I didn't. Gran had that sobering effect on people, including me.

A neat restaurant looked down over the jetty. This was the place for lunch. After parking the car in the dock area we walked back to the restaurant. It looked a nice solid, modern building in black steel and glass. An exciting smell of food cooking permeated the air. We sat close to a window and looked out towards the bay; I think they call it the Sound – the bay, that is.

'So, have you lost your ambition to be a detective, William?'

'No. Now I can afford it. Shall we go take at look at our island, Gran?'

'I don't want to, dear. I don't like water transportation very much.'

As I listened to her, I saw a floatplane begin its run across the water. Quickly, it lifted into the air and headed out over the lake. 'Oh, wow, a floatplane. We could maybe fly there, Gran.'

'No. I really don't want to see this island. I didn't have one yesterday and I'm sure it will cause no change in my lifestyle. After lunch, you go and take a look if you want to. I have things to do here on dry land that I'm sure will bore you to death, dear.'

The waitress came to our table. 'Excuse me, miss,' I said. 'Do you know where Saucer's Island is?'

'No, sir. Where is it?'

'Thanks … I was just wondering.'

'Fiend's Rock,' Gran said softly.

'Oh, Fiend's Rock. Sure, I know where that is,' the waitress said smiling.

'Where?' I asked with enthusiasm.

She pointed out of the window. 'About 20 kilometres that way. What you want for lunch, sir?'

'I don't know. You order, Gran. I'm too excited.'

Gran calmly ordered the food, while my head was buzzing with all the new possibilities. What was the island like? How much cash was I going to get? The lawyer said it would take several days to account for and he would send me the results. My heart suddenly leapt into my mouth as my present pecuniary situation dug me in the ribs – figuratively speaking, of course.

'Gran, I've only got about twelve bucks real money.'

She smiled. 'I'll trust you.'

'What d'yah mean?'

You can't help but admire her calmness. Quietly, she opened her purse and took out a credit card. 'Use this. We'll sort out the details later, I'm sure you can afford it now.'

'Thanks, Gran. I would like to go take a look at our island; sure you wouldn't like to come?'

'No, and that's Saucer's Island.'

'Yeah.'

'After lunch, dear, you go take a look at your island. I want to do a little snooping around here in town. One insular pile of rocks is the same as any other to me, dear.'

Man, I couldn't wait. Lunch suddenly lost its importance. The food was okay, but there were so many other things worth doing. Even so, my gut was twisted and strained with all the excitement and anticipation. As soon as possible, I left Gran and ran down to the harbour. How does one get a boat? Walking into the Tour-line shipping office, I spoke to the girl behind the desk.

'Excuse me, miss, where would one hire a boat?'

'Where do you want to go?' she said with her eyes twinkling lightly. She had some kind of sparkly make-up on her eyelids.

'Saucer's Island.'

Her expression lit up. 'You a detective or something?'

It was my turn to smile. 'Sure, and the new owner.'

'Try Smithers, just up the quay.' She pointed.

In seconds I was at the wooden hut, which had a cloth banner nailed to the roof. "Smithers Boats Self Hire", it said. My hand went for the doorknob, but it opened and swung out of reach. An elderly gentleman from the lawyer's office stood there filling the door frame.

'Hi,' I said weakly.

'Mr Reyner, I presume,' he said and smiled.

'Yes, sir.'

He grinned and pinched his nose, wiping invisible snot from his proboscis. 'What-yah want, son?'

'I, er ... well, I was looking to visit Saucer's Island.'

'There an' back?'

'Yes, sir.'

'It's about an hour there and an hour back.' He looked at his watch. 'It's one fifteen. How long you gonna stay there, son?'

'I don't know, just a look-see.'

'I'd like to be back by five. Hundred bucks. How's that sound?'

'Great,' I said, once more showing enthusiasm. 'I've only got a credit card with me. Will that be alright?'

'I'll bill you. Your lawyer Mr Purvice knows where you'll be and I reckon you can afford it.'

'Sure, yeah, okay.'

He leaned back inside the hut. 'I'm going out to Fiend's Rock, Dot. I'll be back around five. Ernie can take the rest of the rides.' He slammed the door and, staring at me, he slapped his ample gut. 'We'll take the 30 footer. It's the fastest one in my fleet.'

I nodded in agreement, but had no idea what he was talking about. We walked back towards town and then crossed a couple of mooring areas. He stopped at a beautiful blue-and-white open-top powerboat with seating for ten or more. 'This is it,' he said, helping me aboard.

He put his fingers in his mouth and whistled and then sat down and flipped a few switches. A kid appeared and began untying us from the shore as the two huge outboards sprang to life. In moments, we were free of the dock and began a long, gentle U-turn. You could feel the power, even though we were moving at a moderate speed.

Passing the place where the airplanes were moored, he opened the throttle a bit. The bow lifted and we headed out to deeper water.

'An inexperienced hand could get lost forever out here,' Smithers said.

It seemed a lot cooler, what with the breeze from our motion and all. I relaxed in the seat next to my pilot. The lake looked a beautiful shade of green, with islands and rocks breaking the surface all around.

'How do you know where we're going?' I asked.

'I've known the way since I was a kid. Over there is Bob's Point, Parry Island. Remember that, 'cause it's the way in and out of the harbour.' He pushed the throttles forwards and the bow lifted clean out the water. The throb of the motors and the patter of the gentle waves gave me goosebumps.

It was a beautiful ride and a lovely boat. George really knew how to handle it. Kinda made me feel inadequate. All that power was frightening.

'How far?' I asked.

'About 20, 25 kilometres. There's over 30,000 islands around here and in Georgian Bay. Stick to the proper route and you'll stay afloat, not like the *Maria-Bella*.'

'Oh! Who or what was she?'

George laughed and pulled a pipe from his top gun-jacket pocket. It was already stoked and with deft skill, he bent down behind the dash and lit it.

'I guess you'd say the *Maria-Bella* was the cause of all your troubles,' he said with a grin.

'Troubles, I don't have any now. I suppose I'm quite rich.'

George laughed, just as if I had said something really funny. 'That's Two Mile Point,' he said, indicating to our left. 'Keep close to the headland, till we reach Three Mile Point, and then due west.'

'What troubles?' I insisted.

With a wry grin, he pointed to a land mass far ahead of us. 'That's Killbear Park. Good landmark, but don't get fooled. I'm talkin' about your troubles with Jeremiah Fiend.'

'Who's he?'

George chuckled again. ''Tain't my place to tell yah. He were the first, he were the one who started it all.'

'You're not making a lot of sense, Mr Smithers. What exactly do you mean?'

He stroked his chin thoughtfully, checked his instruments and then said, 'Everyone who ever owned Fiend's Rock died and died bad.'

'Uncle Edgar died in an accident.'

George shook his head knowingly. 'Bloody cops couldn't catch shit if it dropped on their heads. No boat blows up when it don't even carry bottle-gas. An' what was the fellow doing in the middle of Georgian Bay? No reason to be 150 kilometres off course. You think he were daft or something?'

'No. Are you saying it wasn't an accident, then?'

He looked at me and smiled. 'Were he a smuggler, drug runner or something the like?'

'Don't know. Shouldn't think so.'

'I don't think so, either. I reckon it were one of the broads – probably that foreign bit. She done for him alright.'

I had no idea how Uncle Edgar died, so I couldn't argue the point. 'So who was this Jeremiah Fiend, then?'

'He were the one who stole the gold in the first place.'

'Stole the gold. What gold?'

'You from another planet, boy? Ain't you ever heard of Fiend's gold?'

I shook my head in serious wonderment. 'No.'

He laughed. 'Three Mile Point. Now we head just left of the land ahead. Well, it's only legend, but they say that Jeremiah Fiend had seven sons. Well, these be dangerous waters, lots o' islands just under the surface. Shoals, rocks; hit them and you's in real trouble. Can you swim?'

'Sure.'

'Not with the ghost of Jeremiah Fiend holdin' you down, you can't. He done for all the rest. I reckon he'll do for you just the same.'

'When? I mean, like, when was this supposed to have happened?'

'In eighteen summat.'

'What actually happened, then?'

'Eighteen, twelve or thirteen. Don't matter. Anyway, a Yankee ship sailed into Georgian Bay. They say that it was going to pay mercenaries to

47

fight the British. Anyhow, she runs aground on Gordon's Rocks. Jeremiah and his boys saw it and took the gold, about 10 tons of it. Them buggers took the gold to Fiend's Rock and while Jeremiah was celebrating on the mainland, the boys hid it, see.'

'They hid 10 tons of gold?'

'Yeah, that's what they say. Anyhow, when the old man came back, he was more pissed than a bear with toothache. He killed them all one by one, but they wouldn't tell where the gold was hid. Then he ups and disappears himself, like.'

'What happened to the gold?'

George laughed. 'That's the question everyone's bin asking for near two centuries. That's the real cause of the troubles. Gold fever. Loony they are, all on 'em.'

I began to understand Uncle Edgar's warning about gold-diggers. 'So nobody's ever found the gold, then?'

'Right. Some think it were hid in the water. They've used magnetometers, metal detectors, sonar, radar and plain old-fashioned divers. Not a sign, not nowhere. There ain't even a hint of the yellah stuff.'

'Well, perhaps it was buried on Fiend's Rock.'

He laughed heartily for several seconds. They don't call it "Rock", Fiend's Rock, 'cause it's made of candy. The island's almost three quarters of a kilometre long, one piece of solid rock. It's frost broke round the edges, but it's one ruddy great lump.'

I was disappointed. I thought my Saucer's Island was going to be some northern form of a tropical paradise.

'Just a piece of rock?' I quizzed.

'You'll see when we get there, boy. I wouldn't advise looking for the gold. That fever is always fatal. I reckon it's all a load of hooey, anyhow. There ain't no gold and never were. Ifan there had bin, well, somebody would o' found it by now, wouldn't they?'

'So what did happen to Jeremiah Fiend?'

'No one knows. He was never found, either dead or alive. An' every treasure hunter who bought the island died a horrible death, just like your uncle. Mysterious, ain't it?'

'Like, all of them?'

'Every single one of 'em. Ifan I were you, I'd sell that rock, take the cash and run as fast I could. Let some other sucker die looking for the treasure that ain't there.'

'What do you think it's worth?'

'That's Killbear Point, see the light? It's only a kilometre wide here. The light ahead is Sister Island. You should remember these places, if you's gonna do your own boating in these waters. Don't need another death, do we?'

'No. So how much do you think Saucer's Island is worth?'

'Edgar paid about five million for it.'

'Five million? Dollars? You mean like five million dollars?'

'Idiots pay that kind o' sum thinking they's gonna be even richer see, cos o' the story of the gold. What's 10 ton of gold worth, boy?'

'No idea.'

'Probably 100 million in today's market.'

'Oh, wow!'

'So now you's got gold fever, eh? Daft as a porcupine pillow. There ain't no gold, boy. All them dead men and not a single gold coin. Not even a smell.'

'Gold coin, what gold coin?'

'The ship was carrying gold coins; yah can't spend bullion. I reckon the old devil ferried the gold ashore and then he killed his sons and buggered off to spend 'is money. That's why there ain't no gold ever found. The old bugger spent it.'

'Wow, so there's no gold, eh?'

'Nah. Ifan I were you, I'd forget all about gold. See that straight ahead, that's Nias Islands. We'll skirt that and your island is directly beyond. The landing is on the west side.'

I looked around. Man, what a wonderful place. Beautiful islands, with trees and beaches, mostly less than a few hundred metres across. Many of the islands had beautiful cottages; some even had small mansions on them. I had no idea that people lived on these little rock lands. Still, yesterday I didn't know there was more than one. We approached a very large island and George throttled down and skilfully brought the boat alongside the jetty. Man, oh, man. I could hardly believe my eyes.

The island had a veritable forest of trees on it, and had a tiny harbour cut into the solid rock, with a large boathouse and ramp at the inland end.

'Wow,' I said standing up and looking around, almost stunned by the grandeur of it all.

George quickly tied off and climbed ashore. 'Well, son. You wanna look at your island?'

'Sure.'

He helped me out. I couldn't believe it. The pier was at least 50 metres long. On the left was a huge house nestling in among mature deciduous trees. It was at least twice as big as Gran's house.

'I thought you said this was a rock?'

'It is. For awhile, they called this place Jim's folly.'

'Why?'

'Well, this guy Jim somebody had two shiploads of earth dumped on the rock. He planted the trees. That was over 100 years ago.'

The south end of the island looked to be almost a complete jungle. The trees were huge and dense. In the north stood the house and eastwards, beyond the boathouse, were four small cottages.

'How many people live here?' I asked.

Smiling, George shook his head. 'None at this moment.'

'Then why all the buildings?'

'Who knows. Edgar wanted to turn this place into a retreat. You know, the brass hats come with their girlfriends for a dirty weekend away from their wives. They'll pay good for discreet service.'

'You're kidding.'

'He told me that some of them CEOs would pay up to five G's for a secret and confidential weekend with a broad of his choice.'

'Wow!'

'Yah got the keys to the house, boy?'

I nodded. The lawyer's secretary gave them to me. At the end of the pier was a concrete path that curved round to the left, straight up to the front patio. The house was a peculiar shape. As you stand in front looking at it, it sort of had the appearance of two houses, a small one in front of a huge one. There were seven windows and a door on the front ground level. The bit that stuck forwards, the smaller house, seemed to have no entrance. The main entrance was just to the right of a very grand double-doored thing. There were two matching covered porches, one on either end. The roof, above the second floor, had more gables and ridges than you could shake a stick at.

'Well, are we going in or you gonna stand here catching flies with yah mouth, boy?'

Fumbling with the keys, I eventually found one that fitted. The foyer was big enough to park your car in, with a huge staircase at the end that curved left.

'I'm amazed,' I said in all honesty.

'An' the ghosts don't frighten you none?'

'Ghosts. What ghosts?'

'Seven Fiends and a dozen others who haunt these halls. It's said you can hear them moan some nights.'

'You gotta be kidding me. Are there really any ghosts here?'

'I ain't seen any, but somethin's gotta be killing the people hereabouts. Ifan I were you, I'd sell this museum and scarper with the money. Don't get tempted by none o' them silly stories of gold coins and sunken ships.'

# *Chapter 6*

## *August, Monday*

The mantel clock began striking ten in the evening as Gran and I returned to the Dundas house. This had been the longest, busiest and most exciting day of my entire life. Falling into bed, my body quickly assimilated unconsciousness. My dreams were filled with the thoughts and actions of the day. Gold, pirates, shipwrecks and murder fleeted through the themes of all my nightmares.

Morning came, but to me it felt like the morning after the night before. Mail was the first thing I thought of. Our lawyer was supposedly sending a letter of confirmation. The smell of breakfast wafted up the stairs, speeding my descent.

'Any snail mail, Gran?'

She looked up from her morning meal and, smiling, she shook her head and then handed me some toast. 'Are you still interested in becoming a detective, dear?'

'Oh, sure. Now I can afford it. You should see our island, Gran. Man, it's great.'

'I will, dear.' She got up and collected my breakfast from the grill and then returned to her seat, handing me the plate. 'I've been doing a little investigating of my own.'

'I figured that's why you stayed ashore. Learn anything useful?'

'It's a very funny business,' she said. 'Did you know that everyone except the police believe Uncle Edgar was murdered?'

'Why?' I mumbled through a mouthful of toast.

'The outfitter told me that Edgar's boat didn't use propane or any other form of natural gas, yet it was supposedly propane that killed him.'

'So?'

'So how could propane have exploded if there is none?'

I shrugged my shoulders. 'I don't know. How?'

'Exactly, dear boy. How? The police report states that the gas he was carrying leaked and while he was on autopilot, the cabin filled with escaping gas and then exploded.'

'I thought you said he didn't use gas?'

'That's right, but his boat was carrying five cylinders. Did you know that there's supposed to be buried treasure on Saucer's Island?'

'I heard about it, Gran.'

'I looked into the house he gave that girl.'

'And?'

'And she's a floozy from Australia.'

'I don't see the connection, Gran.'

She exhaled noisily. 'No. I don't see it, either. But I do think we have our first case. I think we should investigate Edgar's death. It would be a fine start and good practice. There are so many incongruences.'

'So what do we do, Gran?'

She rubbed her hands together and pouted for a few seconds. 'The way I see it is first we should find out why he was carrying propane cylinders. Where was he taking them to or fetching them from? Secondly, we should try to fathom a motive and the reason why he was out on Georgian Bay at that time of night.'

'Motive, that's easy.'

'What?'

'Well, Gran. It's the gold, 10 tons of it in American gold dollars. It's hidden somewhere and Edgar must have found it.'

I could see her brain working as she stared at the ceiling. 'You could be right, but who would benefit from the gold?'

'Anybody who could take it. Gold's pure liquid asset.'

'Exactly. Therefore, it could indicate that Edgar had actually found it. Did you hear the silly rhyme when they read the will to us, dear?'

'Yeah, sure, Gran.'

'I don't remember the words. You know, I think it was a clue. It said something about somebody burying gold in a well under a lamp or something.'

'He also said beware of gold-diggers, Gran. So someone else could know the hiding place. George was right. He reckoned I've got gold fever. I've got a great idea, Gran.'

'Alright, dear, what?'

'Well, August Monday I've got a get-together with the gang. There's strength in numbers. We'll all go to Saucer's Island and have a gold-hunting holiday. What d'yah say, Gran?'

'I don't really want to go to this island. You can have my half. I'll get the lawyer to transfer my share to you, dear.'

'Aw! come on, Gran. What's the harm? You'd love the holiday and then, well … well then you can decide whether you want half or not. Okay?'

'You do as you want, young man. I intend to find out what happened to Uncle Edgar and I don't think the answer lies on Saucer's Island.'

That was almost her final word on the matter. However, August Monday was the second of August and only a couple of weeks away. I busied myself planning and readying for the excursion, buying a metal detector, walkie-talkies and everything I could think of that would help in the search for gold. So Uncle Edgar was dead, what could I do about it? Now, 10 tons of gold is another matter.

The lawyer's letter came and my bank balance jumped from minus $2,340 to plus 3.6 million, cash, money, wampum, moolah, filthy lucre. I tell yah, having that amount of readies takes the shine off gold hunting. I was rich, who the hell needs to worry about coins or gold that may or may not exist? Man, I had wealth beyond my wildest dreams.

Come August Monday, I dressed in my old clothes and hurried to be the first to reach John's Tavern. Grabbing a corner table and ordering twenty beers, that I could now afford, I waited for the others to arrive. Even though it was a holiday, there were very few people in the pub. It was also hot and humid weather, somewhere up in the twenties and uncomfortable. In the bar it was cool and not even much smoke, owing to the poor patronage.

Dee was the first to arrive. With a big smile of recognition, he sauntered over. 'You gonna drink all that yah'self, eh?'

'Come on,' I said, 'get yourself on the outside of some.' He looked good, dressed well and was very tanned. 'Man, you're looking great.'

'Got a neat job, man. I'm working the racing circuit. Would you believe it, eh? I work in the pits. Loads of broads. Man, you name it.'

'I'm happy for you, Dee. I haven't done so badly, either.'

'So, what yah doin'? Anything interesting, eh?' he said, sucking at one of the beers.

I shrugged and almost burst. Not yet, I kept telling myself, not yet. 'Heads up, here's Pete.' I waved and he came over.

'It's August Civic Holiday,' he said, punching me on the biceps in his usual and annoying way.

'Shit, Pete, don't do that.'

He threw himself into a chair and grabbed an unoccupied beer. 'God, it's been hot. So, how the hell have you morons been doing in this cruel world?'

'Dee's got a good position,' I said.

A slow smile spread across Pete's face. 'I hear pumping gas is too hard for you. Had your ass kicked, I hear.'

'No, I quit. I had to go collect my multimillion dollar inheritance. Why would I pump gas, when I can buy the entire station, boss and all?'

Pete roared with laughter. 'Well, Nicholas Nickleby, or whatever your bloody name is, who's the old broad you've been screwing to swing such a wonderful deal?'

'Berk,' I said in mock anger. I knew he wouldn't believe me, but that made it all the more fun.

Gavin Henderson made a grand entrance with half-a-dozen shopping bags dangling from his hands. He waddled over to the table and plonked his load on the corner seat. 'Hi, guys,' he gasped, wiping the sweat from his brow with one hand.

'Sit down and drink, you dork. Anybody seen Alic?' I asked.

Henny brushed his ample blond hair back and with a silly grin on his face, he sat down. 'Nice beer, stinking-hot weather, know what I mean?'

We all nodded and settled in for some serious drinking. The waitress came over and dumped a dozen more bottles on the table. Pete took one in each hand. 'Who's paying?'

'Me. I told you. It's my do. I do the forking out.'

'Oh, yeah.' Pete stood up, took a long suck at his bottle and then announced, 'Bill here says he's now a millionaire and wants to prove it.' He laughed and slumped back in his seat.

'It's true,' I said. 'I own an island with a big house. I'd really like it if you guys would come over and we'll have a holiday, like party every day at my expense.'

Pete roared with laughter. 'Asshole,' he shouted. 'We's all got jobs and work for a living. I say stuff your silly island. If there really is one.'

'I can't go,' Henny mumbled. 'I have work and Doreen wouldn't approve of it.'

Dee pulled a face. 'I could go. Where and when, my old fart?'

Pete jumped up again. 'Friends, McMasterians and idiots. We come here not to praise Bill, but to take the piss. Is there an island or is this his usual crap?'

'Shut up and sit down, Pete,' I said, pulling at him.

'Hi, guys,' came a female voice.

Everyone looked round. Alic stood there, dressed in a skirt short enough to be called a belt, with no bra and a thin, clingy white top.

'Hi,' I responded.

She sat. You know, she really was a fairly good-looking chick. Always had a funny short hairdo and far too much make-up. Nonetheless, she had a nice nature, rather friendly.

'Any of this imbibement for me?' she asked.

'Sure, help yourself.'

'Tell me, Bill, what's all this about you owning an island? Tell us everything. Come on, convince me.' Her eyes sparkled with the delight of teasing.

'Well ... Well, you see, my uncle died. He left me an island with a hotel on it and enough money to keep us all happy for a century. It's no shit, it's real.'

She poured her beer into one of the provided steins and then sipped it delicately. After a short indulgence, she said, 'That's it, that's all there is. Come on now, big boy, where, how big? Come on ... give. I'm sure we're all curious to know the nitty-gritty.'

I had to think about it for a moment. This had to be a selling job if I wanted them to help me find the gold.

'Sure. Well, Fiend's Rock or Saucer's island is —'

Pete interrupted me. 'Is that saucer as in drunk or is that saucer as in cup and saucer?'

'It's named after a famous drunk. It was his island. Anyhow, it's about the size of maybe two city blocks, with a forest, four chalets and a big house.'

'Does it have a swimming pool?' Dee asked with anticipation.

I shook my head. 'No, you pillock. It's in the middle of Georgian Bay – you can swim in that. Like, it's an island, surrounded by water.'

'Does it have a beach, this rock of yours?' Alic said, winking cunningly.

'I don't know, probably. I don't remember seeing one.'

She pulled a face. 'I don't know. It's a hell of a long journey to jump into polluted lake water.'

'It's not polluted,' I barked in response. 'It's Lake Huron; clean, fresh water. The biggest freshwater lake in the world.'

'Second,' Henny mumbled.

'Well, it's bloody big, clean and beautiful. You can see the bottom, it's so clean and clear. I tell you what, as there are four cottages, I'll give one each to you for an all-expenses-paid holiday. So how's that sound?'

Alic smiled, batted her long, artificial eyelashes and said, 'Where will you be staying, my lord?'

'In the house, of course.'

'What about refreshment? You know, sustenance. Are there shops on your island?'

'Refreshment? Sustenance? What d'yah mean?'

Alic leaned over to me and whispered. 'Sustenance, dear boy. Food, you rich nitwit; even with money one has to eat. What shall we eat while we reside at this luxurious resort on Bill's Island?'

'Fiend's Island,' I snapped. 'You lot are thick. I'm offering you a free holiday. I'll drive you there and back. I'll feed you and provide shelter. What the hell more do you want from me?'

Pete thumped me painfully on the right biceps. 'I for one don't believe a bloody word of it. It's a load of twaddle, you little shithead. We've had your pranks before.'

'God damn it, Pete, don't hit me like that. It's all true. Uncle Edgar died in a mysterious boat explosion and left me a fortune. My grandmother has half of it, but she said I could have the island. Come on you lot, how about it?'

Pete giggled as the drink started getting to his mentality. 'Well, it only goes to show that you shouldn't sail on mysterious boats.'

'Listen,' I said, standing up to emphasize my point. 'I need work done. I'll pay as well as keep you for a week. How's that sound?'

'I'll come,' Dee said, clinking his tankard on Pete's bottle. 'You supply the beer and I'll follow you to the ends of the earth.'

I sat down with a thump, trying to think how to attract the gang. The ideal situation would be for them to come with me and enjoy the freedom and excitement of my island.

'Alright,' I said. 'The beer's free. I'll pay you a week's salary to be there and you can help me solve two mysteries.'

'Two?' Pete said with a quizzical glance.

'Yes ... two. First, we'll try to find out what happened to Uncle Edgar. Then, we'll see if five university geniuses can solve the mystery of Fiend's gold.'

Somehow, I must have said the magic word. All at once, there was interest.

'Gold, what gold?' Dee said, showing enthusiasm.

'Alright. I suppose I should have told you about the gold first, as that seems to interest you thieving rebels. You see, there's supposed to be a hidden treasure; 10 tons of gold, which was stolen from the Yanks a couple of hundred years ago.'

Henny did some scribbling on a napkin and then, with eyes wide, he announced, 'That's more than 80 million dollars, man.'

I smiled. 'Okay, so if we find it, I'll share it even-steven. How's that sound?'

A funny, wry grin slowly spread across Henny's face as he mentally calculated the price. 'That's 16 million each.'

To keep the momentum going, I added, 'Okay, so I'll pay for your holiday and give you the chance at 16 million dollars. So who's with me?'

'We have to make sure this is a proper expedition,' Pete said with a slight slur to his speech. 'We'll need the right equipment. And … and as yet, I ain't convinced you're on the up-an'-up, Bill, my old mate.'

'You're not shitting us?' Alic said sharply.

'No. I'm on the level. I promise you, you've got nothing to lose. I'll cover any and all expenses. I can afford it. I'll show you the letter from the lawyer if you don't believe me.'

'Alright,' she said and exhaled. 'And in particular, we'll need someone to housekeep. I don't cook.'

'That's an understatement,' Dee said with a giggle.

'Alright, I know someone who'll do house for us. So is it a deal? Are we going to hunt for lost treasure?'

There was a lot of humming and hawing, heads nodding and face pulling.

'I'm working,' Pete said. 'I can't just up sticks and play Jack Hawkins.'

'So 'm I,' Alic added. 'Was there a Jill Hawkins?'

'Alright, alright. You lot are hard to please. What happened to the idea of going into business together? I thought you lot would be happy to come at my expense. Like, gratis.'

'This isn't business,' Pete said. 'It's … it's gambling.'

'Oh yes it is.' I was determined to finish this argument once and for all. 'I'll pay you all one month's wages for a week's work and at you're present rate. If we find the gold, we'll split it. Now, for crying out loud, how's that sound?'

'I'm in,' Pete said. 'Will that be a written contract?'

'Me, too,' Dee said, nodding. 'I'll take your word for it.'

The others agreed with a nodding of heads.

'Great. Now all I have to do is figure out when and how.'

'And what?' Pete added.

I looked at my ever-right calendar watch. 'Today is Monday the second of August. Let's say Saturday the seventh. I'll pick each of you up at your house.'

'What time?' Henny asked softly.

'What time? Shit, when I get there. Dee lives in Westdale, that's the closest. I'll pick you up, say, 6.00 a.m.'

'Six what?' he said, eyes wide.

'You heard – six a.m.'

'I didn't know they had time that early in the morning.'

'Six a.m. and be ready, Dee. Bring your tools; we may need them. All of you be ready early. I'll phone each one just before I come. You got the date clear in your thick craniums?'

Gran was not terribly pleased with my arrangements. 'You should have consulted me before making such plans,' she moaned.

'Oh, come on, Gran. It's our island; it's not gonna cost anything.'

'Wages for four people, food, laundry. Have you any idea how to look after that many individuals in the middle of a lake? You can't pop to the corner store for milk. If you don't have it you go without. I'm not impressed with the arrangement. Not one little bit.'

I put my arm around her and gave her a little hug of encouragement. 'Please, Gran, it'll give us a chance to investigate Uncle Edgar's death. I know you'll love the place. Think of it as a holiday. Please, pretty please.'

She smiled and agreed. 'You'll be the death of me, young man.'

'So you agree?'

'Do any of your friends know me?'

'No, I don't think so. Why?'

'In that case, I'm Mrs Grantham, your housekeeper.'

'Great. I'm gonna rent a minibus to take everyone. Tonight, I'll phone the gang and tell them it's on for Saturday. Okay?'

'Very well, William, though I don't wish to travel with a crowd of students. I'll find my own way.'

'Do you know where the island is?'

'You found it. I'm reasonably certain I can find it, too.'

It was exciting, probably the most exciting thing that had ever happened to me, up till then. We were going to have a super vacation on Fiend's Rock. That night, I called each of the gang and gave them something to do. Dee had to bring tools. I put Pete in charge of the metal detector, compasses and that sort of thing. Alic could only wonder what clothes she was going to bring. But it didn't matter. I got the impression that they were all as excited about the prospects as I was. My heart fair pounded when I thought about it. Oh, the gold didn't matter; it was the idea of having a worry-free holiday. Money being no object. Now that's a first, for me anyway.

# *Chapter 7*

## *Saturday*

Friday, the excitement and anticipation seemed worse than waiting for Santa Clause to arrive on Christmas morning. I couldn't sleep. Man, the time piddled by so slowly you'd think the clock had stopped. Somehow, sleep eventually overtook me, but no sooner was I away than Gran began banging on my door.

'Come along, William. Today's your day. We don't want to miss it, now do we?'

'Okay, Gran.' I staggered out of bed. Opening the curtains allowed the dismal light to trickle into my room. For the first time in ages, the weather decided to be non-cooperative. What a miserable-looking morning. Grey clouds filled the darkened sky and even a little rain spotted the window. Even so, it remained hot and sticky – choking hot – and the humidity was overpowering.

Figuring that I must have covered every contingency, the sojourn began. The van had been loaded and parked waiting in the driveway out front. After a wash and shave, the aroma of breakfast filled the air. Gran knew how to make a fabulous meal anytime of day. Sitting down to a lovely breakfast, I asked her, 'Are you all packed, Gran?'

She smiled and sat daintily before her plate. 'I won't be going with you, William.'

My heart sunk. 'What?'

'As I said before, I'll make my own way, if you don't mind. Do you have a duplicate set of keys for the house?'

'No, just one for each of the doors.'

'I'll take the back door key, then.' She stuck out her hand in anticipation.

'I don't think there is a back door, Gran. But there are side doors.' I pulled the bundle from my pocket and removed two of the keys. 'I'm not sure what door they fit. I know this one is for the big double doors; I'll keep that one for myself.'

She took the two keys and tucked them into her purse. 'Don't worry about me, William. I do know my way around this world. Now come along, dear, your time is running out.'

By the time I'd stopped farting about and picking everyone up, it was almost quarter to nine. After collecting the gang, we headed out. The traffic on the QEW had turned to pure pandemonium and I was even farther away from my destination than at the start of the day.

'There's a coffee shop near Highway 20,' Pete said. 'Why don't you pull off there?'

''Cause we haven't started yet, that's why. We're not stopping until we reach the 400 at least.'

The volume of vehicles on the 403 Highway increased and had come almost to a standstill by the time we reached the 401. Normally, it would take about an hour to reach the 400; for us, it took us just over two and a half hours. At noon, we pulled off the highway into the service station.

'I had no idea how you lot would slow me down,' I said, feeling a might on the grumpy side.

Pete was sitting beside me. He slapped me on the back. 'Come on, you old sod. This is a holiday. We're having fun, aren't we? What's the rush? That bloody island won't float away, will it?'

'I guess not. But I want to get there this year. That's where the fun begins, not here on the stinking highway.'

'Everyone out,' Pete shouted. 'Worryguts here's going to buy us all breakfast.'

'Lunch,' I said and climbed out.

It was still raining. My stomach was complaining of loneliness and my back ached from doing all the driving. They didn't seem to realize it, but having collected each one of them from their home added more than 60 kilometres to my trip.

'So, when will we reach this haven of yours?' Alic asked. She looked great, relaxed and beautiful, wearing shorts and a flimsy pink top.

'Well, I figure at this rate, say about midnight tomorrow.'

My witty estimate wasn't too far out. We pulled into Parry Sound at just gone three in the afternoon. Man, I thought we'd never make it. More than nine hours for a stinking 300 kilometres.

'Wow, man. Look at the trestle,' Dee said with excitement.

A big railway trestle crosses the town, right over the harbour. We passed under the trestle as I drove directly to the pier, where George Smithers had his dockside office. Parking the van right beside his place, we began climbing out for a stretch. My legs felt like yesterday's French fries.

When I walked inside the shack, a girl sitting by a typewriter busily knitting something with pretty pink wool looked up and smiled at me.

'Hi,' I said. 'I'm Bill Reyner.'

'Yes, sir, we've been expecting you all day.'

'You have? Well, is George Smithers around?'

'He's out at the moment, should be back in about fifteen minutes.'

'Thanks,' I said and walked out again. The rain had stopped and the heat was still relentless. It wasn't too bad down on the waterfront, as a light breeze coming in off the water held the temperature down a bit.

Dizzy had spotted the old fire-watchtower on Tower Hill, just across the bay. 'Wow! Let's go there and climb that tower, eh!'

I didn't want to. My priority was to get to the island before nightfall. 'No, we'll stay here and wait for George. We don't need any more delays. That tower isn't going anywhere.'

'Who's George?' Pete said, leaning against the vehicle.

'He's the guy who's gonna take us to Saucer's Island.'

As I spoke these words, George pulled up in his car. He jumped out with a broad smile on his face. 'D'yah walk?' he said and laughed.

'No. That's our van. Where can I park it for a week?'

'It'll do there. Now, I s'pose you lot want a ride to Fiend's Rock?'

'Yes.'

'Boat's over there. You know the one. Load your gear; I'll be with yah in ten minutes.'

'Come on, guys,' I yelled. 'We've gotta load the boat.'

It was more like moving house than going on holiday. You've never seen such junk. We had suitcases, grocery boxes and even paper bags. We had everything stowed aboard and were seated comfortably, when George arrived on the scene. He smiled and jumped in.

'Your bloody lawyer ain't paid fer the last trip yit. I'm gonna bill you double fer this 'un.'

'Okay, George. That's fair by me. Now, can we get going, before it gets dark or this boat sinks from boredom?'

Smithers whistled and the kid came running. In moments, we were adrift. George started the motors and the last leg of our journey began. Somehow I felt relieved, as my work was almost done. Travelling with that lot was like an infant-school outing. You gotta watch them all the time and you never know when one of them wants a pee. Still, they seemed to be enjoying themselves. It was turning into a beautiful day and the scenery was absolutely unsurpassed.

All the extra weight made a difference to the boat. You could hear the motors working much harder than on my first trip. George lit his pipe and headed us out to deep water.

'Think it's wise?' he said. 'Taking all this lot to a haunted house?'

'Haunted house?' Pete said sitting up.

George chuckled. 'So you ain't told 'em, then?'

'I don't believe it,' I said.

Pete moved closer. 'What about this haunted house, then? Come on, give.'

'It's a load of crap,' I said. 'George is just jerking your chain.'

Dee's eyes sparkled as he said, 'I think it would be great. Oh yeah. A haunted house. This is gonna be a great holiday. You're a pal, Bill.'

'There is no haunted house. Shut up and go back to sleep, all of you.'

Talk about a cartload o' monkeys or, in this case, a boatload. It was around four thirty when we circled the island and headed into the small harbour. It looked even more beautiful than the first time. My island, with trees and a house. Skilfully, George pulled up at the pier, jumped out and tied off.

'Well, you bozos,' I shouted. 'Let's get this boat unloaded.'

The gang was suitably impressed. Once ashore, they stood and looked at the magnificence of the whole estate. Dee was the most excited. He dropped his kit and ran into the woods yelling like a wild thing, whooping and screaming. Alic was more demure and saw the opportunity to get what she wanted.

'Are those private cottages or do you own them, too?' she asked.

'Sure, I own everything on the island,' I answered.

'Well, dearest Bill, I would like to have one of my own, instead of a room in the hotel.'

'Alright, sure thing. That's fine. You can each have a cottage. There are four of them and four of you.' I realized what I had said. Damn, that meant I'd be living alone in that humongous house. 'Course, you can stay in the house if you want to,' I quickly added, thanking George.

Grabbing my stuff, I walked off towards the house. Man, the pangs of hunger and thirst were beginning to gnaw at my innards. The thought occurred to me that there'd be no real food till Gran arrived.

You wouldn't believe it, but as I approached the house the exquisite "perfume" of cooked food assailed my nostrils. The front doors were open and music even emanated from the lounge. Carefully, I crept in, half expecting one of the mysterious ghosts to greet me. Gran was already there and cooking in the huge kitchen.

'Took you longer to get here than I expected,' she said.

'Wow, Gran, how did you manage to pass us?'

'It was easy. I came by floatplane from Hamilton waterfront. Mr Smithers bought me a week's supply of groceries and helped me put them in the pantry. He's such a nice gentleman.'

'How did he know you were here?'

'They even have the telephone this far north,' she said sarcastically.

'Alright, Gran, I get the message.'

'Now, introduce me to your friends and don't forget, I'm Mrs Grantham.'

'Sure. When do we eat?'

'In half an hour. I suppose we could get acquainted during the meal. Remember, I am Mrs Grantham, your housekeeper.'

'Sure, Gran. Er, Mrs Grantham.'

Somehow, the island had a calming effect. Now that all the journeying had come to an end, it was time to relax and enjoy having money. I took all my stuff upstairs. At the top of the left-curving steps was a corridor servicing all the upper rooms. The foyer reached up two storeys tall and had a huge crystal chandelier hanging in the centre.

I chose the room round to the right, it being the largest, with its own bathroom and dressing room. The walk-in closet seemed bigger than my room at old lady Nethercot's. My window looked out towards the north and the lake was visible through the trees. Automatically, my hand flicked on the lights – amazingly, they worked. I couldn't think where the hydroelectric power came from.

The closet was filled with clothes and the drawers were full, too. 'Fool,' I said aloud, 'It's all Uncle Edgar's stuff.'

'William. Where are you, William?' It was Gran calling me from the bottom of the stairs.

Quickly, I ran to the banister and answered. 'Here, Gran. What's the problem?'

'Your friends need to get into their rooms. Do you have the keys for the cottages? And it's Mrs Grantham.'

'Oh, sure. Sorry Gr ... Mrs Grantham.'

I pulled my keys out and separated a few from the bunch and then ran down to distribute them. It was Alic who had come to collect the keys.

'I need a clean-up,' she said haughtily. 'Travelling is such dirty work.' She took the keys and left.

Gran glared at me. 'I thought you said this holiday was for the guys?'

'Sorry, Gran. We always think of Alic as one of the guys.'

'She doesn't look like a guy to me. Luncheon will be served on the back patio,' she said and returned to the kitchen.

I really didn't know my way around. The island was big enough to be complicated. I ran after her. 'Gran, where's the patio?'

'Through the dining room and you'll find it on the east side overlooking the lake.'

There was so much to explore and see. There were buildings all around that I hadn't been in. The patio was great; it was beautiful. Would you believe, a large concrete area, with four picnic tables and chairs. There was also a swing seat and several lounge chairs. The patio stood about 3 metres above the water and to the south was a large beach area.

Dee was the first to find me. He was all bubbly and excited. 'Gees, this is a great place, eh! How much of it is yours, Bill?'

'All of it.'

'Man, wow! Did you see the beach, eh?'

'Yeah.'

'Yah know there's graves over there in the forest. I've got the last cottage. It's great, got everything. Man, I love this place. There's a boat in the boathouse, too. Is it yours, eh?'

'Guess so. If it's here then it's mine. How do you know that there's a boat in there?'

'Not locked; the back door's open. I only looked in, eh! Didn't touch nothing.'

'Go tell the others we're eating here in a few minutes.'

As he ran off, Gran came from the house wheeling a trolley piled with the makings of our meal. 'I suppose this is dinner,' she said and began to unload the trolley. 'By the way, William, I don't mind cooking for this gang, but I don't serve.'

'Sure, Gran, no problem. They'll be here in a minute. I figure we'll work everything out.'

After a while, Pete, Henny and Dee came down the path. What a shower – they were dressed in what I can only describe as beach clothes. They looked like American tourists, complete with cameras.

'Hi, guys,' I greeted. 'This is Mrs Grantham, our housekeeper.'

Gran grunted and marched off back into the house. Pete threw himself down on a chair and said, 'What a funny old biddy.'

'You'll treat her with respect,' I demanded.

The food was good and most welcome. The light breeze made everything seem a little cooler. There were no bugs, which surprised me.

'So, how do we go about looking for this gold of yours?' Pete asked, sitting down in front of the food.

'Dunno,' I replied. 'I've never done any treasure hunting before. There's a sort of cryptic clue.'

'Go on then, what's the clue?'

'I can't remember the rhyme, though its basic message is like this: a wall of gold, something, something in hell. Jeremiah Fiend's buried it in a well. Then find a lamp and lift something up, 'cause the gold's out o' sight.'

'That's not a rhyme,' Pete sneered.

'It goes something like that. The clues are obvious. A well, a wall and a lamp.'

'Well I don't understand it,' Dee said, getting stuck into the food.

Henny was always quiet. I could see the effects of deep thought on his face. He was good at puzzles. If anyone could figure it out, he would.

'Where does the water come from?' he asked quietly.

'Water, what water?' I should have realized what he meant. So I'm thick.

'The water we drink. Where does it come from?'

I shrugged. 'No idea. The lake, probably.'

Alic came sauntering down the path. I swear no one in the world could wear shorter shorts than she could.

'Did you know there's a boat in the boathouse?' she asked.

'Yes, we did.' I pointed to a seat. 'Come on and have something to eat. We'll do some exploring after supper.'

'Lunch,' Pete corrected.

'Dinner,' Dee said.

After the meal, Pete and I walked along the shoreline southwards, towards the beach. Dee ran off in search of answers to Henny's questions about power and water, while Henny remained at the table dreaming and thinking. I don't know where Gran was.

After a short walk, I stood and looked down at the beach. It was an expanse of maybe 25 metres in a bay shape. The sandy beach sloped down into the water, with rocks bordering the inland edges. There was a double changing room off the beach closer to the bungalows.

'Look,' Pete said, pointing.

Beyond the chalets in some trees, about 100 metres or so, was a small cemetery. We wandered over to take a look.

'Funny they would bury anyone out here. There's no church,' I commented.

There were seven weather-beaten headstones in a single row. Pete walked to the first and read the inscription. 'Matthew 7:7. I wonder what that means.'

The next said, "Mark 4:37 and, then Luke 1:62".

Pete smiled. 'I get it. Matthew, Mark, Luke and John. Oh, wow. Peter, Paul and James. I think they were the Disciples of Jesus.'

'No, they're biblical quotes. Hence, the 4:37, etcetera. We should get a Bible and see what the quotes are,' I suggested.

'Do you think it's a clue to the gold?'

'Don't know. Look.' I pointed to where a motor-launch was puttering slowly off our beach with some woman waving at us.

'Oh, neat,' Pete said and waved back. 'Man, see the knockers on that.'

'Don't let Gran hear you talk like that,' I said, trying to create some decorum.

'Gran, what d'yah mean, Gran?'

'Mrs Grantham.'

'Oh?'

The girl in the boat slowly circled round to the western side of the island. We ran through the trees to see what she was doing. With obvious skill, she docked her powerboat at my jetty. Pete and I ran to meet her.

'Good day,' she said in a funny accent.

She was fairly tall and slender, real good shape, and wore a tiny little bikini. She had short blond hair and deep blue eyes.

'Hi,' I wheezed softly, sticking my hand out for a shake. 'I'm William Reyner; they call me Bill.'

'I'm Adeline Reyley,' she chuckled. 'Funny, our names are similar.'

'I'm Peter Gordon. You can call me Pete. Where're you from?'

'Oh, an island just up the way.'

'No, I mean your accent. Is it Australian?'

'Nah! I'm not from Oz, I'm from New Zealand.'

# *Chapter 8*

## *The Weathervane*

It had been a long, tiring day, which left me exhausted, but the others were still playful and excited. Pete and the new girl Adeline played on the beach. I think Alic had her nose put out of joint, as she took the huff, so to speak, and went to her cottage to sulk for awhile.

Dee and I had decided to look around nice and quietly and Henny stayed on the patio. After a short walk, we found a noisy little shed west of the house and about 20 metres from the jetty. There were no windows and only one door. One of the keys on my new bundle fitted the lock and we opened it. Inside were three generator sets. Dee was delighted, well of course he would be, they were motors.

One of the larger generators would run while the other was probably on standby. The noise was a lot less obtrusive outside of the building. Dee explained how he thought it all worked. The little generator was either for idle power or to start the big ones. From there, we walked to the boathouse. It was big, with a workshop and an office. A large 50-foot cabin cruiser sat hauled up on the ramp.

Dee examined the system. 'I figure we can launch it any time you want,' he said with enthusiasm.

'Got to figure out how to open the doors first.' The water came right into the building, with a steep ramp up to the boat cradle, which held the boat.

After a few seconds, the back door opened and Alic sauntered in. She was wearing a short skirt and T-shirt; no bra, of course.

'What yah doin'?' she said and smiled.

'Exploring,' I answered nonchalantly and walked towards the office.

Dee and Alic followed. The office was very plain, with one desk, one chair and a large freezer.

'Weird place for a freezer,' Dee commented.

The freezer was locked with a heavy padlock and the compressor motor was running. There were shelves for some kind of storage all over the end wall and one of almost everything had been crammed on them: boat propellers, engine parts, just about everything you could imagine. Adeline and Pete arrived; Adeline was quite breathless as if she had been running. You could see that Alic didn't appreciate the competition. Man, if looks could kill, the boathouse would have been filled with corpses.

Dee sat on the office-type chair and leaned back, looking at Addy. She smiled and said, 'Anyone for badminton or swimming or anything?'

With a broad smile on his face, Dee said, 'How about moonlight skinny-dipping?'

Alic took a step forwards. 'Dee's with me,' she said and lifted up her T-shirt, flashing her boobs to one and all.

Dee straightened immediately and shot over the back of his chair with a crash. Everyone laughed except Addy.

'That's disgusting,' she snapped.

'I think it's great,' Pete said. 'What's in the freezer?'

I shrugged. 'No idea.'

'Let's find out.' Pete took a metal pipe thing from one of the shelves and walked over to the chest.

Addy quickly intercepted him. 'What are you going to do with that, my strong little Tarzan?'

'I'll show yah.' He took a swing at the padlock.

'Stop it, you stupid bastard,' Addy screamed in a sudden fit of anger and thumped him on the back.

'I'm only gonna break the lock.'

'Stop him, Bill. It's your freezer,' she growled.

''S okay. We'll find out why it's locked.'

The only person upset by the incident was Addy. She snatched the iron bar and flung it to the floor. I couldn't imagine why it annoyed her so much. Pete shrugged and turned to look at the boat up on the ramp. 'Can we get that into the water and go for a spin then, eh?'

I shook my head. 'Tomorrow, we'll do it tomorrow. Let's just relax for today. I'm feeling bushed.'

Addy jumped in the air with girlish excitement. Man, that was sure one way to attract attention; everything, and I mean everything, wobbled. Makes a man break out in a sweat. 'Let's have a barbecue down on the beach. Tell ghost stories and stuff,' she announced breathlessly.

'Come on then,' I said and began the procession out of the boathouse.

We dragged a few chairs down and planted them on the sand. Pete and Dee ran off to find wood in order to build a fire. Addy, Alic and Henny stayed on the beach, while I went to tell Gran of the new plans. She seemed pleased by the news and agreed to help prepare the food for the feast.

Gran grabbed my hand and whispered, 'I don't like that new girl; I think she's trouble.'

'She's alright, Gran.' I figured she didn't like the way Addy dressed or the lack of it. Gran's a bit funny n that way.

'Did you notice the ring on her left hand?'

'No, Gran. What about it?'

'Well, it's identical –' She stopped abruptly and raised her voice. 'Yes, the barbecue is a grand idea. I'll get some food ready.'

Turning round, I saw Addy leaning against the kitchen door frame. 'Hi,' I said and smiled at her.

She flinched, her head nodding towards the beach. 'You comin', mate?'

'Sure. Will you be alright, Gran?'

'I'll follow later with the food, dear.'

When we got to the beach, the base for fire was fairly large and Pete was preparing to light it. I sat on one of the chairs and looked at Addy's left hand. She was wearing a large, unmistakable ring. It didn't mean anything to me.

'We need beer,' I proclaimed.

'I'll go ask Mrs Grantham,' Henny said and walked off.

Addy began acting a little strange, spinning like a child with her arms out. I figured she was showing off or something. She sure was a nice-looking girl, with good curves an' all. Alic was a little pissed off, 'cause we looked at Addy instead of her.

At last, Pete got the fire going. 'How we gonna cook on a bonfire?' he asked.

'We don't,' Dee said. 'We'll make a small fire for cooking.'

It was a beautiful evening and as the sun sank down over the trees, the firelight took over. I guess it was kind o' romantic. Man, what a difference money makes. Screw being poor.

'So what about these ghost stories?' I asked.

Gran and Henny came back loaded with goodies. Addy stood staring into the fire. 'Do you know the tale of Jeremiah Fiend?' she said in a low, spooky voice.

'Only that he buried some gold,' I said and then walked over and grabbed a beer, settling back in my chair to listen.

Adeline stood with her back to the fire facing the rest of us. She looked sort of angelic, with a flickering halo and her hair all silvery and bright.

Dee burped inordinately loudly. 'Sorry.'

'Well, tell us the story, Adeline,' I encouraged.

The light was failing and the heat felt oppressive, but Addy was a spectacle worth looking at. She swayed slightly as if about to go into a trance. 'It was over there,' she said, pointing south-west. The *Maria-Bella*, a privateer once owned by a Frenchman. She was only a small boat with a small crew. Her destination was Penetanguishene. Carrying 10 tons of American gold coins, she crept into Georgian Bay in the dead of night. Towards dawn, the breeze turned into a strong wind and being in strange waters, they ran aground on Skully Stones.'

'I thought it was Gordon Rock,' Gran said.

'No, it was Skully Stones, a submerged island; it's still there to this day. Just west of Gordon Rock.'

'Never mind that, get on with the story,' Pete urged.

'The gold was for General Chandler. They were going to raise an army of mercenaries. Nothing but death was offered them. Fiend lived here with his seven sons; one of whom was fishing and saw the floundering ship. Seeing the opportunity to make a profit, the Fiends offered assistance in return for a reward. Foolishly, the captain tried to bribe Jeremiah. Offering the help of his sons, he rowed back here and collected all seven. When they boarded the vessel, kindness was far from their thoughts. The Fiends slaughtered the entire crew and threw the bodies into the lake. One of the Fiend boys died in the fight.

'To Jeremiah's surprise, the hold was full of gold. Feverishly, they ferried the treasure back to Saucer's Island and then burned the American ship. The story goes that Jeremiah used a small skiff and sailed to Parry Sound to make arrangements with an assayer to value the treasure. When he returned, a sight of horror greeted him. All but one of the boys was dead. Matthew had been stabbed many times with an arrow. Mark had been shot through the head earlier. Luke had been brutally hacked to death with an axe. John lay beaten so badly that every bone in his body was broken. Pete lay over there in the boat slip, drowned. And Paul had been hanged from that tree.' She pointed to a large oak near the beach.

'What about the seventh son?' Alic asked softly.

'James was hiding in the boathouse. He was going to take his father by surprise and kill him, but Jeremiah was hard to do away with and by strength and cunning, he overpowered his son and murdered him. Alas, the gold was gone. Jeremiah went insane trying to find it. His ghost can still be seen at full moon wandering these grounds, looking for his gold. Those who the ghost espy are in danger, for Jeremiah still covets the lost treasure and kills to protect it.'

Alic whispered in the flickering darkness. 'That's a terrible story.'

'And untrue,' Gran said.

'I didn't say it was true,' Addy said and giggled. 'It's the one people prefer to believe though.'

'I'm going to bed,' Gran said and stood up.

I stood up and followed her. 'Me, too.'

Lying on my bed, with cool, quiet air conditioning, I could hear the gang playing, screaming and yelling. It's hard to explain how the happiness swept through me. My body could feel a sort of comfortable, satisfied and welcome indulgence in just being rich and lazy. It seemed 1,000 years since I was sweating my rocks off in uni just trying to make something of myself. Being extremely tired, the happy thoughts brought sleep quite quickly, though the dreams were mixed and varied. Some were nightmarish, but nothing to awaken for.

It's funny how you change when you've got money. My coffers didn't need old man Fiend's gold, I was even losing interest in the silly story. Oh man! The smell of breakfast just walked up the stairs and smacked me in the face. A speedy shower gave me the refreshing energy to run down to the kitchen.

'Morning, Gran.'

She was already seated and the table was set for seven. 'Take a seat, William.'

'Smells good. What is it, Gran?'

'There's oats in the tureen and a variety of flakes in the packets. Under the server is a pile of pancakes. We have both maple syrup and honey.'

'Wow! thanks, Gran. Which is mine?'

'Whichever you want. Sit where you please, dear boy.'

I started loading my plate with pancakes and said, 'Do you have a Bible, Gran?'

'It's a waste of time,' she said with that all-knowing grin on her face.

'What, Bibles?'

She smiled even deeper, expressing that "I know everything" grin and said, 'Silly William. The graves are fake.'

'Fake. How could you possibly know that they're fake?'

She sighed. 'When did the Fiend boys die?'

I shrugged. 'Dunno. Maybe in the early 1800s.'

'And when was the rock given its soil and trees?'

'Oh, yeah. I see what you mean. Almost a century after the Fiends died.'

'You don't think, William. You must analyse the data. Compile it in your mind like a steel computer and reason to the end conclusion.'

'So why are the graves there, Gran?'

'Someone thought it would be a nice talking point for people who don't think too deeply. Or perhaps it's a tourist thing; lends ambience to the place.'

'I don't think there is any gold, Gran. I reckon its all just fairy tales.'

She smiled. 'Well I do. In one way, it all makes sense.'

'You do? But, well ... why do you think there's gold?'

Dee turned up. 'Good morning, everybody.'

'Hi,' I said. 'Where's the others?'

'Caw! This lot fer us?'

'Yeah, get stuck in and shut up. Now, Gran, tell me why you think there is gold here.'

'I didn't say here. I'm sure it's real. That foolish story the girl told is rubbish. The gold ship sank in June 1813. The Fiends lived here until 1816. They were all found murdered, but old man Fiend just disappeared.'

'So Addy's story is true, they were all murdered by the old man and then he ups and leaves.'

'No. A group of treasure hunters invaded the rock and they murdered the Fiends.'

'So what about the old man, Gran?'

'He was taken and murdered somewhere else. He would never divulge the whereabouts of his gold after his sons had been murdered. Think about it, William.'

'How do you know all this?'

'The real story is in the local museum for anyone to read.'

Dee's eyes widened. 'So you figure there ain't no gold eh, Mrs G?'

Gran glared at him and said, 'Is the qualification to enter university an empty cranium?'

Dee shrugged and pouted.

'Well, I never said there was no gold. I believe it has been found. Someone has more than likely found it many years ago.'

Now it was my turn to open my eyes wide. 'You what, Gran? What d'yah mean?'

She smiled. 'A wall of gold as deep as hell, old Jeremiah buried it well. Find the lamp where it burned at night, then move the rock the gold's out of sight.' She looked really pleased with herself.

'How did you manage to memorize the clues, Gran?'

'I phoned the lawyer and asked him for it. One has to use one's brain, William.'

Dee looked around. 'I don't see no phone.'

She opened her bag and dipped in, pulling out a mobile phone. 'If you're with the right company it works, even this far out. Mr Smithers said there're repeaters on some of the islands and we do have a house phone in the hall, dear.'

Wow! You just gotta admire the old girl. She never misses a trick. 'So what about the gold that isn't?' I asked.

'The poor poetry tells us that the gold is hidden in an old well near a light. Well, it's obvious the light is a lake beacon – a lighthouse, perhaps. I believe Edgar found it, or the truth about it, and that's why someone killed him. All we have to do is find the killer or the gold and the case will be solved. One automatically indicates the other.'

Addy walked in; she looked marvellous. Man, only she could wear old jeans, a T-shirt and gloves and still look like a million dollars.

'Why are we eating in the kitchen with the help? There's a perfectly good dining room,' she growled in a low tone of voice.

Gran stood up. 'When you pay my wages, you can give the orders, young lady. Until then, the dog will continue to wag its own tail.' With her nose in the air, she walked out.

Addy pulled a silly face and said, 'Silly old cow. Why don't you fire her? Edgar would have.'

'Uncle Edgar. My Uncle Edgar?'

'Yes. I knew him very well. Now, I want you to count these old coins for me.' She dropped a cloth bag on the table.

I opened it. The little bag had maybe a dozen or so foreign coins in it. 'What d'yah mean, you want me to count these coins?'

She sat opposite me. 'Oh, sweetie, I can't see without my contacts. You wouldn't show me up in front of all the others would you?'

'No, I guess not.'

'Please could you count the value of the coins? I have to know the total value,' she said, fluttering her eyelashes.

I mean to say, well, how can you refuse a helpless, beautiful woman? Dragging the coins out, I quickly counted the total value of the numbers. God knows what they were, but it came to 175 whatevers. Politely, I placed them back into the bag and handed it to her. 'It's 175. What yah want them counted for?'

She smiled and in a sort of hoarse whisper, said, 'I'm not wearing my contacts.'

'Oh!' I said as though I understood the meaning. 'So why you wearing gloves?'

She threw her head to one side and said in a sexy voice, 'I have to help Pete do a little work. What are you boys going to do?'

'How about we get that boat in the water, eh?' Dee said excitedly.

'Sure, why not.'

After we'd finished breakfast, Dee and I ventured out into the beautiful, clear and hot day. Man, I felt good; beautiful women, good friends, money … what more could a man ask? We walked out the main entrance across the path and gardens to the boathouse. Halfway there we met Pete, who was carrying a large weathercock.

'What the hell yah gonna do with that?'

'See that cupola at the top of the house?' he said.

I looked up, 'Sure.'

'Well, me an' Addy's gonna put it up there.'

'What for?'

'Well, that's the place where it should be. Edgar didn't get time to fix it. Addy asked me to do it for him.'

'For him?'

'Well he's dead; he can't ask. Are you going to put the mockers on it?'

'No. Go ahead and be careful. That's a long way up.' Dee and I walked into the boathouse, while Addy and Pete went round the other side of the main house. 'So, how do you figure we'll get that boat into the water?'

Dee grinned. 'Bloody marvellous boat, eh?'

'Sure. So how do we do it?'

Dee obviously knew what he was doing. The boat entrance was the same as a regular garage door. With a flick of a switch, the shuttered door began lifting, like a super-modern portcullis. The waterway was clear, as Adeline had parked way up the other end of the pier. Dee flicked another switch and an electric motor sang out. The boat began to gently run back down the ramp into the water.

'Bloody marvellous, eh?'

'Sure.' I don't know how long we had been trying to launch the boat, but eventually there she was sitting in the water and we were ready to board and release the dolly straps. Suddenly, Addy came running from around the house. She ran across the lawn near the powerhouse, screaming like a mad thing.

Somewhat stunned I jumped off the boat onto the dock and began walking to meet her. 'What's wrong?' I called.

The girl was almost insane, screaming and stumbling. She bumped into me, almost knocking me over. 'Oh, God,' she sobbed. 'Come, come quick.' She grabbed my arm and began dragging me to the rear of the main house. She didn't say anything else, just kept screaming and sobbing. Eventually, I saw the problem. Holy mackerel! Pete was lying at the base of the ladder. Dead still … and I do mean dead. The weathercock was embedded in his back and the coins I had counted were all over the grass. I'd never seen so much blood in my life.

# Chapter 9

## *Inquiry*

At the scene of Pete's accident I was no better than Adeline; my panic felt real enough. Now I know why chickens with their heads cut off run in circles. Gran seemed calm, like a veteran soldier – nothing appeared to faze her. 'Everyone in the sitting room,' she barked like a sergeant major.

Like puppies with their tails between their legs, we huddled ourselves into the sitting room. Addy cried, hugging Dee, and Alic clung to me tighter than a second skin. Henny seemed totally unaffected.

'How the hell can you be that calm, Henny?' I shouted unfairly as a deep feeling of panic gripped my heart.

He didn't smile at all. In fact, his expression didn't change. He sort of reminded me of an undertaker.

'I worked in a funeral parlour once. Dead guys won't hurt you,' he said solemnly.

'But it was Pete, for Christ's sake. Pete.'

Henny nodded. 'Sad, but true,' he said in a low voice.

Gran came into the room, she looked thunderous. 'I don't know what happened and I have called the authorities. I think you all should stay here until they arrive. If anyone needs anything I'll be in the kitchen. I would appreciate it if no one went outside.' She turned and marched off.

'Holy shit!' Dee said. 'What we gonna do?'

'I think we should just relax and wait,' I said, trying to show steely determination.

The time passed very slowly. I can't remember the conversations we had, except that it was pointless gabble. I think we were all afraid. It's unreal how you react in cases like that. I had never seen a dead person before. The fact that it was my friend caused much internal confusion of emotions. I needed to talk to someone with understanding. I wanted to find and talk to Gran, but I couldn't leave Alic.

About an hour and fifteen minutes later, we heard the throb of a power launch as the police approached my island. Even though I'd launched my boat and Addy's was still tied up, there was room for the fuzz. Gran went out to the pier to meet them and I heard the voices as she brought them to the front of the house.

Inspector Spadafora of the Ontario Provincial Police detachment, dressed in his full uniform, gun and all, walked into the sitting room. He was an elderly and very stern-looking policeman. His grey hair gave him that headmaster look.

'I'm Inspector Spadafora,' he said in a deep, commanding voice. 'I'll need a statement from each of you. Please stay here.' He walked out of the room and spoke to Gran in a hushed tone.

I began to shake as the shock started seeping from my muscles. Though, maybe it could just have been the relief of knowing officialdom had arrived. It's always a great relief when someone of authority turns up.

The sitting room was the first room on the right of the entrance hall and the kitchen just behind the stairs, sort of in the middle at the back of the house. No windows overlooked the scene of the accident, except maybe some of the upstairs ones and the family room.

A lady cop walked in. 'I'm PC Gibbons,' she said and stood by the hall entrance.

Spadafora and another cop took Gran over to the family room, in the north-west corner of the house. I guess it was as far away from us as they could get on the ground floor. They walked in and closed the great double doors adjoining the kitchen.

'Sit down, Mrs Hubert. We must have a serious talk,' Spadafora said.

Gran sat. She smiled sweetly at the inspector and composed herself. 'How can I help you, sir?'

An officer sat at the games table taking notes, while another stood by the hall door. Spadafora leaned against the fireplace. 'Quite a handsome house,' he said.

Gran nodded in agreement.

'Where were you when this accident occurred, Mrs Hubert?'

'I was next door, in the kitchen.'

'Did you hear or see anything?'

'As a matter of fact, no.'

'The accident happened just outside here, almost next to the kitchen, and you didn't see anything?'

'If you check the windows of the kitchen, you will find they are all of the frosted-glass type. The original owner disliked his kitchen staff staring out of the windows.'

'Did you hear anything?'

'No, well ... that is, I heard that girl screaming. That's why I went out, to see what was happening.'

'Who was first on the scene, Mrs Hubert?'

Gran had to think for a moment. 'I'm not sure. I suppose it could have been me; that is, after the girl ran away.'

'Please explain, ran away?'

'Well, I suppose she saw the accident and ran to the front side of the house, away from the accident area.'

'What did you do?'

'I examined the boy. Poor child, he was quite dead.'

'And you think you are qualified to make that assessment?'

Gran straightened up. 'I was a nursing assistant before I became a librarian. Besides, any fool knows how to take a pulse.' She raised her eyebrows. 'He is dead, isn't he?'

'Yes, Mrs Hubert, he's dead. I think it's a simple accident. I have to ask everyone what they saw. I have to make a complete report. The coroner's court will decide the cause of death. Until then, I would prefer it if you all stay here on this island.'

'Including that girl, Adeline?'

'She lives in Parry Sound.'

'Is that all? May I go now?'

'Yes, would you send someone else in? Why do you call yourself Mrs Grantham?'

Gran stood and smiled. 'Just a little subterfuge. I'm sure it does no harm.'

'True. You do realize that Adeline Reyley knows who you are?'

'Oh! She does? How are you sure of that, inspector?'

'She was that silly-looking redhead with the false breasts in the lawyer's office. The one who got a house.'

Gran smiled. 'I'll send her in. Good morning, inspector.'

She was and still is a funny old girl. You just never know what's going on in her head. Gran walked directly into the sitting room, smiled a spiteful smile at Addy and said, 'It's your turn, little missy. The policeman wants you in the family room. I'm sure you know where that is?'

'Some cook,' Addy smirked and walked away with a shrug of her shoulders.

Spadafora clasped his hands and with his elbows on his chest, he thumbed his nose. 'So, young lady, we meet again,' he growled.

'You've got nothing on me, copper.'

'True. Please, take a seat. I would like your version of what happened this morning.'

'What d'yah mean?'

'Where were you when Mr Gordon had his alleged accident?'

'Gordon? Oh, you mean Pete.' She shrugged. 'Didn't the old bat tell you?'

'I'm asking the questions. Now, in your own words, would you tell me what happened?'

She shrugged again, pulled a grimace and sat down. 'Well … Bill told us to put that thing on the top of the house. I didn't want to; I thought it was foolish and dangerous. God knows why anyone would want it up there anyway. Anyhow, he said there was no breakfast in his house until it was up, sort of a threat. So me and Pete got the ladder and the weathervane and tried to put it up.'

'How did it come to be stuck between Mr Gordon's ribs?'

She raised her shoulders in hopelessness. 'I have no idea. It was too difficult for us. I went to get Bill to help. I couldn't find him, so I went back to Pete and, well … well, he was there, all dead, like.'

'And then what did you do?'

'I don't know. I reckon I must o' screamed and ran round the house and Bill was there, real close, like. Surprisingly close.'

'Where was Mr Spells?'

'Don't know 'im.'

'So where do you think the gold is, Adeline?'

She was shocked by the question, her eyes widened and she sat up straight. 'Gold, what gold?'

Spadafora smiled, it was just his little game. 'Come along, Addy, dear. You and I both know what you're doing here. This is no holiday for you.'

She snorted. 'You can't pin anything on me, copper. Check the fingerprints on the coins. If it comes to that, check the fingerprints on the weathervane. I never touched any of it.'

'Are you suggesting that this was no accident?'

''Course I am. Someone knocked him off, just as they did Edgar. You cops are thick, you wouldn't know shit if you smelled it.'

The inspector stroked his chin thoughtfully. In his own mind he was certain that Edgar had been murdered, but the coroner's court declared a verdict of accidental death. 'And what was the motive?' he asked.

Her eyes flashed with indignation and anger. 'You bloody lot; you're so … So, sodding dim. The gold, huh!'

'You think he found it, then?'

"Course he bloody did.' Her voice sounded strongly Australian.

'Where was Mrs ... er, Grantham, when you found Mr Gordon?'

'I don't know. In the house, I reckon. She is the bloody cook.'

'Alright, Adeline, would you please send in the next witness?'

'Who?'

'Mr Spells.'

'Who?'

'You probably call him Dee.'

'Oh.' She stood up and straightened her blouse in a meticulous manner and then left via the kitchen door. She walked directly into the room where we were. 'Your turn, smart-arse,' she said, indicating Dee with an immaculately polished artificial fingernail.

'I didn't see nothin'.'

'Well the cops want you. Don't keep them waiting, halfwit.'

Dee walked into the family room. I think it was his first time in there. He looked up in surprise, as the room was two stories high. 'Holy mackerel!' he exclaimed. 'Some room, eh?'

'Please sit down, Mr Spells.'

Dee sat and smiled.

'So, why do they call you Dee?'

'Well, my first name is Dizzy.'

'Dizzy Spells; is that your real name?'

Dee laughed. 'My mom thought it was a real neat joke. See, if the quack asked her if she had any dizzy spells, she could honestly tell him yes, she had one.'

Spadafora was not amused; he frowned and shook his head. 'Well, son, what did you see this morning?'

'When?'

'Where were you when Mr Gordon had his accident?'

'Oh, then. Well, I was in the boathouse, with Bill. We was gonna launch that boat of his, eh! She's a beauty.'

'Yes? Then what?'

'Well, that's it.'

'You didn't see anything?'

'No. We got the boat in the water, eh! Then ... well, I think Bill was on the boat releasing the dolly harness. Yeh, that's when Addy started screaming, like. Bill jumped down and went to see what all the fuss was about; you know what I mean, eh?'

'Yes. Did you go?'

'Oh, yeah. Puhhh! You should o' seen it. Well, Pete was there all dead, like. He looked awful; you know what I mean, eh!'

'Yes. Who was there when you arrived on the scene of the accident?'

Dee shrugged his shoulders, put his hand to his mouth and hissed like a boiling kettle. 'Dunno. Mrs G was there, Bill was there, oh yeah, and Addy. She was all upset like.'

'Where was the other young man?'

'Henny? Dunno. In his room I guess.'

'Thank you, Mr Spells. Would you send in Mr Henderson, please?'

'You don't think it was murder do you, eh?'

'Just send in Mr Henderson, please.'

Dizzy walked away as if nothing bothered him. He looked peaceful and happy, yet Pete had just died.

We were all still in the sitting room with the lady cop, when Dee came in and smiled, 'Your turn, Henny. Just down the hall there.'

Henny was always slow, quiet and unflustered. Sort of reminds yah of an undertaker. In his own good time, he rose and walked to the family room. Closing the door behind him, he walked over to Spadafora and said, 'I didn't see anything.'

'Please, take a seat, Mr Henderson. So, how is it you didn't see anything.'

'I was in my room. I was doing a little homework. One has to keep up, you know.'

'Homework? Please explain.'

'Yeah, well, I'm doing this course on business accounting. So's not to waste time, I did a bit this morning. I didn't get to bed until late last night. We had a party on the beach.'

'Did you get drunk?'

Henny laughed. 'There isn't enough beer on the island to make us drunk. Nah. I guess I went to bed about, oh, maybe one-ish. I heard Addy screaming this morning, like. I didn't see anything. Mrs Grantham shooed me away. We all came here, in the house. I've been here ever since.'

'Which cottage is yours?'

'The third one from the house, right next to Pete's.'

'Did you hear Adeline and Pete leave in the morning?'

'Oh, man. I mean, you couldn't miss Addy. She makes more noise than any six other people.'

'Could you hear their conversation?'

'Nah.'

'Did you hear Mr Spells and William in the boathouse?'

'I heard the winch and stuff. Well, I guess it was the winch.'

'Did you hear Adeline come back to the cottage?'

'I heard her screaming.'

'Thank you, Mr Henderson. Would you kindly ask Mr Reyner to step in here?'

'Sure thing.'

So at last it was my turn. Somehow, I wasn't looking forward to it. I don't know why, but it just seemed very ominous. I walked in and Spadafora indicated the chair with a nod. I sat down. He glared at me in silence for several moments.

At length, he said, 'Well, Mr Reyner?' He exhaled and then walked to the window and stood with his hands behind his back looking out over the place where it happened.

'So, what do you want?' I asked.

He didn't turn. 'Beautiful house, lovely island, very nice area,' he said slowly and then turned to face me. 'Pity there always seems to be a lot of dead people littering up the place. Very untidy.'

'What?'

'What do you think happened to Mr Gordon, William?'

I shook my head. 'He died.'

'How?'

I shrugged and began to feel guilty. 'I don't know.'

'Tell me your version of what happened.'

'Well, I was in the boathouse. Me and Dee were trying to get my boat into the water. Dee figured it all out. We got the winch running and moved the boat into the water. That's when I heard Addy screaming. That's all there was to it.'

Spadafora came over and sat on the seat opposite me. 'When did you tell him to put that vane up on the cupola?'

'Tell 'im? I didn't tell 'im. I was against it. They wanted to do it. Thought it would be a lot of fun.'

'They, who are they?'

'I didn't think much to the idea of anyone going on the roof, it's high up there. Addy and Pete were all excited about it. It was their idea. I just wanted to get the boat in the water. Who needs a weathervane?'

'The angel of death resides here on the island, Mr Reyner. Did you know that since the days of the Fiends, every owner had come to a violent end?'

'No. Well, maybe.'

'If I were you, I'd sell this place as quickly as possible. When I heard there was another death here, I felt certain it would be you.'

His words were cold and forced shivers through my whole body. 'You're serious,' I said in a mousy voice.

'I am indeed most serious, Mr Reyner. I do not want any more dead men on my patch. If it were my decision, I would send you all home right now. But the chief constable wants you all to remain here until after the coroner's inquest. Then I want you all to pack your bags and get the hell out of here. Do you understand what I mean?'

'Sure, like this town ain't big enough fer the both o' us,' I said, putting on my best cowboy accent.

'No. I just want you to live a normal and long life.'

'That's just superstition. I don't think the gold really exists.'

He smiled a sort of sardonic smile. 'You may not, but others do. As long as that silly story of treasure persists, people will die. The inquest will be Wednesday. I want you out by Thursday. Now, I can't order you to leave your own property. How do you think I can best protect you and your grandmother?

'Protect … protect us. I don't know. Do you want to stay here with us? There's loads of room.'

He laughed. 'Thursday, I'll call your grandmother on her mobile phone. Alright?'

'I guess so. What'll happen to Pete?'

'We'll take care of him, don't worry about that.'

# *Chapter 10*

# *Monday*

Just before he departed from my island, Mr Spadafora came into the sitting room and addressed us all.

'I'm going back to the mainland to finish these reports. Tomorrow, I want every one of you to come to the detachment and sign your own statements.'

When the inspector had finished with us, all the police left the island and took Pete's body with them. Spadafora walked to the jetty and boarded the police boat. It was real queer, strange like. I mean, we were all still the same and in the same place, but Pete was no more. I wasn't sure whether to cry or scream. Gran returned to the kitchen and began yet another meal. She more than likely needed to do something just to take her mind off the awful thing that had happened on my island.

'Alright,' I said. 'We'll go into town tomorrow. Dee and I will ready the boat. What about you, Addy?'

'I'm going home right now.'

She didn't say goodbye or anything, just walked off into the distance. I looked at the others and shook my head in disgust. 'Well, guys, what now?'

Henny smiled. 'It's a shame about Pete, but ...'

'Shame, shame? It's a hell of a lot more than a shame.' I felt angry, indignant. Somehow, calling Pete's death a shame was sacrilege.

Henny shrugged. 'It is a shame; I'm not pleased about it. But, well ... life goes on, you know. It was an accident.'

'What the hell are we gonna tell his parents?' I snapped. 'Oh! It's a shame, but old Pete's kicked the bucket. Still, never mind, it doesn't matter, you could always have another kid.'

'I didn't mean any disrespect,' Henny said slowly. 'Don't put words in my mouth. We'll finish this holiday in his memory.'

'Now that the bitch has gone,' Alic said, 'I'm going to catch some rays before the sun falls off the edge of the sky. Anyone want to join me?'

We all shook our heads in the negative. 'I don't feel like doing anything,' I said.

'What if she's gonna sunbathe naked, eh?' Dee said with a silly grin on his face.

'Oh come on, Dee,' I moaned. 'You've seen her tits before.'

'Yeah. See yah, Bill.' He quickly followed Alic.

'Well,' I said with a sigh. 'That leaves you and me, Henny. Wanna try out the boat?'

He shrugged. 'I guess so. You drive. Okay?'

'Sure.' I walked to the kitchen door. 'We're gonna get the boat operational, Gran. When's supper?'

'In about half an hour, William. Make sure there are no more accidents.'

'Come on, Henny. Somehow, it just isn't the same without Pete.'

The cradle was still attached. I am not a boat person, but there is a brain in my head, no matter what Gran says. We quickly undid the straps that held the boat to the submerged trailer. Oh, sure, we could tell when the last strap was off, as the boat began to slowly drift away from the dolly cradle.

'Do something,' Henny said slightly more excitedly than usual.

I sat at the controls in the open cockpit. It was almost the same as a car and needed a key. I searched my bundle as the wind pushed us up against the dockside. We hadn't put out the fenders, so the wooden pier began banging against the painted side of the boat.

'I can't find the key, Henny. You jump off and tie us up, before we do some damage.'

Henny jumped ashore and after a few moments, he managed to tie us to the dock. 'Where'd you figure the key is, then?'

I shrugged and joined him ashore. Gran yelled from the front door. 'Supper's ready.'

It had been a terrible day, hot, uncomfortable and nothing had gone right. After supper, I ransacked my room looking for the key and didn't find it. Dee offered to jump the ignition, but that idea did not appeal to me. After an extensive search, I found it in the desk in the office of the boathouse.

Damn it. Man, you should have seen the dents and scratches in the side of the boat. You know – that really pissed me off. 'Get in, you dummies,' I yelled and untied the rope. Didn't make any difference, it still kept bumping against the dock. Impatiently, I put the key in and turned it.

Sure enough, the lights came on. There was one starter button and two switches.

'Flick the first and press the starter,' Dee suggested.

I flicked the switch and pressed the button. The starter whined, but no engine. 'I don't know how to start it,' I said angrily. 'Push us away from the dock and throw out the fenders.'

Henny went up on the front deck to follow my instructions and Dee to the rear. Alic was relaxing on one of the plush seats, almost wearing clothes. An idea came to me – there were two other switches. I flicked the first, threw both starter switches and pressed the button. Instantly, one engine started and the instruments sprang to life. Flicking the other switch I did it again and "varroom" – the second engine started.

We still didn't go anywhere. There was a handle with the letters "F" "N" and "R" and two levers, like an airplane throttle. I pushed the throttles forwards. The engines screamed as froth and water spewed up at the back end, yet we hadn't moved. I snapped the lever to "F". That was a mistake.

The front of the boat leapt up and we left the dock like a 6 ton rocket. Henny fell off the front deck and disappeared into our wake as we sped out into the lake. I throttled back and after a few hair-raising moments got control of the boat. Alic sat back and enjoyed it as if all was normal.

After a while I was able to run the thing properly. It just required practise with the "FNR" lever and the throttles. Eventually, the boat learned to do as it was told and we slowly steered our way back to the dock. Henny was ashore by this time and he didn't look too pleased, but he helped me tie her up with the fenders out this time.

'Well, children,' I said. 'We're ready to make our first run ashore tomorrow.'

'Reckon you can find it?' Dee asked.

'Sure, it's that way.'

It seemed quiet; the air felt thick and sound absorbing. Wasn't quite the same without Pete, even drinking seemed pointless. I didn't sleep well that night, either. You just wouldn't believe the nightmares. My whole body began to sweat as if the air conditioning had quit, yet I felt cold.

Breakfast was welcome and, as usual, fantastic. Dee, Henny and Alic were at the table before me. That had to be a memorable first. As I sat, Alic squinted at me and said, 'Can I have a room in the house, instead of a cottage?'

'Why?'

'I can't sleep out there. Please let me sleep in the house tonight.'

91

'Sure,' I said. 'Who's coming to Parry Sound this morning?'

'I am,' Dee said. 'I wanna see that tower; you know, the one we saw when we first reached the town.'

Henny shrugged. 'Sure.'

'Well, I'm not going to stay here all alone,' Alic snapped.

Gran walked in dressed in her going-out dress and for the first time was carrying a handbag. 'Can you operate the vessel in an orderly fashion, William?'

'Sure, I think so, Gran.'

'Very well. Let's go. I trust we are all going?'

I nodded. 'Sure, Gran. I'll meet you all at the pier in ten minutes.'

I gulped down the rest of my breakfast and ran back to my room. It felt good having something to do. In the closet was Uncle Edgar's captain's hat. I grabbed it and the boat key and set out for the pier.

Gran was already there, standing near the boat. 'You'll have to help me aboard, William. I don't appreciate boats as well you know.'

'Sure, Gran.' I took her hand and eased her weight as she stepped up to the gunwale. 'You can sit inside if you like, Gran.'

'I really don't like boats at all, William. Does this one have a toilet?'

I shrugged. 'Dunno.'

The other three came wandering across the grass. Alic was dressed properly for the first time. I think she was even wearing a bra. She looked nice, sort of sultry and sexy. Holding her hand, I helped her aboard.

'Henny, you release the rope at the front ... and don't fall in the water this time. Dee, you cast off the back one.'

My crew quickly released the ropes and then, with a little trepidation, I turned the key and went through the procedure to start the engines. They sounded good. I pushed the lever into "F" and eased the throttles forwards. Even so, the boat took off rather sharply. Thank goodness no one fell into the water. Opening the throttles to a nice comfortable setting we swung round the island and headed for Rose Island. The instruments were a little confusing. It had three fuel gauges, two heat, two rev counters and several others no one recognized.

'Can I drive?' Dee said all excited.

'Sure,' I pointed to Killbear Park and the way we needed to go. 'Now, take it nice and easy. I'll see how Gran is.'

Gran had entered the cabin. It was very nautical, with bunks and round windows, a nice mahogany table and book shelves. There were several closets.

'What's in there?' I asked.

92

'That one's the toilet. And through there is the little kitchen. Shouldn't there be a passage to the engine room?'

I smiled. 'The engines are under that hatch at the back, Gran. How are you feelin'?'

'I shall be alright, the water's smooth. Who's driving?'

'Dee.' Being worried about my helmsman, I went back to the cockpit. 'Everything okay, Dee?'

'Sure. It's great, eh?'

'Have you driven a boat before?'

'Sure. Not this big, though. It's great, eh?'

'Sure, Dee.' I walked back to the rear deck to see if Alic was alright. 'Hi, Alic, you alright?'

She glared at me for a few seconds. 'Oh, I'm just stupendous. Should we sacrifice someone just to jazz up the ride a bit?'

'I'm as sorry as you are about Pete. I just wanted to make sure you were all right. You don't have to bite my head off.'

'I'm sorry, Bill. I feel lost and lonely. I want to go home and that cop said we have to stay.' She sighed deeply. 'How're we going to get to the police station?'

'The van's at the dock. We'll drive in style.'

Dee was good, probably better than me at driving the boat. Just like a professional, he coasted us into the harbour and, using the thrust reverser, he pulled up to the dock real sweet and gentle. I put the fenders out, but the dock had rubber tyres along it to protect boats.

Henny learns quickly. He jumped ashore and tied us off as if he had been born to it. You'd think he'd spent his life on boats. We moored in what I figured was George Smithers' berth and I walked to the office just to let him know. George was out, but his secretary was sat there doing her fingernails.

'Hi! Is it all right if I park my boat in George's spot for awhile?'

She looked up from doing her manicuring. 'Oh, Mr Reyner, sure.'

'I'll be taking the van. Okay?'

'Sure, Mr Reyner, no problem.'

We all loaded into the van and I sat in the driver's position. 'Where to, Gran?'

'The OPP detachment.'

I nodded thoughtfully. 'Sure, where's that?'

'I don't know. I thought you did.'

'Alright,' I jumped out and ducked back into the shack. 'Excuse me, miss. How would I get to the OPP detachment?'

She pulled a facial contortion as she put her brain into gear. Obviously, maps were a lot more difficult than coloured talons. 'Well, sort of up the hill and left on Seguin. On the corner you'll see a sort of church and the fire station. Straight up Church Street and then, well ... Well, from there it's a bit difficult. Go up to Issabella, turn right and ask again. Okay?'

'Great, sure, thanks.'

It wasn't difficult, I'm from the city. I asked one other person and drove almost straight there. We all piled in and asked for Inspector Spadafora. It was neat and simple. Turns out we weren't there for more than ten minutes. After the signing we again boarded the van.

'So where to, Gran?'

'I would like to do some snooping. Will you come with me, William?'

'Sure. Where do you guys wanna go?'

'I want to look at the tower,' Dee said like an excited child.

'Okay, I'll drive you all over there. Let's say, five o'clock at the boat. Is that okay by everybody?'

They nodded and mumbled. It was easy to find the way to the tower. We dropped the crew and began the return to town. 'Where to now, Gran?'

'The lawyer's office.'

'Right.'

I stopped on the lawyer's driveway. If they didn't like it, I'd buy the place and pull it down. 'I'll wait for you here, Gran. Unless you really need me inside.'

'Very well, William. Do not go away,' she said, emphasizing every word.

It was a stinking-hot day, but the van had air, so I sat twiddling my thumbs trying to plan the rest of my life. The old girl was only gone about fifteen minutes.

'Well, William. It's all very interesting. Drive out to Columbia Street.'

'So where's that, Gran?'

'I'll guide you. Turn right at the courthouse, then left on Seguin.'

'Where are we going?'

'Uncle Edgar gave that girl a house.'

'I know that – I was there in the room when it all happened.'

'No. He gave her a house several months ago, even before the accident.'

'So where are we going, Gran?'

'To take a look at the house.'

'Why not just ask Addy?'

94

She exhaled noisily through her nostrils. 'Let's call it snooping. Why would she need two houses?'

'You've got two – one on the island and one in Dundas. Why shouldn't she have two?'

'Because it's suspicious.'

I shrugged and drove. Gran knew the way. I guess the lawyer had primed her and she has a great memory. Anyhow, we stopped outside this nice modern little bungalow with a well-kept garden. Gran was in the height of her glory as if about to catch someone in the act, so to speak. Feeling like a conspicuous daylight bandit, I followed her round to the back door. It was locked – as one might expect. We peeked in through the windows. The place looked very nice, neat and clean.

'Open the door, William.'

'It's locked,' I insisted.

'Force it, boy.'

'You what, Gran?'

'Goodness me, boy. Break it or something. What do you have those magnificent muscles for?'

I walked over to the patio doors, took a quick look around and then tried to break in. Being no burglary expert, they yielded not one iota for me. The doors were flimsy, but withstood everything I could throw at them.

'You're hopeless, William. Stand aside.' She took a thing that looked like a can opener from her purse and with deft and experienced hands, Gran jemmied the lock.

'Come on, follow me,' she said, pushing the door inwards.

We walked in. Man, you could tell it was a woman's house, what with all the frills and dead, dried-out flowers everywhere. Gran searched the drawers of the sideboard and generally snooped around. After a while, she said. 'I don't understand it, William. I think she must have moved to the new house. But why did she leave everything like this? Come along, let's go.'

We walked out of the back door and just got it shut, when this old geezer next door leaned over the hedge and said, 'She ain't there, missus.'

'No,' Gran said haughtily. 'We surmised that.'

'No, missus, she ain't never there. Used to was, but not no more.'

'How do you mean?'

'Well, there were two of 'em.'

'Two?'

'Ah. I ain't stupid. I knows there's two of 'em.'

'What exactly do you mean, Mr, er ...?'

'Takouski. I've seen 'em – two of 'em.'

You could tell that the old man had tweaked her curiosity. She smiled sweetly. 'I was looking for Adeline Reyley.'

'Oh, I knows who yous looking for. As I said, there's two of 'em.'

Gran walked over to the hedge that separated the two properties. 'How do you know there's two of them, sir?'

'I looks after the garden, see. I likes things that grow. I looks after Miss Reyley's garden, oh, fer maybe a month. Well, on this day I seed her in the backyard. She weren't wearin' too much, neither. So she goes in the house, see. I walks to the front, to see if there's any mail. Then guess what I seed there?'

'Don't know. What did you see?'

'I seed her comin' up the path, fully dressed, hair done and all. I ain't daft. There had to be two of 'em. I asked her how her sister was. She got all hot under the collar. Told me to mind me own business. "Silly old bugger," she says. "How could there be two of us?" But I knows better.'

'Thank you, Mr Takouski. You've been a great help.'

'Ah. Them's both got that silly accent, as if they's from Australia or somewhere. But I knows. I knows.'

'Yes, thank you, Mr Takouski. You have a nice day.'

# Chapter 11

## Tuesday's Gun

We let Dee pilot us all back to the island, as he was better at it than me. The weather felt sweltering, so Gran and I sat in the cabin, with the comfort of air conditioning. Gran seemed smug with her inner thoughts and she had that self-satisfied look on her face. You could tell she'd figured something out just by the way she held herself.

'So what yah thinking, Gran?'

'I'm thinking, William, we have found our murderer. We just don't have any evidence as yet.'

'How d'you figure that, Gran?'

'Your friend Miss Reyley is prime suspect in my view.'

'Addy?'

'Yes. I do believe she is the murderer or murderess.'

I laughed aloud. 'Come on, Gran, that skinny little broad. What would be her reason? You gotta have a motive.'

Gran thought for a few moments. 'If I knew the reason, I would probably have the proof needed to have her arrested. If one were to suppose that Edgar actually did find the gold then his silly little rhyme would make sense. Little Miss Tight Britches wanted it all to herself, ergo, she killed him.'

'But how does that give her the gold and why's she still hanging around our island?'

Gran scratched the back of her neck with the little finger of her left hand, all sort of delicate and feminine. 'I would surmise she didn't get time to remove it – 10 tons of gold is not something one could hide in one's bra, as big as hers is. I would say she needs time. Probably thought Edgar was going to leave the island to her. Then she would have had all the time in the world.'

'Sounds good, Gran, but I don't believe a word of it. Little Addy's too flimsy, too polite.'

'So was Crippen.'

'Nah, not Addy.'

'Hmm. And too large breasted for you to actually see the truth, young man.'

'Oh come off it, Gran.'

'You could be her next target, William. Inspector Spadafora said she knows who I am. That could explain her insulting remarks and indifferent behaviour. We must watch her carefully, very carefully.'

'She's not even on our island, Gran. She left freely.'

'Well, I wouldn't trust her. I'm sure she's trouble. You can see it in her eyes.'

'What about that old geezer's theory of there being two of them?'

She shrugged. 'Don't know. Really doesn't make a whole lot of sense. No one else has seen two of them. Only one was mentioned in the will and both houses belong to the same girl. I think the old man isn't quite as sharp as he thinks he is. Perhaps he is confusing two different occasions.'

I wasn't worried and certainly didn't think Addy could be dangerous. It seemed to me that Uncle Edgar could have accidentally blown himself up trying to do something none of us knew about. The cops thought it was an accident. It was only Gran and Smithers who insisted it was murder.

'So you still think Uncle Edgar was knocked off then, Gran?'

'I most certainly do, but do we have to use such lowly terminology?'

'But the cops don't?'

'Maybe. Did you know that Edgar was allergic to the perfume they put in propane gas?'

'No. I didn't even know they put perfume in propane gas.'

'None of his boats or even the barbecue used propane. Yet, by coincidence, the very boat he was travelling in, and in the middle of the night, blew up. A propane explosion was the cause. Now, why do you suspect he was carrying gas cylinders, when nothing he owns uses it?'

I thought for a few moments. 'Well, surely the cops know this. You found it out. They can't be totally stupid.'

'They do know it. Inspector Spadafora said the coroner returned a verdict of accidental death, because there were no clues to the contrary. As to why he was carrying cylinders of propane, no one knows. Where he was going at that time of night, no one knows. But there was no evidence of any form to suggest foul play. Edgar was the sole occupant of the boat.'

'The question remains, Gran. Who?'

She looked out the window at the passing scenery. 'I'm convinced the gold is the key. If Edgar actually found it, and the rhyme describes it, then he didn't want just anybody to know. Maybe that's a clue in itself.'

'How do you mean, Gran?'

'Beware of gold-diggers. I wonder what he meant by that statement.'

I shrugged.

She held my hand. 'William, time is running out; we only have until the inquest to solve this riddle.'

She was probably right, though it didn't seem important any more. I was falling out of love with the thought of owning an island. What Spadafora had said worried me.

'Gran, did you know that all the owners of Fiend's Rock died, sort of quick, like?'

She opened her bag and removed a small notebook. 'What you said is not entirely true, William. After the Fiends disappeared ...' she thumbed through the notebook and stopped at a page. 'The Fiend's house was destroyed by fire in 1816. There's no history recorded until Robert Jardine bought the place in 1850. He built a shack and was found dead in it, in 1858. In 1861, James MacInnes bought the island. He built the first portion of the existing house. He was the one who put the soil on the island and planted the trees. He was there for thirty-seven years and then died of old age. The house lay empty and deserted for another thirty-odd years, when it was bought by Mr Putnham in the year 1935. He disappeared without trace in 1937 and the island was deserted until just after the war.'

'Where on earth did you get all this info, Gran?'

'I've been busy. Alexander Coldwater purchased the island in 1946 and spent thousands refurbishing the house. He died of a heart attack in 1984. Your Uncle Edgar bought the place in 1987 and moved in a couple of years later. So you see, not every owner died unexpectedly or even under mysterious circumstances.'

'I'm amazed, Gran. So where'd you get all that info?'

'Even Parry Sound has a library, dear boy. Inspector Spadafora was just trying to frighten us. He would like to see this island ...' she stopped and stared at the cabin ceiling. 'Oh dear. I don't suppose ...'

'What, Gran?'

'No ... it's too silly for words.'

'What, Gran?'

'Inspector Spadafora knows the history of the island as well as I do, if not better. He knows the story of the gold. He was at the lawyer's office. He seems to be a central figure in this entire unfolding drama.'

Dee docked the boat like a professional and even Henny did his bit by tossing out the fenders. I helped Gran off the boat and then addressed the others.

'Alright, guys, listen up. Gran says the key to this mystery is the gold. Today, we're gonna find it. I want every nook and cranny, every hole and every hillock looked at. Every rock looked under, there has to be a clue somewhere.'

'I'll get the metal detector,' Dee suggested with a gleeful grin.

'I'll start at the south of the island,' Henny said and walked off in that direction.

'How about you, Alic?'

She shrugged her shoulders and grimaced. 'I'm not in a gold-hunting mood. I think I'll move my things into the house. Which room can I have?'

'Any, except mine or Gran's. Help yourself.'

Dee came running across the lawn with the detector in his arms. 'Where'll we start, eh?'

I shrugged. 'What the heck. It doesn't matter. Get using that metal detector, start sweeping, forty-niners. Let me know if you get a reading.'

We started walking south. I don't think I'd ever been to the south end of the island before. About halfway to the shoreline and just about parallel with the tombs stood a very small shack. It was only about a metre in height.

Dee immediately got a good reading and began excitedly sweeping the area.

'You twit,' I said. 'It's the well. There's bound to be lots of metal around here, piping an' all that.'

'Didn't that rhyme say something about the gold being buried in a well, eh?'

'No. It said the gold was buried well. On the other hand, maybe you've got something. Where else would you bury gold, but in a place where people would expect to get a metal detector reading? Maybe you've got something alright.'

'And look there, eh. See, look.'

I looked in the direction he was pointing. About 100 metres south-east, almost at the very end of the island, was a mound of rocks, with a stone slab path all the way round it.

'So?'

'So, my fellow friend and gold hunter. What do you think it is, eh?'

'A pile of bloody rock, clag-head.'

'Not just any pile of rocks, eh? It's a beacon hill. The place where they lit fires to warn ships. "Find the lamp where it burned at night", get it, eh?'

'It's too sodding simple, Dee. So we've found the lamp and the well. So where's the goodies? I don't see any gold.'

'And move a rock, the gold's in sight.'

He was right on the money as far as the rhyme was concerned. But which rock? Where?

'Go ahead then ... move this rock.'

He pulled a funny face and smiled. 'The bloody place is full of them, eh.'

'Well,' I said with a sigh. 'We could always dig up this end of the island. But it's funny no one else ever found it.'

'Your uncle did, he found it, eh?'

Gran's voice sang out like a yodelling Swiss mountain farmer. 'Dinner's ready, come and get it.'

'Well, that puts the kibosh on gold hunting for the time being, Dee. Let's go get tucked in. It'll be dark soon. Tomorrow, we'll all put some effort into the search and dig up our long-lost treasure.'

'I'm with you, buddy-boy.'

It was a cold supper. Meat slices and bread, with canned soup. Even so, it tasted great. Gran was a genius when it came to throwing a meal together. Alic seemed very quiet and dressed quite soberly, hardly anything showing at all. Dee was excited about the possibility of having found the treasure.

'I'm gonna dig that sucker up tomorrow. Any of you guys gonna help, eh?'

I put my sandwich down and looked at Gran. I figured I should put her in the picture. 'You see, Gran, we think we've sort of maybe found the gold.'

She pulled a funny face. 'I doubt that very much, William.'

'Well, the rhyme says he buried it in the well near a lamp that burns at night.'

'Yes?' She looked expectant and gesticulated a clear question. 'What?'

'Well, there's a big metal detector sounding near the well and that's where the shipping beacon was.'

Gran smiled sweetly. 'Then what's the problem?'

'Well.' I kind of felt stupid. 'Well, the whole area seems to give a reading, the detector goes wild. The rhyme says to lift up a rock and the gold's in sight. But which rock?'

'Out of sight,' Gran corrected.

'Out of sight? That doesn't make any sense.'

'We'll see what happens in the morning. Now, where's that girl, Adeline?'

The mention of that girl sparked Alic's interest. 'That bitch, where?'

'That's what Gran asked.'

'Thank God, I don't like that, that … Well, her. If she comes back, I want to go home immediately,' Alic groaned.

I figured it was time to change the subject. 'Did you find yourself a room in the house, Alic?'

She nodded. 'It's close to yours and has a very large lock on the door.'

'Great.'

'Oh, shit,' she said. 'Listen.'

I listened and there was the unmistakable sound of a powerful boat reversing its engines. 'Sounds like Addy,' I said.

Alic stood up. 'I'm going to my room. Tell her I died or something. The funeral will be next week.'

Moments later, the front door banged and Addy appeared all smiles and dressed in shorts and khaki shirt.

'Hi, gang,' she greeted with a circular wave.

We were, of course, pleased to see her. She's really something to look at.

'Hi,' I said. 'Take a seat. Want something to eat?'

'No thanks, mate. I'd like a tea, though.'

Gran picked up the teapot. 'Sugar and milk?'

'Nah, just cream, please.'

Gran poured the tea and handed it to Addy. 'What are you going to do with your house on Columbia Street?'

'Why? Wanna buy it?'

'No. I wondered why you needed two houses, or maybe there are two of you.'

Addy looked thunderclouds at Gran. 'It's my bloody house. I do what I like. I don't need the home help telling me what to do with it.'

Gran frowned, stood up and slowly walked out of the room, with her head held high. Not a single word was said.

Addy shrugged and sat. 'Now the old bag's gorn, shall we have a rave-up?'

'Pete's dead,' I said in an admonishing tone.

'So he's dead. Being all miserable won't bring him back. Where's that poncy sheila?'

'What?'

'That "be nice to me and I'll show you me tits" girl.'

I smiled and said, 'You mean Alic.'

'So where is she?'

'In her room.'

'Great, let's go out to the beach and have some fun. The water's nice.'

'I think it's a great idea,' Dee said all wide-eyed.

'No. I'm going to bed and tomorrow there's plenty of hard work needed doing. We think we've found the gold.'

'Can I stay the night?' she asked in a slinky sort of voice.

'Sure.'

'I'll bunk down in one of the unused cottages. Don't want to bother the old bat, now do I?'

If she wasn't such a pretty girl, I think I would have gotten annoyed at her remarks about Gran. All the traipsing around with Gran had sort of tired me out, but I walked to the beach to watch the kids for a while. Dee and Addy played volleyball. Man, I hate that game. The walk back to the house gave me a melancholy feeling, sort of sad and lonely. The thought struck me that maybe I'd watch a bit of TV for a little while.

There's never anything on when you want to watch it. Disgusted at the state of the entertainment business, yours truly decided to retire for the night.

'Goodnight, Gran,' I yelled and walked up the stairs.

Hell, it was only around eight or shortly after. Nonetheless, Uncle Edgar's room felt like home. It represented security and homely comfort.

After showering in that lovely, soothing water, I dried myself off and put my PJs on. Then, for something to do, I started looking through the dresser drawers. Funny thing, there were some photos of Addy and a man I can only guess at as being Uncle Edgar. He looked like a Reyner, having that strong jawline and being handsome like me. After a while, a soft "tap-tap" was heard on my door.

'Come in. It's not locked.'

Surprise, surprise, it was Alic. She walked in quietly and closed the door behind her.

'Hi,' I said. 'Come in why don't you?'

Somehow, she looked forlorn, almost frightened. Typically, she was wearing a flimsy nightie that was just long enough to hide everything.

'I'm afraid,' she wheezed almost inaudibly.

'What you afraid of, Alic? Nothing frightens you.'

'There's evil around here, death in disguise. I can't sleep alone. Please let me stay here with you in this room.'

My immediate thought was what would Gran think? Then I figured it was my house, what the hey.

'I don't think that's a good idea, Alic.' I couldn't believe that I actually said it.

She began to whimper. It was hard to tell if it was real or a put-on, but she managed to produce a few tears. Like a sucker, I put my arms around her to console her. Oh man, I'm telling you, she has that feminine magic.

'Alright, I guess you can stay. I'll sleep on the floor.'

In a very sexy way, she pulled herself close to me. Man! Phew! I suddenly felt all hot and shy. I ran away from her and dived into my own bed. Not that it was intentional, more panic or shock. She followed me.

The sun was well into the sky on another hot summer's day when consciousness crept into my brain. For the first time, I slept absolutely dreamless. Didn't need to dream, the real thing was there. My arm was still around Alic and she was completely naked. What a wonderful and beautiful girl. Even after a night's sleep she looked magnificent and felt wonderful. The softness and exquisite smoothness of her flesh was breathtaking.

Gently, I tried to disentangle myself in order not to wake her. She opened her eyes and for a moment, couldn't focus them.

'You won't leave me, will you, Bill?'

I smiled and kissed her gently. 'Stick with me and you'll be alright.' Listening to myself, it sounded a bit like Humphrey Bogart.

Breakfast was over and Gran smiled as I descended the stairs with Alic.

'I'll run you up a little nourishment,' she said. 'Do you want pancakes or cereal?'

'Pancakes would be great, Gran,' I said and Alic just nodded, giving me a little hug at the same time. The sound of frivolity going on outside drifted in through the open window. 'Go with Gran, I'll be back in a moment. I just want to see what those children are up to.'

I can tell you, there was no pleasure in what confronted me. Dee was furiously digging in one of the old graves. He was already down a couple of feet. Addy was playing the fool, making fun of everyone, by giggling and making crude Australian jokes. Henny was the greatest shock. He was playing with a shotgun.

'Where the hell d'you get that gun?' I yelled.

Henny smiled and waved it. 'It's a pump and takes five rounds.'

'Where'd you get it?'

'Addy found it in one of your cottages.'

'Then give it to me. I don't want any more accidents on this island. Besides, I can't stand body parts lying around.'

Addy came over. 'Scaredy-cat,' she teased.

'I'm not scared. I just don't want any accidents. There's been too many on this island already.'

'It's Tuesday's gun,' she said, twirling round like a dizzy child.

'Tuesday's gun. Who's Tuesday?'

'Stupid fool. Monday's gun is filled with fun, Tuesday's gun is free to you and every one. Wednesday's gun is loaded with lead and Thursday's gun will shoot you dead. Friday's gun –'

'Alright, alright, I get the message. And why the hell is he digging in that grave?'

'Gold, oh foolish Bill.' She began to act tauntingly. Somehow, she didn't look as beautiful as I thought she was. She seemed to have an aura of cruelty.

Addy finding that gun really annoyed me. The last thing we needed on the island was a loaded weapon. Acting rather like a stiff-neck, I took the shotgun to the house and presented it to Gran. She was even less pleased than myself. She said she was going to lock it up in her room. I figured the case of Tuesday's gun was all over.

# *Chapter 12*

## *Gold-diggers*

After taking the shotgun off Henny and giving it to Gran for safe keeping, I returned to the gang, where digging was still in progress. 'Alright, alright,' I said, raising my voice. 'Quit the digging already.'

'The gold has to be here,' Dee said excitedly.

'No it bloody doesn't. I told you last night. The gold's in the well or near it.'

Addy stepped into the arena. 'I think Dee's right. The gold has to be in one of the graves.'

'Jesus, Addy. Do you have any idea how big 10 tons of gold is?'

She shrugged he shoulders and shook her head.

Dee threw the spade down and climbed out of the hole. 'Ten tons of gold, well that's about 10,000 kilograms. I think it's about 5,000 kilograms per cubic metre. So we're looking for a couple of cubic metres of gold,' he said, leaning on his spade with a big grin on his face. 'Henny should have a closer estimate.'

'I know its value, not its size,' Henny mumbled softly.

'Well,' I said. 'If it's coins, you can double that estimate for size. If they were scattered 10 centimetres deep, they'd cover an area about of about 20 square metres. You wouldn't find it in that grave, now would you?'

'I still say some of it could be here in a grave,' Dee said. 'Just look at the headstones.' He stood where he could read the stones. 'See, look. Matthew 7:7. Mark 4:37. Luke 1:62.'

'Alright, alright,' I shouted. 'You nitwit, these graves were made 100 years after the gold disappeared. Like, duh?'

'I believe you,' Addy said softly. 'But did it ever occur to you that James MacInnes could have found the gold and he re-hid it somewhere?'

I looked at her and thought for a few seconds. 'No, it didn't.'

'Well, Mr Know-it-all, I have a theory, one I shared with your uncle, before he threw me off this island.'

'He did what?'

'We had a row and he banished me from this island. I wouldn't come across, if you know what I mean. Men!'

'No.'

'He wanted me to sleep with him and I wouldn't. He banished me from the island and then he went and blew himself up. Suicide I shouldn't wonder.'

'Crap. So what's this theory you shared, Addy?'

She sat on the grass facing the row of tombstones. 'You see,' she said. 'I thought about it a lot. Why would anyone go to so much trouble to build monuments to some people who died years before? Well, I solved that mystery.'

I walked over and sat beside her. 'Well, go ahead, enlighten us.'

'Okay. James MacInnes bought the island for the sole purpose of digging up the gold. Well, he found it. Then he had to hide it again, so the gold hunters couldn't figure it out as he had. He created these graves, one of which was blasted out of the solid rock. That's where he put the treasure. The other tombs are for confusion. When the earth was put back, they all looked the same, except for the headstones.'

'Well, if that's true, how did you come to figure it out?'

She sighed and waved a very feminine hand towards the tombstones. 'Edgar figured it out. He tried to keep me in the dark and I'm not stupid.'

'So explain it to us.'

Lying back, she recited from memory. 'The first stone, Matthew 7:7. "Ask and it shall be given you; seek, and ye shall find". Does that ring a bell in your wooden head?'

'I guess so.'

'Second, Mark 4:37. "And there arose a great storm of wind, and the waves beat against the ship, so that it was now full". The third grave is Luke 1:62. "And they made signs to his father how he would leave him".'

'You mean the boys gave their father the finger?'

'Use your brain, Bill. It's code. Then we have John 5:8. "And there are three that bear witness in the earth, the spirit, the water, and the blood, and these three agree in one". Are you getting the message, college boy?'

'Yes, I think so, but your last quote is wrong. I looked it up in Gran's Bible.'

Addy laughed. 'You fool; you fell for it like everyone else. Check your Bible index; there's three books of John. "And the three that bear witness, and these three agree in one". You see, *one*, book one is the only one that agrees.'

'If you say so.' Personally, her explanation left me out in the cold.

'I'll continue. The fifth grave is Peter 3:15. "But sanctify the Lord God in your hearts: and be ready always to give an answer to every man that asketh you a reason of the hope that is in you with meekness and fear". See.'

'Well ... I don't really understand that one.'

'Have patience, William Reyner. The seventh tomb is James 1:11. "For the sun is no sooner risen with a burning heat, but it withereth the grass, and the flower thereof falleth and the grace of the fashion of it perisheth: so also shall the rich man fade away in his ways". Now do you see?'

'No, I bloody don't. And you missed out the sixth brother, Paul 3:21.'

She rolled over and smiled sweetly at me. 'There is no book of Paul in the Christian Bible.'

'So that's where you should be digging, then.'

'No. It has to be John, for he's the only one who bore witness. Paul is there to fool the weak-minded.' Her voice was soft and sort of sing-song. With her peculiar accent, it was almost a mystic experience listening to her.

I had to think, but couldn't quite remember the biblical quotes and neither was the interpretation of them anything like obvious. She must have spent a long time thinking about it.

'How do you know Edgar figured it out?'

She stroked my knee softly. 'Where were you last night?'

'What?'

'Where were you last night, college boy?'

'I was, er ... I was in my room asleep, why?'

'Who with?'

'Well.' I began to feel a little prickly. 'What's it to you?'

'She's a bonehead. No brain, just tits. You would find me much more exciting and interesting, William. I'm a real woman.'

Funny, the thought flashed through my head: beware of gold-diggers. I wondered if that was what Uncle Edgar had meant.

'Alright,' I said in a raised voice and jumped to my feet. 'Stop all the digging. Dee, get the metal detector and test the hole you've made. If it's down there, it should show.'

He looked at me sort of cockeyed. 'I wouldn't have done any digging if I hadn't tested the ground first, Bill.'

'And?'

'And it fairly jumps out at you. There's something down there alright an' I'm gonna dig it out.'

I sighed a deep sigh. Maybe Addy was right and Gran was wrong. 'So what you gonna do with your other house?' I asked, changing the subject.

She glared at me. 'Mind your own bloody business, mate. I don't like people poking around in my affairs.'

I pouted and shrugged. 'Alic doesn't mind.'

'I don't care what that bitch on heat likes or dislikes. I'm my own woman. No one owns me.'

Just the mention of Alic made Addy's spine prickle, like a hedgehog in a defensive mood. I smiled at the thought and wandered away from her in the general direction of the well. I felt sure that the treasure was there and not in the graves. Addy came running after me breathlessly, like a puppy after its mom.

'Why don't we get rid of all these layabouts?' she whispered.

'What do you mean?'

'Just me and you. Send that old bat Gran back to her toadstool and the other idiots home. Just me an' you, what d'yah say, college boy?'

I stopped walking and looked her in the eyes. She was a strange girl, one minute all lovey-dovey and then hellfire and brimstone.

'Nobody can leave until after the inquest on Thursday. And don't call me college boy, okay?' I said and began walking again.

'So let's have some fun. Let me stay with you. I'll make it worth your while. Anything she can do I can do, but I can do it better.'

'Oh! How?'

She smiled a coy smile and moved her head to one side, fluttering her eyelashes. 'Surely you're a big boy. You understand these things.'

I didn't fancy her. At first sight, she looked wild and sexy, but now she frightened me, kind of like a witch. There was that underlying volcano and you just never knew when she was going to spew hot ash and start casting evil spells.

'I can't hurt Alic. Let's play it cool until she leaves on Thursday, how's that sound?'

'You'll be sorry you turned me down, William Reyner,' she growled and ran back to the others.

I felt relieved, at least she didn't explode. Now, the only thing left to do was find the gold. Suddenly, the treasure had taken on a whole new life of its own. Finding the bullion would solve all my problems – everyone's problems. Somewhere out there it was laughing at us, hiding and giggling. How did Edgar find it and what did that silly rhyme really mean?

Standing near the pile of rocks they had christened Beckon Hill, I looked around. If only there was such a thing as a gold diviner. Slowly and deep in randomly confused thought, I walked around the circle of stone slabs. The beacon mound looked like an impregnable natural fortress.

'If only you could talk, you must have seen everything,' I said aloud.

Compared to Beacon Hill, the well head looked a lot newer – a small wood shack on a low pile of rocks. The door was for a midget and none of the rocks could be lifted. I almost jumped out of my skin as Addy grabbed me from behind. She intended it as a friendly gesture, but it almost stopped my heart.

'Shit, Addy, did you have to do that?'

She laughed, as my shock was her amusement. 'You mustn't let your mind wander out here; it's a bit too small to be out on its own. You might meet the ghost of Jeremiah Fiend, who will inhabit your body if you don't watch out.'

'Don't be so daft, Addy.'

She ran around to the front of me and held my head in both of her hands. 'Let's have a seance. See if we can get any information out of Jeremiah himself.'

'Seance?'

'Yah, as in talk to the ghost of Jeremiah Fiend,' she said in a spooky, wailing voice.

The very thought sent shivers down my spine. 'You've gotta be kidding me.'

'It's set then, tonight. We'll set up in the cemetery. Oh, it's going to be fun.'

She spun round like a little girl and skipped off to tell the others. The only thing that really frightened me was the thought that Gran would go ballistic when she found out. This millionaire holiday was turning into a continuous nightmare. Roll on Thursday; maybe I could get shot of this entire place, ghosts and all.

Feeling a bit like a weary soldier returning to battle, I began walking back to the house. The sun was bright and the weather stinking-hot, while the colours were brilliant and the lake sparkled. It looked like a wonderland of beauty – almost paradise. Yet, I myself was beginning to hate it all. Somehow, there seemed to be evil on this island. Alic was right.

I found Gran working in the kitchen, as usual. She always kept herself busy, cleaning, cooking and scurrying here and there.

'Where's Alic?' I asked.

'She's in her room. Says she doesn't want to meet that witch with the boat.'

'God, I hate all this, Gran. It's like a living nightmare. I want to go home. Can we sell this place?'

Gran stopped working and sat leaning against the table opposite me. I sat and looked at her. Obviously, she was about to give me a lecture.

'William, I do not relish this place, either. I have concluded that the problem is a clash of fiery personalities. There is nothing wrong with this island or the trees that inhabit it. I have noticed that even our flowers wilt when Miss Reyley sets foot here.'

'Oh, Gran, you're exaggerating. She's kinda fun.'

'She's the angel of death. I'm certain Edgar died at her hands.'

'I really think you're barking up the wrong tree, Gran. She doesn't like you and I think the feeling is mutual. You know, she's quite honest when you're not there. She admits everything. She says she's got two houses and she used to date Uncle Edgar. She's lived in this house. Why do you suspect her?'

Gran reached across and took my hand. 'I believe Uncle Edgar suspected her. I think she's the gold-digger he warned us about.'

'So you reckon Addy blew up his boat?'

'Yes. I haven't worked out how, though I'm sure she did. And that gun is just another ploy of hers. Heaven only knows what she intends to do with it.'

'Oh, come on, Gran. You don't think she's gonna run amok and gun us all down, do you? Well, do you?'

'A weapon in the hands of a fool,' she said. 'She brought it here to create a little jealousy and boom – more dead people.'

I laughed. 'No, Gran. You've got it entirely wrong. I don't think there is any gold and I'm sure Addy's as innocent as I am. You've just got it in for her.'

Gran eased herself up. 'I want her off this island as soon as possible. I'm not joking, William. Make up some excuse and get her off. Do I make myself clear?'

I thought for a moment. Gran must have it all wrong. She'd obviously got the wrong end of the stick. Addy had to be innocent, but I couldn't go against the old girl's wishes.

'So what'll I tell her?' I said with a sigh of resignation.

Gran smiled. 'I don't know, you think of something. Tell her you've got AIDS or something.'

'Not bloody likely,' I snapped.

'Well, I'll leave it up to you, William. You decide how you'll get rid of her. I don't want any more murders on this island and please mind your language.'

'Murders. Who's been murdered?'

'Please, just do as I say, William.'

Filled with thought, I wandered back to the dig. Dee was still trying to prove Addy's theory. Henny was watching and Addy was shouting words of encouragement.

'Alright, you guys. Heads up. Listen.' Amazingly, they paid heed. Dee stopped digging and all stood looking at me. 'Well. I don't think there's any point digging this hole in my backyard. The gold's not there. Let's throw more effort into the well, so to speak. I figure it has to be there. Addy, Gran said she wants you off this island.'

Addy's eyes sparkled with anger. 'You mean the old bat's going to toss me out?'

'Sorry, Addy. She gets the last say.'

Her attitude suddenly changed. Calmness wiped over her like a magic wand. 'Okay,' she said politely in a sweet voice. You'd think I'd just offered her a candy. 'I want to stay long enough to complete the seance. Will you let me, huh? Please, college boy.'

'Sure. But stop calling me college boy. I don't want you off the island, but Gran's taken a dislike to you. Don't blame me. You seem to go out of your way to upset her.'

'Oh no I don't. It's a pity, William Reyner. I figured we could make beautiful music together. Will you agree to come see me on the mainland before you go back to Hamilton?'

'Dundas. Sure, I'll come see you. So when's this seance of yours?'

She smiled. 'Soon, Billy boy. It'll work better when it's dark. Are you going to tell the old bat?'

'I'll tell Gran you're leaving after the last party. How's that sound?'

She blew a kiss and moved her head in a sexy way. There was something really peculiar about that girl, but I hadn't figured it out yet.

# Chapter 13

## The Séance

Time really began to drag, as I was in a hurry to get Addy off the island. It's obvious that Gran would be pleased and relieved to see the back of this particular girl. Unfortunately, the gang seemed excited about Addy's idea to hold a seance. Well, only those who knew about it. Man, how do you tell people to just clear off, without causing a fight?

In disgust, I walked back to the house with the near jungle heat and humidity gnawing at my every nerve. At least indoors we had comfort and coolness. Alic sat in the sitting room doing nothing in particular. She had been watching me through the window.

'Hi,' I said and walked into the room.

'Oh, Bill. I thought you were going to get rid of that girl.'

'Sure. She's leaving tonight. Don't worry. I don't like her, I never really did and Gran wants her off the island, like ASAP.'

'Come, sit with me, Bill.'

I walked over and eased myself down onto the love seat. She took my hands and looked into my eyes expectantly.

'What is it, Alic? What's wrong?'

'I have to go home, Bill. I'll go mad if I stay here any longer. Please help me. I must get out of here.'

I sighed and said, 'Sweetie, I would take you myself, but the cops say we have to stay. Would you rather stay in a hotel on the mainland?'

Her grip tightened. 'No, I don't want to be alone. Please, you won't leave me, will you?'

'No. I'll be here for you. I tell you what, the minute the inquest's over I'll hire a plane and fly you to Hamilton. How's that sound?'

She smiled weakly. 'Oh God! My nerves are shot. I keep seeing Pete just lying there and all that blood. I'll never get over it, Bill.'

'It was an accident, Alic. Try to put it out of your mind. Relax – take deep breaths. We'll be going to the funeral when the cops give the go-ahead, maybe that'll put an end to it.'

She put her arms around me and hugged me. 'I do need you, Bill. Please don't leave me, not for a second.'

'No problem, Alic. They're going to have a sort of party tonight, after dark, and then Addy's going to leave on her boat, never again to return. Is that okay?'

'You won't let her in this house will you, Bill?'

'No, Gran would eat my shorts with me in them if I did. Believe me – we'll all be happier when she's off this island.'

'I don't want any of that gold, Bill, even if you do find it. I think it's haunted. Fiend guards his treasure from beyond the grave. I can feel him just about everywhere.'

I wanted to laugh but didn't, because it's not nice to laugh at someone as worried and scared as she was. 'Don't worry, Alic. We're all safe in this house. Nothing will harm us here, not even Fiend himself.'

'What if the power should fail?'

'It won't. Even if it does, we've got emergency lighting. If you're really scared, you could lock yourself in your room.'

'I saw Mrs Grantham with a gun. Where'd she get a gun from? What's she going to do with it?'

'I gave it to her – took it off Henny. It's alright, Gran's hidden it. No one's going to use it.'

'Don't leave the house, Bill. Please stay with me, until this thing is all over.'

'Sure, but I have to go to the do tonight. Just to keep everyone in line. Then I'll protect you day and night till we leave here. Is that alright?'

'Do you have to go outside?'

'Well, just tonight for awhile. I'll stay with you till then. As soon as Addy's off the island, I'll be back. Why don't you lock yourself in your room till then? You'll be quite safe there.'

'Are you trying to get rid of me, William Reyner?'

'No, of course not.'

With a sound a little less than a whimper, she stood up and walked out of the room. I figured she was beginning to crack-up. There was this underlying stress that even I could feel. Maybe it was the ghost of old Jeremiah Fiend reaping his revenge. The day dragged on and I didn't want to go out, but didn't want to stay in, either. With a sigh and a shrug, I left. The others were still farting around in the cemetery. Addy was a driver, she could always get people to do things for her. She was so self-confident and a real know-it-all.

'Addy,' I shouted.

**116**

She stopped prodding the others and began slowly walking towards me. 'Do I hear my master calling?'

'I was wondering. Do you really want to do this seance thing? Like, I mean ... well, can't we wait a couple of weeks? Say, till after the inquest anyway.'

Her eyes flashed with glee as she giggled at the thought. 'I know all about the dead. My mother was a medium. She used to rustle up the dead all the time. Necromancy, it's called.'

'Oh shit, Addy. I don't like the idea. We've had enough trouble as it is. Do we have to awaken the dead as well?'

Addy laughed and took my hand. 'Don't be afraid, my old mate. I'll be here to protect you. I've got one of those Ouija boards on the boat.'

'A what?'

'Oh, come on, you can't be that thick. Come, I'll show you.'

We began walking towards her boat.

'So, where we gonna do this thing? The seance, I mean.'

Addy's boat didn't have a cabin as mine did, just a coop over the steerage. The seats down each side were storage bins. She raised the lid on one and removed a thing like a small, flat tea tray. It had letters of the alphabet arranged on it.

'We'll need a glass drinking tumbler. You can get one from the house. Okay, Billy boy?'

'Sure,' I shrugged. 'What's that?' I pointed to a thing in the bin that looked like a small torpedo on a stick.

She snickered. 'You a real sailor, mate?'

'Well, what is it?'

'It's an electric outboard. You clip it on the transom and motor off using battery power.'

'Why would you do that?'

'As I said, you a real sailor? Well, Billy boy, if the engine conks out for any reason, I stick that in the water and poodle away, sort of a spare engine, see? It'll give me about two knots for two hours.'

'Hmm! I don't have one on my boat.'

'No, you dummy, your boat's got two engines. This is my second engine. It's real neat, can hardly hear it working. Good for creeping up on somebody.'

'Well, I'm new to all this marine stuff. What's a transom, anyhow?'

She smiled and did a Pete on me, thumping my biceps painfully with her clenched fist. 'It's the arse end of a boat, mate.'

'So, what are you going to do for supper?' I said. 'Gran doesn't really want you in the house.'

'Stupid old cow. I don't care about her. I've got tuck aboard. I'll eat here. See all you blokes on the beach after dark. How's that sound?'

It was my turn to smile. Talk about "The Unsinkable Molly Brown". Nothing fazes Addy; she could take everything in her stride if she wanted to. Even Pete's death only upset her for a few minutes.

'Alright, I'll help you set up after supper. Please don't antagonize Gran. I have to live with her.'

'Don't worry, Billy boy. We'll have a ball and find that gold if it's the last thing we do. Tonight's the night,' she nudged me hard. 'How's that silly bitch with the flyaway sweater?'

'Alic is sick, she's not well at all. All this excitement is too much for her, poor kid.'

'Poor kid my arse. She's a scheming little bitch. Don't like me, 'cause I'm competition. I'll match my knockers against hers any day. What you say, Bill?' Her funny accent made what she said almost humorous.

'Well, I have to go help Gran. Don't start any fights and keep you shirt on. See yah.'

Walking back to the house, my mind was deep in thought. I could feel a black cloud slowly encircling me, like an evil fog had descended over my life. It felt really weird as if old Jeremiah Fiend was walking in my shadow. As I walked in the main entrance, Gran was coming from the kitchen. She could see the worried expression on my face.

'What's biting you, William?'

'Oh, God, Gran. I don't know. I just can't get things under control. The kids want to hold a seance after dark. Want to contact Jeremiah Fiend's ghost.'

'Not in this house, they don't.'

'No, no, Gran. It's on the beach or in the cemetery. Addy said she'll go home afterwards, but the whole thing worries me.'

She walked over and stood in front of me. 'William. A seance is pure fiction, nothing will come of it. Tell her to leave now and stop dilly-dallying.'

'Well, I'm sort of committed, Gran. She thinks we're going to find the gold by talking to Jeremiah Fiend's ghost.'

Gran laughed – the first laugh of the day. She walked into the sitting room and I followed. 'Come along, William, sit and be comfortable.'

I walked in and sat. 'What, Gran?'

'Ghosts, William, are an aberration of the psyche. Generated by the viewer through external stimulus.'

'What?' She spoke pure gobbledygook.

Gran sighed and sat. 'Living creatures have mental energy and under certain circumstances, they can actually record their thoughts in the form of mental waves, which are stored in solid objects.'

'I don't think we're talking the same language, Gran. I have no idea what you're on about.'

'Now come along, William, you're not that dense. You've heard of telepathy?'

'Yeah.'

'Mental waves passed from one person to another. It's fairly rare, but it's factual and has been proved scientifically.'

'So?'

'The same waves can be recorded in wood, metal or even stone. Sensitive people can detect these recordings, either willingly or unwillingly. Either way, the net result is the supposed creation of a ghost. It is all in the viewer's head, there is nothing physical.'

'Well, I don't see what all this has to do with a seance. All we're gonna do is rustle up a few spooks.'

'You don't listen, William. I just explained to you that there are no ghosts; it is all in the head of the persons involved. The living persons, that is.'

I had to think about what she'd said for a few seconds. 'If there aren't any ghosts, then what do people see?'

'I thought I had explained that. Mental waves, telepathy, recorded information. Am I getting through, William?'

'Well, if there aren't any ghosts, then it won't do any harm, will it?'

She sighed. 'Very well, go ahead. You won't learn anything. Nothing can be learned at a seance that is not already known by one of the participants.'

'How can you be sure, Gran?'

'Mediums are misguided people, dear. They think they are contacting the dead. They're not. All they do is tap into the subconscious of those present. Never in history has information come forth in any seance that was not already known by at least one of those present.'

'Oh. But, what if they tapped into some of this recorded stuff you were on about?'

'I don't wish to argue, William.'

She stood and walked haughtily out of the room. I figured that must be one point for me – a real first. If she was right, and she usually is, then there could be recorded information embedded in something on the island. Something that the seance may spark to life. Excuse the expression.

Supper was a sombre affair and Alic joined us. The poor kid didn't look too good at all. Her usual vibrancy had gone and she looked a little drawn and pensive. I'd already asked everyone not to mention the seance, because there was no point putting her though more agony. The trouble being, it didn't get dark until way gone nine and supper was at seven.

Who could tell what Addy was doing out there all alone? I felt myself becoming mistrustful of everyone and everything. Gran's theory of the cop Spadafora also worried me. I really hadn't thought about it before and then it hit me. He was always there. Whenever anyone died, he was there and seemed to know everything. What the hell, we'd soon all be off the island and safely in Dundas many miles from here.

We'd finished supper by around twenty minutes to eight. The guys were in a hurry to get out and help Addy prepare. Alic was upset, because I wouldn't go to bed.

'It's too bloody early,' I complained. 'As soon as I get rid of you-know-who, I'll come up. Alright?'

'You promised,' she said mournfully.

'I'm keeping my promise. Don't worry, Alic, there's nothing going to happen in this house, Gran wouldn't let it. Would you, Gran?'

With difficulty and a quick peck on the cheek, I managed to get out of the house.

As expected, the others were setting up in the cemetery. They'd carried a picnic table over and were setting up lawn candles in a circle.

'I thought this was to be a beach party?' I said.

Addy was in her twirling mood, childlike and silly. She spun with her arms outstretched. 'No,' she said softly. 'Cemeteries have the best atmosphere. They're full of dead people.'

'Not this one.' I noticed that she never actually did any of the work. She always managed to get some other sucker to do it for her. 'Stop spinning, Addy, you're making me feel dizzy. No disrespect intended, Dee.' The remark struck home and caused much laughter. Even Addy stopped her incessant gyrations. 'Have you had anything to eat, Adeline?' I asked.

She shrugged.

'Well have you or haven't you?'

'No.'

'I'll get you something from the kitchen. You can't go all day without food.'

Talk about children, if I didn't look out for them they'd forget to wash behind their ears. Gran was not in a mood to make any more food, so I took a pot of jam, a loaf of bread, some butter and a knife. Reaching the cemetery with my load, I placed the goods on the table.

'Oh man, that looks good, eh!' Dee said and began attacking the meagre offerings.

'Lay off, Dee. I brought it for Addy; you've eaten.'

Eventually, it got dark, the lawn candles were lit and the four of us were ready to start the seance. We turned a drinking tumbler upside down and placed it on Addy's Ouija board. Then we all sat around the table.

'Have any of you done this before?' Addy asked.

I shook my head and so did Dee, but Henny nodded and smiled. 'Sure, all the kids on our street play this game.'

'It's not a game,' Addy snapped.

I tossed my pennyworth in. 'Gran says seances are a waste of time, 'cause you won't find out anything that one of us doesn't already know.'

'Granny Hubert is an arsehole,' Addy snapped.

I was shocked by her language and the fact she knew Gran's real name. 'How did you know her real name?' I asked.

'Oh, do me a favour, Bill. I was at the lawyer's office when they gave you this place. Do you think I'm thick?'

'I don't remember seeing you there.'

'No, you wouldn't. Mom always said if I wanted not to be recognized, just stuff my bra and no man will look at my face.'

'That was you, the one with the big ... er. Her?'

'Shut up and put your fingers on the glass. Come on, all of you.'

I looked at Addy in the dim, flickering light. I swear I didn't recognize her. Gran had, she'd said as much.

'This is stupid,' I said. 'Nothing's gonna happen.'

'Shut up, Bill,' Addy hissed. Then, with refreshed energy and a wailing voice, she said, 'Is there anyone there.'

I almost laughed. It seemed so comical. She said it again several more times and then suddenly, the glass shot across the board. I can tell you, my hair stood on end. For a few seconds, the tumbler shot around aimlessly. It wasn't me pushing the glass and I don't think it was anyone else.

'What is your name?' Addy wailed.

The glass sort of snapped from letter to letter. Henny read it as the thing stopped. 'O-M-A-H.'

121

'Omah,' I said in puzzlement. 'What sort of name is that?'

'Ask sensible questions,' Addy snapped. Then she said, 'Do you know Jeremiah Fiend, Omah?' The glass shot to the word "yes" and stopped. 'Omah, ask Jeremiah Fiend if there is anything we can do for him.' The glass flew around the board aimlessly for a few seconds and finally stopped on "yes", then nothing. 'Are you still there, Omah?' Addy wailed. Nothing happened. 'Are you there, Omah?' The glass moved to "yes" again. 'Is there anything we can do for him?' It circled and stopped at "yes" once more. 'What can we do for him?' The glass became really violent, flying back and forth, and then jumping to letters: "K-I-L-L-T-H-E-O-N-E-W-H-O-S-E-E-K-S-M-Y-G-O-L-D".

'Kill the one who seeks my gold,' I said.

Suddenly, there was an ear-piercing scream. Leaping to my feet and knocking the glass off the board, I then fell backwards over the chair.
Alic was standing by the tree behind me, her hands to her head. She screamed again and fainted into a heap on the ground.

# Chapter 14

## Henny's Final Curtain

To say the very least, Alic had ruined the mood for a seance. Her scream echoed through the silent night, making everyone's hair stand on end. The poor kid collapsed there and then onto the lawn. I rushed to Alic and picked her up in my arms; she was at the end of her tether. If it wasn't for the seriousness of the situation, there would have been much laughter. The other three dummies were still sitting around the table. Talk about the three proverbial monkeys.

'The seance is over. It's time for you to go home, Addy,' I shouted back at them.

Alic began to moan and whimper. I marched directly to the house carrying the girl and got her into the bright light as soon as possible. As we entered the main doorway, she suddenly became all clingy and excited. Gran met us and you could tell by her expression that she was not very pleased.

'What's going on?' she demanded.

'Alic fainted.'

'What was she doing out there?'

'I don't know, Gran.' I walked into the sitting room and put Alic down on the settee. She clung to me and wouldn't let go.

'I saw him, I saw him,' she sobbed.

'Who? Who did you see, Alic?'

She hugged me tight and began to cry. 'I saw that old man who murdered his sons. He was there watching you. Oh God. It was terrible, Bill. It was simply terrible.'

'There, there, Alic. Don't worry, it's all over now. You're safe in here with us.'

'I'll get her something,' Gran volunteered.

Alic clutched at me again. 'Oh, Bill. He was so ugly. He's the one who's killing the people who live here. He wants to kill you.'

'Don't worry, Alic. Ghosts can't hurt anybody. Oh, here's Gran.'

'Come on, dear,' Gran said. 'Drink this; it'll calm your nerves.'

'I have to go make sure Addy's leaving, Gran. Look after Alic for me.' As I tried to disengage myself, she held on all the tighter. 'Come on, Alic, you'll have to let me go. I've got work to do.'

'Don't go, please don't go.'

With difficulty, I managed to extricate myself from her arms. The tears were streaming down her face in small rivulets. I've never ever seen anyone so distressed as she seemed to be. Gran took over trying to calm her down. I straightened my clothes and shrugged. God, she looked bad and I still had Addy to contend with.

The whole atmosphere on Fiend's Rock had changed. There was an icy silence in the air. The trees had lost that friendly look and were more like monsters hiding something sinister in their shadows. The candles were still burning in the cemetery, but no one appeared to be using their light. I walked through the trees towards the dock. Addy's boat was still there and still tied up.

Suddenly, I heard a crashing sound from the boathouse. Running over to it, I entered through the back door. Addy stood with a stick in her hands, excitedly egging on the other two. Henny and Dee were rolling on the floor engaged in mortal combat.

'What the bloody hell's going on here?' I shouted.

No one answered as they all continued doing their own things.

'Alright, alright. Come on, pack it in.' Being bigger than either of them, I waded in and tried to separate the pair of them. 'Come on, quit, you two assholes.'

'Let them finish,' Addy shouted. There was real fire in her eyes. She looked wild and overexcited, like a cat ready for combat.

Eventually, I managed to part the two idiots. If necessary, I was prepared to take both of them on. Breathing hard and blood nearing the boil, I got one in each hand by the scruff of the neck. 'Now lay off, you guys, or I'll pound the pair of you.'

'He started it,' Dee said.

'Alright, alright. Now back off and cool down. What's it all about?'

'He started it,' Dee said again.

'How?'

'No I didn't. All I said was Addy's too loose for my liking.'

I had to jump in again, as Dee tried to take a swipe at Henny. 'I'll not warn you guys again. Now quit it. I don't give a shit who said what to who. Henny, apologize, now!'

'I'm sorry, Dee.'

Dee shrugged and straightened his shirt. 'I'm going to bed.'

'Alright,' I barked. 'Dee, you sleep in the bungalow. Henny, I want you in the house. Go get your things and move into the house. Now! Addy, I think it's time you went home.'

'I'm going, killjoy.'

'What room will I be in?' Henny asked.

'This end, the front one. Alic's in the one opposite. Are you going, Addy?'

She shrugged and then began walking towards her boat. I couldn't believe how the day had ended. Alic had a fainting fit and the other two were fighting over some stupid remark to the Aussie broad. I stood trembling with anger as Addy fired up her boat engine. In moments, she cast off and the boat roared away into the darkness. I could see her navigational lights disappearing into the distance.

Henny arrived with his bedroll in his arms. 'Yah, gonna show me the way, Bill?'

'Sure ... follow me. I'm really glad Addy's gone. She's nothing but trouble. What the hell were you two fighting about?'

'I don't know. I guess she was egging us on; she's like that, you know.'

I showed him to his room. Gran had already turned in and Alic's door was locked. I went downstairs and locked the doors and then returned to my own room. The shenanigans had tired me right out. The day seemed to have lasted a week. We still had to get through tomorrow and the inquest and then, thank God, home.

Nightmares rolled in one after the other. Tossing and turning in my bed, I spent more time screaming and running in my dreams than the competitors at an athletic meet. God! what a night.

At last, morning came and the sun woke me, the light streaming across my room. Dragging myself out of bed, my body ached from the nocturnal exercise. That lovely water falling on my body from the shower nozzle made be feel much better, though the memory of those dreams was enough to ruin the rest of the day.

Gran wasn't up yet, though Henny's door stood open. I poked my head in and took a quick look around. No Henny. Alic's door was still locked. The thought struck me that it would be best not to wake her. Breakfast seemed a good idea and Gran was not there to get it for me. Before becoming a millionaire, I'd always made my own, if I had any that is. Though, toast always tastes much better when Gran makes it. Even the jam has more flavour when she serves it. After a miserable repast, I wandered out onto the patio. The air seemed sweet, damp and warm. A slight mist hung over the island. You wouldn't think that such a pleasant place could house the evil ghost of Jeremiah Fiend.

It sort of seemed funny that I was the only person awake, but it felt good to be alive. I wandered down to the cemetery to see what damage those idiots had done. What a mess; one grave was completely vandalized and there was a great pile of dirt on another. With a sigh I decided that the two fools who had done it would have to put it right before we went to court the next day.

The mist hung around the trees like gossamer wisps, giving the graves and the house a spooky ambience. Even so, the fresh morning air felt invigorating. A speedboat skimmed over the water almost on the horizon and a couple of seagulls squawked at me as I neared the old Beacon Hill. The thought came to me that the attitudes of last night could have been a little more adult. The kids were only burning off a little steam. Everyone needs to blow off steam every now and again.

I walked towards the boat, which was still moored at the dock. The top and deck were wet from a heavy dew or maybe it was the mist. A smug, proud feeling came over me just looking at that marine monster in the knowledge that she was all mine and not a penny owed. Gloating is not my forte, but what the hey. Turning, I admired the huge house as it, too, was mine and it, too, was debt free. No mortgage and not a single bill that couldn't be covered with a smile.

Stepping into the boat, I spotted something floating near the front end. Quickly making my way to a better vantage point, the object became clear. I couldn't believe it. God! It was awful. Henny lay in the water face down. Without a second thought, I jumped in the cold lake water.

Struggling with the heavy and limp body, I dragged him to the pier and climbed out, pulling him with me. He was dead alright, not an ounce of life anywhere. Oh God! For a moment, panic rushed to my head, making me run to the house. Bursting in the front door, I screamed for Gran.

She came down the stairs grumbling. 'What ails you, boy? Make a little less noise. Some of us are still sleeping.'

'It's Henny, Gran. He's dead. Henny's dead.'

'Oh, my Lord. What happened? When? Where?'

'I don't know. I found him in the slipway by the boat.'

'Don't move him. I'll call the OPP. Oh, my Lord, where's my phone?'

I didn't stop to help find the phone, I just ran back out of the house like a mad thing. When I got back to the boat, Henny was still lying there.

It felt like a cruel joke. It had to be a joke. Surely he'd get up and laugh in a moment, but he didn't.

'What's all the noise?' came Dee's voice from over by the cottages.

I turned and found Dee walking round the boathouse. 'It's Henny; he's dead.'

Dee almost collapsed with the shock. He could see the body at my feet. 'You killed 'im?'

'No, stupid. I found him in the water. Gran's phoning the police right now.'

'Where's Alic?'

'I don't know. In her room, I guess.'

'What about Addy?'

I shrugged. 'Don't ask dumb questions, Dee. I don't know anything.'

'What are we gonna do, Bill? Do yah think it's Jeremiah Fiend's ghost? Has he come back to kill us all?'

'No. Go get Gran. Hurry up.'

I stood looking at Henny lying there, all wet and very dead. I rubbed my head in wonderment, how could this have happened? The sound of a powerboat attracted my attention. Turning round, I saw the police patrol boat throttling down to make a landing at my jetty.

'How could they get here so quick?' I said aloud to myself.

Officer Spadafora stood on the foredeck. He waved as if it were a neighbourly meeting. Like a dummy, I waved back and then walked over to help tie them off. He stepped off the boat all smiles.

'I hear you've had a little trouble again.'

'A little trouble? A little trouble? No, we've had another bloody disaster. How did you get here so quick?'

'Almost here when the call came through. What happened?'

I indicated Henny. 'I found him in the water over there. I dragged him out. He's dead. He's bloody dead.'

'Touch anything else?'

'No.'

'Alright ... let's go into the house. They'll take care of him.' He walked back and whispered something to another cop and then hustled me towards the house. 'How'd it happen?'

I shook my head. 'I don't know. There was a bit of a scuffle last night, but then he went to bed ... I don't know – before midnight, I guess.'

We entered the house as Gran opened the front door for us. 'Good morning, inspector. Would you like a bite of breakfast?' she said, all calm and normal.

'No, no thank you, Mrs G. I'm here on official business. Is that Miss Reyley here on the island?'

I shook my head. 'No, she left just before Henny went to bed last night.'

The OPP officer stroked his thin moustache with one hand and thought for a moment. 'I'm getting tired of collecting dead people from here. Can anyone tell me what happened?'

We all shook our heads and mumbled in the negative.

'I wouldn't mind a cup of coffee, Mrs er-em, Grantham.'

'Oh, you can stop the pretence,' Gran said. 'We all know who I am. I'll make coffee. Would you all come into the kitchen?'

'Where's the other girl, Miss Alicia Morris?' Spadafora asked.

Again I shrugged. 'Alic was locked in her room when I went outside this morning.'

'Would you fetch her, please?'

'I'll go,' Dee said, skipping off towards the stairs.

Spadafora eased his weight down onto one of the kitchen chairs. 'I was hoping to end the lunacy on this island once and for all. I do hope the lot of you are going to be at the court tomorrow. I would like each of you in turn to come to the detachment to make a statement on this affair. So, nobody saw what happened, eh?'

I shook my head. 'I found him in the water this morning. Looks like he maybe fell off the boat again.'

'Again?'

'Well, yeah. He's done it before.'

'In the middle of the night?'

'No, no. The last time was in daylight. Well, I mean, the last time I saw him do it, it was daylight. If you see what I mean?'

'I just happened to be nearby when the call came through. I was looking for Adeline Reyley. She's usually here and at the centre of disturbances.'

I looked the cop straight in the eyes. 'I think it's suspicious that you're always around when someone takes a nosedive. How come you're so quick off the mark?'

He cocked his head sideways. I realized I'd said the wrong thing. He stroked his moustache thoughtfully for a few seconds, with his eyes looking right through me.

'Are you a troublemaker, lad, or just plain stupid?'

'I, er … Well. I mean you, you, er, you should look at it from my point of view.'

'Go on. What's your point of view, Mr Reyner?'

'Who found Uncle Edgar?'

'The coastguard.'

'Oh, I thought you did. Well ... well.' I sat down, trying to think. I guess it was the shock of finding Henny, it must have scattered my brains.

Gran placed some coffee on the table. 'Help yourselves, boys. So what has happened?'

Spadafora smiled. 'Always the calm little housekeeper, eh, Mrs Hubert?'

'Someone has to be in command, officer.'

Dee came flying down the stairs as if the devil were after him. 'I can't get Alic to open her door and guess who I saw through the hall window?'

'I don't know, who?' I said angrily.

'Addy's here.'

'Addy,' I said, jumping up. 'Here?'

'Yeah. Well, her boat's just out in the water. She's watching us, like, with binoculars, I think.'

Spadafora took his communicator and mumbled a few words in it and then he looked at me. 'She wasn't here all night, eh?'

'No. She left before midnight.'

'Well,' the cop said, 'she'll be here in a minute.'

He was right. After only a few minutes, the door opened and Addy walked in as bold as brass.

'G'day all,' she said in her funny accent.

'Hi, Addy,' I wheezed.

'Please sit, young lady.' Spadafora said. 'Where were you last night?'

'I was here.'

'All night?'

'No, I left. I don't know, probably before midnight. The old bag there threw me off the island.'

Gran pulled an expression, but she didn't say anything.

Spadafora continued. 'Did you sleep in your house?'

'Yes. Well, no – not really. I went there grabbed a few things and then slept on the boat.'

'Why?'

'I don't know. I suppose I was upset. I wanted to find the gold. And those blokes had a fight. A right old brawl. You should have seen the wingding.'

'Which house did you visit?' Spadafora asked without blinking.

'What's all this about, cop? Dumb questions. What's happened?'

'Well, miss. Just tell me which house you were at and what time.'

'My new house on Gibson. I suppose it was maybe … oh, I don't know, one or so in the morning, I suppose.'

'Well, someone torched your other house last night.'

She jumped up, eyes wide. Then glared at me. 'You?'

'Me, why would I do that?'

'You and the old bag were sniffing around. I know what goes on. I hate you bastards. It's jealousy. None of you like me, do you?'

'Honest, Addy. We never left the island. I found Henny dead this morning.'

She slowly sank to a chair. For the first time I swear I saw tears. She looked real knocked out. I thought for a second or two she was going to be sick.

'Henny's dead?' she gasped.

'Yes.'

'His final curtain,' Addy said and then began to cry.

# *Chapter 15*

## *The Inquest*

Eventually, Inspector Spadafora and the rest of the cops left my island and took poor old Henny with them. It was no celebration, though. Addy was a burden – she suddenly became another Alic. With two weepy broads who hated the sight of each other, life was becoming unbearable. Alic locked herself in her room and refused to emerge until Addy had gone. Addy wanted to stay, because she had no other friends in North America and she felt terribly sad and lonely.

Gran sighed and conceded that Addy could stay under our care for a while at least. To prevent any further trouble, Gran ordered us all to stay indoors and within each other's sight. If there was to be trouble on our island, then she figured there would be safety in numbers.

'You three stay here,' she growled at me and marched away.

'What the hell are we gonna do?' I asked, looking at Dee.

Addy sniffled. 'I've got clothes upstairs. Can I go dress? I need a change.'

'No. You'll stay here, just as Gran ordered. Only one of us at a time is permitted out of sight. Have patience or take your boat and go.'

'You're very hard, William Reyner. I lost my house last night or had you forgotten.'

'Sure and I lost a good friend. We'll do as Gran says. Alright?'

Everyone nodded in agreement.

Dee put his arm around Addy and said, 'I'll look after you, we'll be alright. What'll you do after the inquest?'

She shrugged. 'Don't know, sell my one remaining house maybe and go home.'

'Where is your home, Addy?' I asked.

'New Zealand. I don't have any parents. They're dead, killed in a diving accident. I wanted to stay here, as I loved Edgar, even though all he thought about was that bloody gold. What are you going to do, Bill?'

'I'll sell this dump and retire to Dundas with Gran. I don't ever want to spend another night on this island or, come to that, any flaming island.'

'What about the gold?' Dee quizzed excitedly.

'Screw the gold. I don't need the money. Let some other moron fight and die over it. I want out.'

We all looked up as Gran led Alic into the lounge. She pointed to a seat and growled orders. 'I don't want any trouble. You girls will have to get along until tomorrow. Any trouble and you'll have me to contend with. Is that clear?'

'What'll we do to pass the time?' I said, standing.

'How about a game or something?' Dee suggested.

Alic sat on the settee by herself and just kept sniffling. Eventually, I walked over to her and sat. Putting my arm around her in an attempt to comfort her, I said, 'Come on, Alic. We'll be going home tomorrow.'

'I saw that evil man, Bill. I saw him. He wants us all dead. Everyone who tried to take his gold is dead.'

'Sure, not to worry, Alic. We'll be off this island tomorrow. First thing, we're going to the courthouse on the mainland. Then we'll have to go to the detachment. After that, I'll take you home, okay?'

She cuddled close. 'This is the worst time of my life. I can't believe what has happened here, Bill. I just can't believe it.'

'Don't worry, it'll be alright.'

'I'll stay with you all night. You won't leave me, will you, Bill?'

'No, I won't leave you, Alic.'

Gran excused herself from the room and went to prepare some food. After a while, she came back and told us all to move into the kitchen, where she could keep an eye on us. Although at first everyone was reluctant to move, eventually we sort of wandered into the kitchen. Gran barked orders like a regimental sergeant major.

'All of you sit at the table. I don't want any of you wandering off. Is that clear?'

'Sure, Gran.'

'Very well,' she said. 'Help yourselves to the food. Adeline, I need to know more about you. Where exactly are you from?'

'Wellington, New Zealand.'

'Why did you come here to this island or even to this country?'

'Edgar invited me.'

'How could Edgar invite you if you were in New Zealand?'

Addy smiled a sort of sickly smile. 'Mail order.'

'Mail order?'

'He was looking for a wife and he put an ad in the *Wellington Journal*.'

Gran thumbed her nose for a moment. 'I don't believe a word of it. Edgar had all the money in the world. Why on earth would he advertise for a wife and particularly in New Zealand? Think of another excuse, young lady.'

Addy snickered. 'You silly old bat, what do you know? I answered his letter. He put an ad in the *Gazette*. I answered it. He wanted a house-servant. I figured he was looking for a wife. An' I like me comforts.'

'I thought it was *The Times*.'

Addy's eyes flashed with anger. 'You'll have to get up early in the morning to catch me out like that, missus. *Journal* is the local name for the daily paper and *Gazette* is the advertising section. We don't have a *Times*. So why the hell are you picking on me? Have a go at that tit-flasher there. She's far too quiet to be real.'

'I'm sorry,' Gran said. 'You see, I don't trust anyone except, perhaps, William. There's too many strange goings-on around here. There is the stupid story of gold and ghosts and we've had two people die on this island in less than a week. And what about your house? Why would anyone burn it down?'

Addy flashed pure hatred. 'Stupid old cow. How the hell would I know? I don't even know why you were there. What did you expect to find? Another body, maybe.'

'Well, I am sorry about that. I was trying to get some background information on you. Where you came from, how and why you came here.'

'Well, now you know. Edgar wanted to marry me. I would have, too, except he died in an accident and left you the island. It should have been mine. All this should have been mine by rights.'

'Well,' Gran said with a sly smile, 'you can seduce the next owner. William and I are going to get rid of this place as soon as is humanly possible. There's no point getting your claws stuck into William, he won't own this place in a few days.'

Addy shrugged and began eating her sandwich as if nothing had been said. I was left cold, staggered at what had been said. There again, no one had told me that I was selling the island. Still, if Gran said that's the way it is, then that's the way it is. It sure hadn't been a fun holiday. Funny though, it seemed like we'd lived on the island for years – forever, even.

I'd never been to court before, for any reason. The inquest turned out to be a complete waste of time. They hashed over everything that everybody already knew. It dragged on for hours and hours. The magistrate was thirty minutes late to start with and the only person he really listened to was Inspector Spadafora. Everybody else's evidence was merely a mechanical portrayal of what had happened earlier.

An hour was put aside for lunch and we all went downtown and found a restaurant for a midday meal. Addy seemed subdued, Alic seemed withdrawn and Dee was his usual excited self. He wanted to look at, touch, taste and poke his fingers into everything. Gran was quiet and regal, her eyes keeping a close watch on all of us. You could almost see her thinking. Addy invited us all back to her new house on Gibson Street for a drink. Gran declined for us all, without making any excuses.

The last half of the inquest went more or less the same as the first half. It too was a total waste of time, just like the first half. Boring questions and even more boring answers. The thing that really pissed me off was at the very end, the magistrate gave a lecture that went on for best part of twenty-five minutes.

To sum it up, he had decided to reserve his decision until the following day. I mean, what an anticlimax. After a full and mind-numbing day of hogwash, nothing happened, nothing, until tomorrow, that is.

Spadafora came over to us with his face all smiles. 'I want you off the island ASAP,' he said with an ear-to-ear grin. 'Report to the detachment, give your statements and then get the hell off my turf.'

'Are you kicking us out of the county, inspector?' I said jokingly.

'Yes. If I have any trouble from any of you, you'll be examining the inner walls of our nice rustic jail.'

'What about Addy?' I asked.

He looked her directly in the eyes. 'You, young lady. I have feelers out on you. I don't like you or believe you. I'll dig until I nail you. Illegal immigrant, anything. Whatever it is I'll find it and then I'll nail your hide to the wall.'

As he walked away, Addy pulled a face. 'Stupid old bastard,' she growled. 'He won't find anything on me. I'm squeaky clean.'

'Gran,' I said, changing the subject. 'What'll we do now?'

'I suppose we should get this thing over at the OPP detachment. Why don't you drive us all over there right now?'

'Then what, Gran?'

'Home,' she said, her eyes flashing. 'I think it's time we left this place and pretend it doesn't exist. I'll contact the lawyers and let them get rid of it for us.'

'So what's the story for now, Gran?'

'First the detachment, statements and all. Then I want to do a little more snooping. We'll have to go back to Fiend's Rock to collect our things.' She looked at her watch. 'I think it's a little too late to go home today. We'll leave first thing in the morning.'

'I want to go now,' Alic moaned.

'Well, if you can think of a way of doing it, dear, you go. I won't stop you,' Gran said. 'But I need William here for the time being.'

'I have to get my things from the island,' Alic said and suddenly jumped at me and hugged me. 'Promise we'll leave first thing in the morning.'

'Sure thing.'

For some reason or other the cops at the detachment were not as friendly as they had been the first time. It was almost as if they were reluctantly doing us a favour or something. It seemed to take forever to get the statements out of the way. They were almost rude to Addy, as if they wanted to bait her.

Alic stuck to me like glue and tried to keep Addy on the opposite side of me. After the signing fiasco, Addy left to examine her burned-out house. The rest of us went downtown for a meal. After eating at the dockside restaurant Gran told us to go back to Fiend's Rock; she would find her own way back to the island.

Dee drove the boat, while Alic stayed with me in the cabin. The scenery was still beautiful and the ride exhilarating, but my heart wasn't in it. A dark shadow hung over the world, like the angel of death just waiting for his next victim.

'I want to leave first thing in the morning, Bill. Please,' Alic reiterated.

'Sure thing. I'll phone for a plane. Would you like to leave tonight, maybe?'

'Yes, that would be great.'

'I'll phone the tour company. We could have you back in Hamilton in a couple of hours. How's that sound?'

She gave me a hug. 'Oh, thank you. My nerves are shattered, I'm terrified. You know, I did see that terrible man, really I did.'

'What man?'

'Jeremiah Fiend, at the seance. Even a locked door won't keep him out of a room. Please don't leave me alone tonight, not for a moment.'

'No sweat. I'll phone for a plane as soon as we land. You stay close to me. It'll be alright, I promise you.'

She was right in some ways. As Dee pulled our boat into the small harbour the island looked sinister. It appeared as if there was some terrible phantom just waiting for us to return. Even at twenty-five degrees C there was a chill in the air.

Dee was good and managed to tie us off all by himself. He jumped back on board and shut down the engines. The silence felt choking; even the birds didn't have anything to sing about. The house looked dark and uninviting. The trees were motionless, like deathly still sentinels, and even the water lay calm. Funny, although it was a long way away, the dig in the cemetery was the first thing you noticed.

'And then there were three,' Dee said in a deliberately spooky voice.

'Shut up, Dee. Come on, let's get into the house and get the lights on. I've got a phone call to make.'

I half expected the lights to fail. It was just one of those days. However, the lights did work and they gave some cheer. Guess what? Right, the phone was dead. Dead as a dodo. I didn't know how to break the news to Alic. God! it could send her right over the edge. No sweat, Gran had a mobile phone. I'd just make an excuse and wait for Gran.

At least Addy wasn't there – that alone was the only comforting thought. I put the kettle on for a coffee. 'You better collect your things together, Alic. We'll be leaving as soon as I can get you a plane.'

She smiled weakly. 'I would rather you come and help me.'

'Oh, come on, Alic. I'll make the arrangements. You go get ready. It's just a couple of hours to Hamilton.'

'What about the ghost of Jeremiah Fiend?'

'He doesn't come in the house. You go get ready. Dee and I'll stand guard here.'

Reluctantly, she wandered out of the room. Dee looked at me and pulled a stupid expression. 'You don't really believe in that crap about Jeremiah Fiend, do you, Bill?'

'No.'

'So what's this about a plane?'

'I'm sending Alic home by plane.'

'Why?'

'She's had it. Her nerves are shot. I want to get her out of here, before she has a complete breakdown. I'll use Gran's mobile to call.'

'Why not use the house phone?'

I shrugged, pretending it wasn't important. 'It's not working. Gran's got a mobile, that'll do.' The kettle began whistling. 'Yah want tea or coffee?'

'Coffee, I guess. Beer would be better.'

'Not till we get home.'

'What about the gold. You gonna keep it all for yourself?'

'I don't think there is any gold, Dee. It's mystic crap, spread by Addy. There isn't any.'

'What a rip. I expected to be rich ... what a rip.'

It seemed hours before we heard the sound of big engines doing a reversing bit out at the pier. 'It's Gran,' I said and ran out of the door.

Oh, crap, it was Addy. She parked her boat with obvious expertise and tied it up. She was dressed in jeans, a denim shirt and silly-looking gardening gloves.

'Hi,' I said weakly as she walked towards me.

'G'day, mate. Where's the old bat?'

'Gran's not an old bat. She's on the mainland checking something.'

'And that other flashy bitch?'

'Alic's in her room. She's going home as soon as I can get a plane for her.'

'So ... when's that?'

'The phone's out. I can't call anybody.'

'You got a boat, don't you?'

I looked at her and she was serious. 'I have a boat, but what the hell's that got to do with anything.'

'Bloody hell, mate. Does the word radio mean anything to you?'

'Oh, yeah, I guess so. But who will I call?'

'Come on, dummy.' She turned and marched towards my boat. I followed her.

Though Gran had a real dislike for Addy, I found her helpful and willing. To me, she seemed honest. She walked into the cabin, opened a cupboard and flicked a few switches. 'This is papa, sierra, nine'a, nine'a, five. Calling ship to shore.'

'Go ahead, papa sierra nine, nine, five,' came an answer almost immediately.

'Hi, Ken, this is Addy, can you patch me ship to shore. I wanna talk to Buz; need one of his planes.'

The radio began making noises like a telephone and then a voice said, 'Hargrieves Flight Tours. This is Buz, can I help you?'

'Sure, this is Addy. I'm at Fiend's Rock. We need a plane to go to Hamilton. The boss here can afford it, he's loaded.'

'Sorry, Addy, one plane's out of business and the other two are booked; one's way up north.'

'So when can we have one?' she asked.
'Sorry, girl, but tomorrow afternoon at the earliest.'
'Roger, over and out.'

# Chapter 16

## Nowhere to Hide

There was no way of getting Alic off the island. What a panic; I felt like screaming and running wild. We were stuck on that bloody island, with no Gran and God knows what dangers. I put my hands to my temples, needing to think clearly. Addy was back on my island and she seemed quite pleased that there was no transport available. She had that sickly grin – it just had to mean trouble.

'We'll be leaving Fiend's Rock first thing in the morning,' I said as an opener.

She tossed her head to one side and smiled. 'I can't see why. Just get rid of little Miss Titties and we'll have a ball. You and me, Billy boy, you and me.'

'You don't like her, do you?'

'No. I don't like women who try to manipulate men by exposing themselves. I think that's as low as prostitution. Don't you?'

I shrugged and said. 'Gees ... I don't know. I never thought of it. Anyway, I promised I'd get her home tomorrow.'

Addy leaned against the side of the boat and stared blankly into the water. 'I tell you what, mate. Let's take her to the mainland right now. Buy her a taxi; you can afford it. Get the bitch out of our hair tonight. What d'you say?'

'Good idea. Great idea. I'll go tell her.' It seemed to me to be an excellent solution to the problem. Addy had that funny effect on people. She was so innocent and quick-thinking. We walked over to the house and found Dee sitting in the kitchen scoffing some of Gran's leftovers.

'Hi,' he growled, clutching a round of bread in his grubby paws.

'Where's Alic?' I demanded.

Dee flipped his shoulders in a gesture of ignorance. 'Dunno. In her room I guess.'

'Alright, you two, stay indoors and no fighting. I'm going after Alic. Be back in a minute or so.' I ran up the stairs two at a time. Alic's door was closed. I tapped gently.

'Who's there?' she growled.

'It's only me,' I yelled.

Moments later, there was a rattle of a key turning in the lock and she opened the door. She looked so sweet and pretty, unlike Addy. I figured she'd been doing her hair or something.

Alic smiled sweetly. 'All set. Did you get me a plane?'

'No. There's no plane until tomorrow afternoon. But –'

'But nothing, Bill, you always let me down. I wish I hadn't come on this stupid outing.' She seemed quite angry.

'Oh, come on, Alic. I can't help it if there's no planes. Addy suggested we go back to Parry Sound and get you a taxi home. I can afford it. You can go in style.'

Her eyes narrowed. Man, you could almost hear the hate boiling up. 'I don't give a fig what that … that person thinks. If I go by taxi, what'll happen to you?'

'Well, nothing. I'll stay. I've got Gran.'

'Oh, sure. You'll stay; you'll stay with that witch from down under. You always did like the ones with big, with … well girls like her. I want her to go. Get her off this island. I won't go till she's out of here.' She slammed the door and noisily turned the key.

Oh God! I was beginning to realize why some men stay single. It was easier to store pins in a balloon than please two women at the same time. Gran would have to help me sort this one out. I couldn't see how to throw Addy off the island; yet, if she stayed, there'd be no pleasing Alic. With a shrug of determination I turned and wandered back down the stairs.

'So where's Alic?' Dee asked.

'Don't talk to me about her. She won't come out of her room. You lot are slowly and surely driving me insane.'

'Cheer up, mate,' Addy said with a big smile. 'We don't need bitchy sheilas. Why don't we play somethin'?'

'Like music?' Dee said.

'No, dummy. How about a game of gin or, better still, poker; a good old Yankee game.' Her eyes lit up at the thought of poker.

Dee stretched his neck in surprise. 'Strip poker?'

'No, stupid,' Addy growled. 'For money.'

Dee slithered down and sank back into his seat. 'I don't have any money.'

'You can play for your share of Fiend's treasure,' she said, all gleeful and giggly. 'Get the cards, William.'

I shrugged. 'Don't think there are any.'

'Oh, come on. Follow me.'

We followed her into the family room. She knew her way around alright. Without difficulty, Addy opened a table. It sort of flipped over, kind of like a secret storage thing that contained cards, crib boards and chips.

'Well don't just stand around, you blokes. Grab a chair and let's get to it.' She sat down and began shuffling the deck. 'You wanna play five or seven?'

I shrugged.

Dee smiled. 'What will you be playing for?'

'Your share of the gold.'

'No, I mean, what will you pay with when you lose?'

She laughed. 'I ain't losin', mate.'

'What if you do?'

'Money, then.'

Dee pulled a chair over. 'Real money?'

'Of course, nitwit. Is there any other kind?'

'Alright, deal me in. We'll play stud. High card deals.'

'I don't want any of this shit,' I said. 'I always lose at cards. I don't think it's a good idea and Gran wouldn't approve.'

'Oh, come on, Bill,' Addy begged. 'Be a sport, mate.'

'No.'

'Oh, rats. Know what I mean, eh? Come on, Bill. Let the girl have her fun. Tell you what. Let her play for her clothes. If she loses, she strips, eh?' Dee grinned.

'No,' Addy snapped. 'Money.'

I shook my head. Then we heard the engines of a powerful boat. Relieved at the distraction, I walked quickly to the front door. To my relief, it was Gran. George Smithers had brought her home. He didn't stop, just held the shore until Gran got off and then drove away into the night.

'Oh boy. Am I ever glad to see you, Gran,' was my greeting.

'I see that girl is here again.'

'Yah and Alic won't come out of her room. Say's she won't leave the island until Addy does. What am I going to do, Gran?'

Gran came into the house and closed the door. 'Well ... tomorrow, we'll all go to the mainland. Adeline can go wherever she wants. You are driving us home. Do you understand me, William?'

'Yes, Gran.'

'Very good. You tell Adeline, while I make a little supper. Now move.'

I walked back to the family room, where the terrible twosome was playing cards. 'Adeline,' I blurted out.

She looked up from the cards she was holding and by the expression on her face, man, you'd think I'd just sworn at her. 'What?' she growled.

I moved closer and sat on a vacant chair next to her. 'Gran says we're leaving this island for good and all, tomorrow. You can go where you like, but we're all going back to Hamilton and then Dundas.'

'What about the gold?'

'There isn't any gold.'

She threw her cards on the table in a gesture of anger. 'I'll buy the island off you. Sell it to me. How much are you asking?'

'Oh God!' I sighed. 'It's not up to me. Gran will take care of all that.'

Addy just sat there staring at me. You could almost see her thinking. After a while, she said softly, 'Alright, I'll apply through my lawyer.' Then she smiled and her eyes twinkled. 'But tonight, we'll play cards, Billy boy.'

We didn't, or at least I didn't. I wanted to go to bed, while the terrible twosome played their god-awful card game. Gran made her annoyance obvious and then retired for the night. I kept looking at my watch. 'Oh, for Christ's sake, haven't you finished that bloody game yet? I wanna go to bed.'

'He's a bit of a shit,' Addy said into her cards.

Dee laughed. 'Come off it, eh! Why don't you join in, Bill?'

'Because I bloody don't want to.'

Addy giggled and whispered something to Dee.

'What did she say?'

Dee giggled. 'She said you're only in a hurry to get a hold of Alic's tits.'

'You guys are assholes,' I shouted and stormed out of the room. I'd had it up to here with those two. Alic and Gran were right; the island was a sinkhole, a place that sucked the fun out of everything. 'I'm going to bed,' I shouted back over my shoulder.

I went upstairs and knocked gently on Alic's door. 'Alic, are you alright?'

'Go away, traitor.'

'I'm sorry, Alic. This is the last night. Addy'll be going in the morning and we'll go home. Alright?'

'Go away, traitor, I hate you.'

I sighed and wandered to my own room. It turned into a bad night, filled with horror and nightmares. Bad dreams must have awakened me at least a dozen times. It got to the point where I couldn't tell reality from dreams. Voices and screams, devils and demons – even old man Fiend came to see me. Man, was I ever glad to see that sunlight in the morning.

The sky looked a vivid shade of red – blood red – with yellow clouds scattered about like bile on a blood-soaked blanket. God! I hate that place. A shave and shower made me feel a little better and dressing in clean, laundered clothes was soothing. I walked over to Alic's room and banged on the door. 'Come on, sleepy, it's time to go home. Today is the day.' There was no reply. I banged several times with the same result. With a sigh of resignation, I walked downstairs. Gran was in the kitchen. The fabulous smell of bacon acted like a magnet. 'Morning, Gran.'

'Good morning, William. I thought we would have a nice breakfast and then head for home.'

'Sure. Seen anybody else yet?'

'No. Have your breakfast and then we'll start the process of moving. You can go wake what's his name, Dizzy? Is that girl still here?'

'Don't know, Gran. I'll check when I've got stuck round the outside of some of that fabulous bacon.'

After breakfast, I walked over to the bungalows. Man! I couldn't believe it. Addy's boat was tied up where she'd left it yesterday, but mine had gone. I walked over to the dock and just stared. I couldn't believe what was not before my eyes. Foolishly, I ran into the boathouse, but of course it was empty, or at least empty of boats.

Quickly, I ran to Dee's cottage and banged on the door. After a few seconds he arrived, all bleary-eyed. 'What's all the noise, eh?'

'Where's Addy,' I demanded.

Dee shrugged. 'Dunno.'

'When did she leave the island last night?'

His eyes opened wide in surprise. 'Leave the island. She said she was gonna sleep next door in that cottage.'

I ran next door and banged on the door. It was the bungalow Henny had used. The door was locked. After a few moments, I heard stirring inside and then Addy came to the door. She looked fresh, clean, sweet and, as usual, beautiful and unruffled, more like a cut-out doll than a real person.

'What's up, mate?'

'Where's my boat?' I demanded.

She looked out towards the slipway. 'Where'd you leave it?'

143

'Oh, come on, Addy. You know bloody well where I left it.'

She displayed an expression of surprise and puzzlement. 'Well, you'd think I'd hear the engine on a big bugger like that one. When did you miss it, mate?'

I shook my head in disgust. 'Just now. For God's sake! Gran'll kill me. We'll have to use your boat to get off the island. Will you run us to Parry Sound?'

'Righto. Don't give it a second thought, mate.'

'Breakfast's ready,' I said and ran back to the house and into the kitchen. 'The boat's gone, Gran,' I yelled breathlessly.

'Gone, gone where?'

'I don't know, someone must have stolen it during the ...'

I stopped, a terrible thought flashed through my mind. No, it couldn't be. Without saying another word I ran upstairs and banged on Alic's door. There was no reply. In anger, I kicked the door. The damn thing wouldn't yield to me. It was built of good, solid Victorian wood. Instantly, I flew down the stairs and ran to the back of the boathouse. Addy and Dee were just coming across for breakfast.

'What yah doin', Billy boy?' Addy called.

'I'm getting the ladder. Come on, you guys. Gimme a hand.'

We picked it up and carried it to the house, placing it up against Alic's window, and then I climbed to the top. I half expected to find yet another dead body. Instead, I found an empty room. There was no one in there.

'I don't believe it!'

'What?' Dee yelled.

'She's gone. She's ripped-off my boat. I don't believe it, she's gone.' As I slid down the ladder, the others could see the expression of bewilderment on my face.

'She's hiding; you just can't see her, eh?'

'The room's empty. She's bloody gone.'

'Let's go break the door down, eh? We've gotta make sure. I don't reckon she could drive the boat; besides, we'd have heard the engines.'

I agreed and, leaving the ladder where it was, we all marched into the house and up the stairs. I kicked the door several times. Man, it was a tough one. It would not yield a single centimetre. Dee and I threw our shoulders at it and all we got was painful shoulders.

'Use the shotgun, blow it open, eh?'

I was tempted, but then figured it to be a bad idea. 'Go get an axe or something,' I demanded.

Dee ran off just as Gran came up the stairs. 'You could always use this key,' she said, handing me a single key.

'Where'd you get it, Gran?'

'There's a spare key for every door in the kitchen cabinet, silly boy.'

I grabbed it and unlocked the door. We entered and there was no sign that the bed had even been slept in. Her clothes were gone and the room was neat and tidy.

'I don't believe it,' I growled. 'I just don't believe it. Why would she do such a crazy thing?'

Addy shrugged. 'Maybe to teach you a lesson. But I thought she didn't know anything technical. Could she drive a boat?'

I brushed my hair back with one hand. 'I don't know. She can drive a car. I've seen her licence.'

'Call the cops,' Addy suggested.

'No. She's gone. My boat'll be safe. You can take us to Parry Sound.'

'Alright,' Addy said with a smile. 'You get your things together and I'll go get my stuff from the bungalow.'

I was angry, but what the hey. Anything I needed I could buy. Addy and Dee walked off, leaving Gran glaring at me.

'So what did I do now?'

Gran peeked out the door then walked back into Alic's room and spoke in a low voice. 'What if Alicia is dead? She could have been murdered.'

'So who took the boat, Gran?'

She thought for a moment. 'I think Addy was right, we should call Inspector Spadafora and have this mess sorted out professionally.'

'What mess? Alic's run off with my ... our boat. So what. We'll buy another one or collect this one ashore. I think we should gather our things, keep our mouths shut and get the hell out of here, before someone else dies on us.'

Gran smiled. 'Hasn't been much of a holiday, has it, William? Alright, let's get off this blessed island and as soon as we are ashore, we will report Alicia missing. That'll put everything on a legal footing.'

'Alright, Gran. I'll buy that. Now, let's get out of here ASAP.'

Of course, nothing is as simple as you think. Dee was waiting for us in the kitchen.

'Bill,' he said excitedly.

'What?'

'Addy sent me over here. She says there's a basement in this house and you should check it before you leave, eh!'

'A basement. I haven't seen it. Where is it, then?'

'It's off the family room.'

We all walked into the family room and looked around. I couldn't see any basement. After several minutes' search I got annoyed. 'This is crap, Dee. Now, grab your junk and let's get the hell out of here. You ready, Gran?'

'I'll just run up and get my things. Be with you in five minutes. Meet you at the dock, dear.'

She went upstairs, while we wandered to the front door. You could almost feel the ghost of old Jeremiah clawing at us to stay. I felt there was a great need for speed. When we reached the front door, Addy was just coming in.

'So, did you look in the basement, mate?' she asked.

'No ... there isn't one.'

'Sure there is. I'll show you.' She marched off towards the family room.

I followed her with a sigh of resignation. 'So where's this mysterious basement?'

She walked over to a bookcase on the east wall. It was obvious she had been there before. By moving one of the books, a panel opened to reveal a secret passage, just like in the movies.

'Wow!' I exclaimed.

'I'm too nervous to go down there. You blokes go. What if there are more dead bodies down there?'

I breathed out in a loud hiss between my teeth. 'Come on, Dee.'

The basement was the size of the family room; clean but dusty. There was nothing down there. After a quick search, we ascended to the family room again.

We found Addy and Gran in the kitchen. Gran had just come down the stairs. 'William,' she said, 'grab my mobile and let's go.'

I looked around. 'I can't see it, Gran. Like, where is it?'

A full-scale search ensued, but no phone. After a good five minutes searching the kitchen and ten more searching the house, we decided to forget it and leave.

As we rounded the corner heading for the dock, Addy suddenly stopped, put her hands to her head and screamed. I almost fell over with the shock of it and dropped the bags I was carrying.

'What the hell's wrong now?'

'Oh, my God!' she yelled. 'My boat's gone.'

146

# Chapter 17

## Boredom

It is difficult to relate my emotions of that moment when the realization swept over me that we were marooned. My heart came into my mouth and almost choked off my breath. We had no phone and no boats.

'What are we going to do, Gran?' I said with a slight quaver in my voice.

She slowly placed her bags on the ground and looked around. 'We will signal a passing boat, what else do marooned people do?'

'Boats don't pass close by here, Gran. We're not on a shipping lane and tourists don't usually come this far out.'

She stroked her top lip thoughtfully for a few moments. 'Not to worry; Inspector Spadafora will surely notice your vehicle in port at Parry Sound and come out here to blow his horn and exercise his jurisdictional muscles.'

I smiled. 'You're right, Gran. How long do you figure before he comes out here to gloat?'

As she was thinking of a reply, Addy said, 'What if that bitch took your car? The cops will figure all is well. How they going to know there's trouble here?'

'You have a disquieting habit of being bluntly obvious, young lady,' Gran said with a sigh of resignation.

I began wandering back into the house. My mind was doing overtime trying to solve the puzzle of how to get off this rock.

Dee came running after me. 'We could still look for the gold, eh! Know what I mean?'

I felt more like slugging him than digging for gold. 'For God's sake, Dee, there ain't any gold and I doubt there ever was. It's a stinking myth.'

'Oh yes there bloody is, mate,' Addy said in a grouchy tone. 'I reckon it's a perfect heaven-sent opportunity now that flashy bitch's gone and there's just us kids. What you say, mates? Let's give it our best and hunt that yellow metal down.'

I walked across the entrance hall and tossed by bag down. 'What the hell, we're here anyway. It'll give us something to do.'

Dee's eyes lit up as his whole personality changed. He became the old excited and animated friend I knew before all our troubles. 'Great, I'm gonna run over and chuck my junk in the bungalow, eh?'

'Sure, Dee. I'll meet you in the kitchen.'

Gran arrived with her bag and after a few minutes, we were all beginning to settle into the house again. Dee came running into the house as if the devil were after him. He threw himself into a seat.

Addy was quiet and thoughtful. She took up a seat near the table. 'I love this house. Sure you won't sell it to me?'

Gran sat opposite Addy. 'Young lady, I don't care who buys it. I've arranged for the lawyers to handle the sale. If you're interested, you should contact them and put in your offer.'

'Alright, don't get grouchy. Where do you think the gold is, missus?'

'If there is any gold, it has to be in the well near Beacon Hill. It's the only place that matches the rhyme.'

Addy laughed as though a good joke had been executed. 'No. Edgar found it, I know Edgar found it and I know he didn't find it in the well. Wherever it is, it has to be somewhere in the primeval rock. Fiend put it there. I figure a cave or a natural hole, probably covered by the dirt when it was dumped here.'

'Absolute poppycock,' Gran snapped. 'No one could find the gold for years before the soil arrived. If it's not in the well then it's not on this island.'

'Well I say it is an' I've been here a lot longer than you. I worked with Edgar. I've seen his diagrams and stuff. The gold is here on this island. I tell you what – give me the island, with the agreement that I'll give you half of all the gold found here. What d'yah say?'

'No,' Gran snapped. 'Not at all. The lawyers will sell it for me. If you want it, go see them. Now, I don't want to hear any more about it. We will go about our normal daily business while we wait for Inspector Spadafora to come rescue us. Should we have to spend another night here then everyone will sleep in this house.'

'Bossy old bugger,' Addy moaned.

'Come on, Addy,' I said. 'Be nice to Gran, we're all in the same boat.'

'Alright, mate. Gran, I apologize, I'm sorry.' She did not sound very convincing.

Gran smiled and you could see her relax. 'Is anyone hungry?'

We all shook our heads. 'No, Gran,' I said. 'We'll go down to the beach and see if we can flag a boat down.'

'Very well, you children run along. Take care and stay together. I'll start lunch. Would you like a cooked meal? After all, we may be here some time.'

'Sure, Gran.'

We wandered outside into the sweltering heat. It was so hot you couldn't see Killbear Island for the heat haze and the sun was lifting vapour up off the water, almost like a summer fog. Addy pulled off her jeans and T-shirt. Underneath, she was wearing a very skimpy swimsuit. Dee's eyes opened up and looked as large as saucers.

'Well?' Addy said, sauntering off towards the water.

'Very,' Dee gasped. He watched her without blinking.

Addy ran down the beach and dived into the crystal water. I lowered myself down and sat on the hot sand. She swam until she could barely be seen. This was kind of worrying. My heart began to pound as the girl vanished into the haze. Where the hell was she going? Nervously, I stood and shaded my eyes and then, at the top of my voice, I yelled, 'Addy, don't go so far.'

She obviously didn't hear me. 'For Christ's sake, Dee,' I said angrily. 'She'll drown out there.'

'Ah, she's a good swimmer; she's probably going for help, eh?'

I couldn't settle, knowing that Addy was out there in the water. 'It's fresh water, not salt,' I said. 'It's a lot easier to drown in fresh water.'

'So?'

'So it's harder to swim in fresh water, you nitwit.'

'Ah! You worry too much, Bill. You'll see; she'll be back, probably in a big, fast rescue boat.'

I sighed in total hopelessness and sank back down to the sand. 'Man! I'm sick of the stress and I wanna go home.'

'Why don't we hunt for the gold, Bill? See if we can find it before she gets back, eh?'

'After a couple of hundred years, just what do you suggest?'

'How about Addy's theory? I'll get a shovel and we can attack that grave again.'

'Alright, I'm with you if you do all the work. It's too bloody hot for digging.'

We walked over to the old graves and a chill ran through me. It seemed that old man Fiend was watching us. I could feel his eyes burning into my back. Dee grabbed the shovel and attacked the soil. I don't know where he got all the energy in that heat. For awhile I stood like a fool just watching. What a ridiculous situation. Alic's missing, Henny's dead, Pete's dead and now Addy is trying to commit suicide.

I didn't want the gold, even if it was there. Thinking back, perhaps Dee was just working off his nervous energy. Some people are like that. After a while, I realized that some of the sweat on his face was actually tears. Dee was weeping and hiding his emotion in physical labour.

'Let's go have a coffee or something,' I suggested.

Dee threw the shovel down. 'I can't leave,' he said softly. 'Addy needs me.'

With a lump in my throat, I walked over to him and gave him a brotherly hug. 'I don't know where Addy is. But I figure she's gone for help. She wouldn't just leave us stranded.'

'I'll sit on the beach and wait for her, Bill. You go get yourself a coffee, eh?'

We both walked back to the beach. Addy's clothes were just lying there taunting us. The water was calm, but there were no boats and no swimmers visible.

'This has been a bloody lousy holiday,' I mumbled.

'Do you think Addy will marry me, eh?'

'Marry you? Did you ask her?'

'No. I was gonna do it on the boat going home. God, I wish I'd stopped her going into the water like that. Do you think she's alright?'

'Don't worry, Dee, she knows what she's doing. It's Addy we're talking about, not Alic. I'm sure she knows her limitations. You keep a lookout for her or any likely boats. I'll go get us a couple of cold beers. Alright?'

'Yeah, sure.'

I figured Dee needed a couple of minutes alone to get control of his emotions. Going to get a beer was as good an excuse as I could come up with. Gran had a pinafore on and a silly-looking hairnet. Her hands were all covered in flour.

'Where are your friends, William?'

I threw myself onto one of the chairs. 'Gees, Gran, I wish we'd never come to this place. I can't understand how so many things can go this wrong.'

'Yes, indeed, William. I'm sure it's not supernatural. A very physical being is pulling the strings. I haven't figured out how, who or for that matter why, though it surely is a living person.'

'Well, it's not Addy. She's gone; she swam off into the distance.'

150

'She did? Why?'

'I think she's gone to get help, either that or drowned. Oh gees, Gran, where's your mobile?'

'That's the clue, William. I'm sure that's the clue.'

'The clue, whatever do you mean, Gran?'

'Ghosts have no use for mobile phones. A physical being took it, the same one who disabled the house telephone and the same one who ran off with our boats. Someone with an axe to grind.'

'No one can drive two boats, Gran. I figure it must have been Alic who took mine.'

'What about Adeline's boat, did she take that one, too?'

'Of course not, Gran. You can't drive two boats at once.'

'Then who did?'

I realised where her train of thought was going. Holy mackerel, it had to be someone on the island. However, if they took Addy's boat then we were all safe, until he or she came back.

'Gran,' I said slowly.

'Yes, William.'

'Well, if it's not you, which it isn't, and it's not me, which it isn't. Well, that only leaves Addy and Dee. I don't see how they could be the cause of all our troubles. Dee's still here and Addy's gone swimming.'

'I have put a lot of thought into it, William. I've also done a bit of snooping on the mainland.'

'Alright. So what's your theory?'

She walked over and filled the kettle for another cup of tea, talking as she worked. 'Well, I checked on the supposed other girl, the one the old man told us about. No one has actually seen her; that is, no one I talked to. A couple of people swear that they encountered her or them in quick succession. Just as the old man did. But no one has ever seen them simultaneously.'

'So?'

'The house was burned while we were all here on this island, except for Adeline.'

'So are you saying she burned her own house down?'

'Stop prompting me, William. I am thinking aloud. Listen or say something constructive.'

'Sorry, Gran.'

'Inspector Spadafora is the only person that fits the bill. He had the opportunity and the capability. That only leaves the motive. I think he was quite capable of murdering Edgar in a manner that would slip past the

151

coroner. See how quickly he swept over the facts about Pete's death. I think he just didn't want to stir up a full inquiry. That might bring in outsiders and bring his little plan to a halt.

'What about the boat disappearance?'

'I think the bad person could be hiding here on this island. The boats were put adrift, the wind took them.'

'Alright,' I said, joining in with the spirit of the thing. 'First, what happened to Alic? And second – now this is a big one – the wind is in the wrong quarter to allow the boats to drift off. They would be blown ashore, right into our dock.'

She sighed deeply. 'True, William. Let's hope Alicia took your boat, as that will only leave the complication of Adeline's boat. What happened to it?'

'Yeah, I guess a man could push the boat to the end of the pier. But I don't think there was time. I was out there only a few minutes after it went. We would have seen it drifting...' I stopped and had a terrible thought. 'Nah, couldn't be.'

'What, William?'

The kettle suddenly started whistling as if calling for half-time. I looked at Gran. 'Well, what if they were sunk instead of stolen?'

She poured the water into the teapot in silence, obviously thinking. Then she brought the pot over, put it down on the table and sat down. 'How quickly would a boat sink?'

I shrugged my shoulders. 'Dunno, Gran. Even if they were sunk, what's it mean?'

Gran straightened up and thought for a few seconds. 'If the boats were sunk, William, it means the criminal is here on this island. All our lives could still be in danger. Call Adeline and Dizzy in. I think we should stay close to each other and indoors.'

'Addy swam off, Gran. I can't call her,' I said softly.

'What?'

'She sort of swam off. Gone for help, I think. I told you.'

Gran was silent and deep in thought. After awhile, she said, 'There are only four of us left, all the others were victims of accidents. If there is no outsider then our nemesis is one of us.'

'What do you mean, Gran?'

'I don't know. I'm just thinking aloud again. You do see what I mean, though? If there is someone hiding on this island, arranging accidents and preventing us from communicating, it has to be either someone we don't know or someone we do.'

'Gee, it don't take a rocket scientist to figure that out, Gran.'

'No, what I mean is it has to be one of us four or a person hidden somewhere on the island.'

'I don't think so, Gran. The boat thing is the only bit I don't understand. Alic stole mine, Addy's must have, well, I don't know, just drifted off. Maybe the wind was in the opposite quarter and she hadn't tied it off properly and later it changed again.'

'It makes no difference; I believe we are all in danger. We must await the authorities or wave down a passing boat. I am sorry about Adeline, maybe I've misjudged her.' She stopped to think for a moment. 'Go collect Dizzy. I would like us all to stay close to each other ....' she sighed deeply, 'now there are only three of us.'

I didn't even stop to drink my tea. Like a schoolboy when the bell goes, I ran out of the house and down to the beach. Dee was still there, kneeling on the sand looking out over the lake. 'Dee,' I yelled. 'Gran wants us all back in the house.'

'I can't leave Addy; you know what I mean, eh?'

I walked up to him and touched his shoulder in a gesture of friendship. 'Dee, if Addy swims back here, I'm sure she'll be able to find her way to the house. Gran wants us all in the house, where it's safe.'

'Safe. What yah mean, safe?'

'Oh, come on, Dee. Gran is worried that the loss of the boats is more than an accident. She thinks there's some sinister force trying to kill us all.'

'That's what Alic said. She saw it, she saw it. You was there.'

'Well, I don't think ... oh well, never mind what I think. Let's go to the house and keep an eye on Gran. Alright?'

'Sure.'

I didn't keep track of the time, but it sure as hell dragged. None of us felt like playing any games. I stood in the living room looking out of the window towards the beach and couldn't help but think that Addy must have drowned in the lake somewhere. If I'd known she was going to attempt swimming to another island I would have tried to stop her.

Dee lay on the settee staring at the ceiling, grumbling every now and again about my unsporting attitude. Gran was preparing lunch in the kitchen. Suddenly and very unexpectedly, I saw someone move near the beach. I watched in stunned silence.

A person came into clear view. Unreal. It was Addy. She was dressed in blue jeans and a denim sleeveless shirt. The wet, flimsy costume was in her hand as she skipped lightly towards the house.

# Chapter 18

## The Break-up

We all thought Addy must have been lost at sea, so to speak, but as if nothing at all had happened, the girl came wandering into the house. Her face looked all smiles and her hair still wet. I just stood with my mouth open, looking at her shocked and confused.

Her eyes twinkled as she said, 'Water's lovely. You should've come with me. You'd love it, mate.'

'Where have you been, Addy? We've been worried sick. I'd no idea you were going to swim off like that. What were you doing?'

She tossed her wet swimsuit into the hearth. 'I went to get help. There's an island just over there; it's only about a kilometre and a half. You do get excited easily.'

'So what happened?' I asked.

Dee stood in the doorway unblinking. He was even more shocked than me. 'I thought you were dead,' he said in an angry voice.

'Oh, Jesus. You blokes are a load of old women. I swam to Bob's Island. There was nobody at home, mate. The boathouse was locked and there's no window in it. I was going to break into the house to use their phone, when I remembered they only use a mobile phone. So what you blokes bin up to while I was gone?'

Dee ran off to inform Gran of the good news.

'Sit and rest,' I said in a soft, friendly voice. 'You must be tired after a swim like that.'

'Not really. I usually swim every day. I probably could have made it to Foster Rock, but I'm not sure of the currents out there. Could turn out to be tricky.'

'Don't do anything like that again, Addy. You really had us all worried.'

Gran came into the sitting room. 'Well,' she said with real expressiveness. 'I am pleased to see you, young lady. I thought for sure you had become another victim of the Fiend saga.'

Addy laughed. 'Not me. I tried to get help, but failed. Tomorrow's Saturday. It's the tourist season and the weekend. I reckon there'll be plenty of boats around. We'll be able to flag one down. Do you have a distress rocket or a flare pistol?'

Gran shook her head in the negative. 'I'm afraid not. I've been cooking. I hope you'll join us for supper.'

'Right yah are.'

Dee suddenly became enthused. 'Alright. What say we banish that old bastard Fiend and dig up his gold, right after supper?'

'Great,' Addy agreed.

'Any idea how anyone could have moved your boat without us hearing it, Addy?' I asked.

She shrugged offhandedly and with a big smile, said, 'Could have used the dipper.'

'What's a dipper?'

'The electric drive, maybe, or a paddle. Though we should have heard Alic drive yours off. Your boat makes enough noise to wake the dead, if you get me drift.'

'True. I guess we were all asleep. It's a wonder it didn't wake us.'

Gran called from the kitchen. 'Come and get it. Supper's ready.'

I think Addy felt good, as Gran had accepted her as a sort of hero for trying to save us all. She was given a seat at the head of the table. I sat next to her and Gran at the other end. 'Well, I'm glad you made it back alive,' I remarked.

'So tell us what happened,' Dee suggested. 'You've been gone three or four hours.'

'Well, I swam directly to the island that Mr Franks owns. It's not that big. The real problem was that I couldn't see very well from the water. I was a bit afraid of getting lost out there. It's a big bloody lake.'

'Not to worry, Addy,' I squeezed her hand. 'We can live comfortably here until someone misses us.'

The meal was, as to be expected, near perfect. I don't know how Gran does it, but she could whip up a feast on a desert island. A good meal always makes a man feel better, though I still felt worried about being a prisoner on Fiend's Rock. No matter how I racked my brain, I couldn't think of any way to escape.

Suddenly, Dee sparked up with a bright idea. 'I've got it, I've got it. We could build a raft and sail to freedom, eh?'

'Brilliant,' I encouraged. 'We've got everything we need: tools, materials. Great. When do we start?'

'Straight after this meal. We'll build it in the boathouse, what you say, eh?'

For the first time since the catastrophe, we were all encouraged. Even Addy was enthused. I couldn't help but notice there was something peculiar about her. She looked beautiful in a strange sort of way, yet her eyes reminded me of pools of acid. She seemed the type who would stab you in the back if it was to her advantage. Her attitude was flip-flop, pro-and-con. Anything for a laugh and yet there seemed this underlying fire, waiting to break out and consume everything in sight.

After a good feed, Addy and Dee set out to build our escape vehicle. I stayed with Gran to give her a hand in the kitchen. While she cleared and tidied-up, I put the dishes in the washer. Gran came over and handed me a large basin. 'Put this in,' she said.

'Sure, Gran.'

'You do look very serious, William. You know, there is nothing to worry about. Tomorrow's Saturday and I'm sure Mr Smithers will call the police.'

'Why should he?'

'Your car is still there.'

'Not if Alic took it.'

She looked serious for a few moments. 'Oh well, there's always Dizzy's raft. Shouldn't you go out there and keep an eye on them?'

'Will you be all right on your own, Gran?'

She smiled sweetly. 'I'll be perfectly safe. You go and help. The sooner we're off this island the better.'

Eagerly, I closed the dishwashing machine and flicked the switch. As soon as I was sure things were working okay, I took my leave of Gran and ran over to the boathouse. You should have heard the noise. There was yelling and screaming coming from inside the boat storage area, so I ran round and in through the back door.

Dee and Addy were on the floor at the end of the boat ramp. Dee was on top of her pinning her down. I yelled at them, 'What the bloody hell's going on here?'

'I'm gonna kill this broad,' Dee shouted angrily.

'Get off,' I screamed and went to the girl's aid. I pushed him over. Instantly, he got up and tried to take a swing at me. Being bigger, stronger and probably fitter, I quickly subdued him. 'Now stop all this crap! What the hell is going on?'

157

Dee wiped the blood from the scratches on his face. 'It was her, it was her,' he shouted excitedly. 'The filth, the things she says shouldn't be said by anyone, never mind a woman.'

'Alright, alright. Words are words. Grow up, man.' I turned to Addy, 'You get in the house. Dee, clean yourself up and don't let Gran know what's been going on. There's no excuse for any man to strike a woman. It's cowardly. Now, get out of my sight. Get your stuff from the cottage. You're staying in the house until further notice. Git.'

Dee scuffled off in the direction of the house without replying. I turned back to Addy. She could see the anger in my eyes and smiled sort of coyly – a weak, embarrassed sort of smile. 'I'm sorry,' she wheezed hoarsely.

'I'm sorry, too. I don't want any fighting. We're marooned on this place and I'd like us all to survive to be rescued.'

'I'm sorry,' she said again. 'I'll stay out here. I can't go in the house. I think I might start fighting again. He's really insufferable, you know.'

'Gees, Addy. I don't think it's a good idea you staying out here all alone.'

'So … will you stay with me?' Her eyes lit up and her countenance changed.

'No, no, I can't. But if you have to, you can stay out here. Stay in your cottage and don't let anyone in.'

'I'll let you in, William,' she said in a hoarse whisper. 'I'd always let you in, Billy boy.'

'Come on. Let's get out of here.' We walked out into the daylight. Would you believe, not a single boat on the horizon. Everyone in the world was staying at home. 'Nothing,' I said, indicating the lake.

'Maybe we're flying the yellow peter.'

'The what?'

'Oh, nothing. I'm feeling very tired. I think I'll go have a sleep. If a rescue ship comes, wake me, or if you want to come over, don't hesitate. I'm sure there's something we could do together.'

Somehow or other, I managed to escape her clutches and walked back to the house. It was getting late and not a sign of outside help. When I walked in the kitchen, Gran was still working.

'Don't you ever rest, Gran?'

'I'm just keeping busy to keep my mind active, William.'

'Where's Dee?'

'I thought he was out there with you.'

'Damn. So he hasn't come in the house yet?'

'Well, if he did, I haven't seen him.'

With a sigh and a shrug, I walked outside again. A shiver ran down my spine, for there was a figure of a person near the Beckon Hill. I ran down there and found no trace of anyone. As I started to return, Dee came out of his cottage with a large bundle of things in his arms. I ran over to him and asked, 'Everything alright?'

'Sure. I can't sleep in the same house as that, that ... well, her. You know what I mean, eh?'

'Oh, shut up, Dee. Come on. I'm getting the creeps out here.'

Eventually, Dee settled in the house. You just wouldn't believe how difficult he could be. Gran wasn't very pleased, either. She stopped me in the hall.

'William, where is Adeline?'

'She's outside. Well, that is, she's in one of the cottages.'

'I think everyone should be in the house. Tomorrow, someone will rescue us for sure. Now, you toddle along and persuade her to come stay with us in the safety of this building.'

With a sigh, I walked out of the house and over to the bungalows again. Addy was in the one Pete used. I knocked and waited. Eventually, the door opened.

'Hi,' she said, wide-eyed and bright. Quickly, she pushed me away from the door and closed it. 'Let's walk,' she said.

It was almost rude of her, but what the heck. I allowed myself to be led. 'Where to?'

Addy put her arm around me and walked toward Beacon Hill. 'I like you, William. I don't see why we can't be close friends, very close. If you get rid of old Grandma, well, just think about it. You and me all alone on this beautiful island, if you know what I mean. Wouldn't that be great?'

'No. Not until all this trouble is over. I don't like being held prisoner. Haven't you thought about it? Whoever got rid of the phone and the boat wants us here. Why?'

She stopped walking and confronted me. 'I want the gold. I want the life it will give me. I want you. Why can't you work with me on this, instead of acting like a shit?'

'Work with you? What d'yah mean?'

'Get rid of Grandma; get rid of that dingo, Dee. Just you and me, together. We could be a great team.' Her eyes looked almost glossy.

I shook my head. 'It's getting dark. Don't worry, Addy, I'll see you're all right. Tonight, I would like you in the house. Tomorrow, this nightmare will be over.'

'Ignorant bastard,' she said sharply and slapped me across the face. 'You stupid dingo. I want that gold and I'll get it, with or without you. Stuff your bloody house. I'm staying in the bungalow, 'less you want to chuck me out of there, too.'

'No.' I turned and walked back to the house. The sun was going down, casting a gorgeous red banner on the lake. Sadly, it reminded me of blood. 'I'm gonna lock the door, Addy,' I shouted. 'You'd better come now or face the consequences.'

'Stuff off, dingo.'

With a sigh of resignation, I walked to the house and closed the door. Leaning against it for moral support, I tried to weigh up the pros and cons. Then I turned the key and left it in the lock. Gran was in the kitchen, as usual.

'Hi, Gran.'

She smiled sweetly. 'She wouldn't come in?'

'Right, Gran.'

'Not to worry, William. I'm certain she knows how to look after herself. What are you going to do?'

'What am I going to do? What d'yah mean?'

'I think we should remain awake tonight, probably in turns. Vigilance, I do believe, is essential.'

'Why?'

'I just feel there is great danger here. Awake, we can control it or at least not be taken by surprise. The one awake should be down here. In fact, we could both stay down here and take turns. Just you and I.'

'What about that shotgun?'

'What about it, William?'

'I figure we should have it close by.'

She sat thoughtfully for several moments. 'I don't like weapons of any kind. Besides, what use would it be against a ghost?'

'A ghost, what ghost?'

'William, I was joking. I thought you would like to shoot the ghost of Jeremiah Fiend.'

'No, Gran. The thing that worries me is the loose cannon that could be hiding on this island. I thought I saw a man near Beacon Hill. I just thought that the gun would be handy if kept nearby. For one thing, we'd know where it was.'

Again, she thought for a few moments. 'Very well. Do you know how to make certain the thing is not loaded?'

'Sure.'

'Very well. I'll collect the weapon and you can make certain it is not loaded. It can then be used for intimidation, without anyone actually being in any danger.'

I had to chuckle, she was a genius. 'Okay, Gran, I'll buy that. I'll set up watch by the window in the family room. From there, I'll be able to see the cottages as well.'

'You're a good boy, William. I'll get the shotgun for you.'

I pulled the furniture round to face the window at the south end of the room. Although it was a long way from the exit, I figured it would be the best place for a night vigil. Turning the lights out made the windows stop reflecting; I could see all the way to the end of the island.

Sitting on the comfortable settee, I pulled a few cushions around me and settled in. After a few moments the door opened, allowing a flood of light in from the hall.

'Are you there, William?' came Gran's voice.

'Sure, Gran. Close the door.'

'I can't see without light.'

"Click," and the light came on. I looked round; she was standing there with the gun across her arms.

'Come on in and settle down, Gran. Give me the gun.'

Not being an expert on weapons, I wasn't sure how to tell if it was loaded or not. A few pumps on the ejection lever and three cartridges popped out. No more followed, which made me think it must be empty. Standing the weapon by the small reading table, I indicated the light. Gran smiled and walked over to the switch.

'I'll stay here with you, William. If you wish, I'll take the first watch.'

It seemed a little ridiculous, but both Gran and the gun gave me a little courage. The island looked beautiful in the moonlight. A slight wind had got up and the trees were gracefully waving. The water had small whitecaps that glistened in the eerie light. Without difficulty, I fell asleep, leaving Gran on duty.

Almost scared out of my skin I jumped, responding to Gran shaking my shoulder. 'Gees, Gran. What's wrong?'

'Nothing, William. It has been a quiet night. It's your turn. Are you ready?'

'Oh, sure.' I sat up straight and stared out of the window into the darkness. 'What time is it, Gran?'

'Just gone three. Now, may I sleep?'

'Sure, you go ahead.'

Amazing as it may seem, within minutes she was snoring. God, if only I could sleep like that. I guess it comes with age. The trees swayed rhythmically and the only sound was that of a clock ticking somewhere and Gran's throaty chorus.

With a start, I leapt to my feet and the gun fell to the floor with a crash. God, it was daylight. Holy mackerel, I'd slept the night through.

# Chapter 19

## Blood on the Path

I'd slept right through my watch, leaving no one on guard. Gran still lay snoring like a trooper. Even the crash of me knocking the shotgun to the floor didn't wake her. The sun was, as yet, not fully above the horizon, but the sky had that morning brightness about it. My heart pounded in my chest from the shock of suddenly awakening. I tried to relax my nerves by breathing deeply; after all, nothing had really happened. Nothing moved out there – even the trees were still. It was as if the snoring grandmother and I were the only living things in the world.

Quietly, so as not to waken Gran, I walked to the kitchen. She needed the rest, poor old girl. Somehow, she made me feel kind of sad. Gran had come to this island filled with excitement and glee and it had turned out to be a total disaster. Mayhem would be a pleasant description. How could we attract a ship, boat or even a passing skier, plane or satellite?

Toast is the easiest thing to make. Sure doesn't require too much skill to scorch a piece of bread. We had some bread in the refrigerator; frozen, though. Doesn't taste the same as when Gran makes it. I sat at the table with my buttered, semi-burned bread thinking. Somehow, there had to be a way off this haunted island. I had learned to hate this place. Gees, it was so beautiful at the beginning; a real dream, but now the dream had turned into a nightmare.

I wondered what really happened to Edgar. Did he die by accident? When you start to think like that, you begin to wonder whether anyone died by accident. I mean, Pete could have been bashed and then stabbed by the weathervane. Then there's Henny, he could have been bashed on the head and dumped in the water. And what about Alic? Where did she get to? Just suppose she was murdered and thrown into the lake and then the killer escaped on the boat. Nah, crap. Addy's pessimism was rubbing off. Edgar died as a result of an accident and so did the others. That still leaves Alic. I somehow couldn't imagine her stealing my boat. I'm positive she would have at least said goodbye, if only to rub it in.

I almost jumped out of my skin as Gran came into the room. 'Gran, you scared me. I was just having a little breakfast.'

'Is everyone all right, dear?'

'What do yah mean?'

She sighed. 'William, what was the purpose of spending the night looking out of the window?'

'Oh well, nothing happened, Gran, if that's what you mean.'

'Good. I'll make breakfast. Would you like something cooked?'

'Yes, please.' I sat back and relaxed. Gran is the finest woman in my life. I can't imagine why I never appreciated her before.

Gran smiled and told me to go upstairs and clean up. A nice hot shower would make me feel better. After a quick shave and shower, I put some clean clothes on and then looked out of the window. Not a bloody boat on the horizon. Unreal, this place is usually lousy, with stupid tourists rushing about in their expensive vessels.

Breakfast was excellent – what else?

'Thanks, Gran, you're the greatest. Do you figure we'll get off this rock today?'

Gran chuckled encouragingly. 'I think I will give up this detective stuff. I cannot make head nor tail of this story, William. Perhaps things will look clearer when we are safely at home. As regards escaping this place, I would think someone will miss us today.'

'I sure as hell hope you're right, Gran.'

'I think you should wake up your friends. I'll give them breakfast and we can make plans to leave this place. And please modify your language, young man.'

'Sure, Gran.' I wandered upstairs again. What was the hurry? Banging on Dee's door, I yelled, 'Come on, you lazy dink. It's time for breakfast on this, our last day.'

A few groans came from the other side of the door, indicating that he was still alive. 'Bugger off, Bill.'

'Breakfast is being served. Come and get it.' I walked away. Addy was sleeping out in the cottage. I figured maybe she should be awakened, too. She'd kill me if I let her sleep through breakfast – figuratively speaking, that is.

The sun was climbing into the sky for another relentless day of heat. The birds sang and the crickets chirped. Nothing could go wrong – it was a perfect morning. As I rounded the corner of the first cottage, it looked like someone lying on the grass just over by the boathouse. My blood froze in my veins as my heart pounded, fit to burst. For several moments I stood and stared, unable to accept that which was obvious.

Addy lay on the grass face down. She was still wearing the clothes she had on last night. There was no mistaking it; she was dead – dead as mutton. Suddenly, I panicked and fled back to the house, screaming for Gran.

'Gran, Gran, Addy's dead. Come quick, Gran, come quick.'

She met me at the front door. 'What's all the noise, boy?'

I almost leapt into her arms. I could feel my strength failing. 'Addy's dead, Addy's dead,' I blurted out.

'Where?'

I pointed and then leaned against the wall for support. My knees were beginning to buckle underneath me.

Dee turned up and said, 'What's up, Bill?'

'It's Addy, she's ... she's been ...'

I stopped and Dee took off at a trot towards Gran. I looked at my hands and they were shaking uncontrollably. 'I can't believe it, I just can't believe it.' Pulling myself off the wall, I followed Dee. Gran was bending down over the girl. 'Is she ... is she dead?' I whispered.

Gran nodded. 'I'm afraid so. Stone cold and I do mean stone cold.'

I guess it was too much for me, all the blood, that awful mess. Somewhat out of character, I fainted. Consciousness returned to me in the sitting room. Gran held out a glass of water for me.

'Drink this, William.'

'What happened?' I asked foolishly.

'You fainted, dear. Dizzy and I and brought you in here.'

'I did? You did? Yes, I did. How's Addy?'

'She is dead, William. This time, it is definitely murder.'

'Oh God! I don't feel at all well. I think I'm going to be sick.'

'There are only three of us left alive,' she said slowly. 'You, me and Dizzy. I didn't kill that girl, how about you, William?'

'Christ, Gran. What d'yah take me for. I didn't do it.'

'Exactly.'

My head was spinning and all I could see in my mind's eye was Addy lying there, her face blown from her head by a shotgun blast. The memory overshadowed every conscious thought. All I could see was poor Addy lying there in all that blood.

'I don't understand, Gran. What do you mean?'

'I sometimes wonder about you, William. You did not do it. I did nt do it, so who would you suppose did?'

165

'Holy shit, Gran, you don't mean …?'

'As far as we know, there is only one other person on this island. I'm fairly sure Jeremiah Fiend wouldn't use a shotgun.'

'What are we going to do, Gran?'

'You left that weapon in the family room; go get it and the cartridges. I suppose it is the only gun on the island?'

'Don't know.' As quick as I could and controlling my stomach as best as possible, I got up and ran into the family room. The gun was still there along with the cartridges, all three of them. I grabbed it and ran back to Gran. 'Where's Dee?'

'He seems to be extremely upset. I think he's with the dead girl.'

'I don't understand, Gran. I didn't hear any gunshots last night. I mean, you'd think you'd hear a noise that loud and that close to the house. What are we going to do? We can't leave her out there.' My head began to spin again. The whole situation was like a never-ending nightmare.

'We'll have to bring her in. Vermin will try to eat the body.'

'For the sake of all that's holy, Gran. It makes me feel sick to the stomach. As if I didn't feel bad enough. I don't know if I can touch her, Gran, what with her being dead and all.'

'Pull yourself together, William. You're a Reyner, not a mouse.'

'Do we have to have her in the house? I don't think I can take it.'

'Don't be so foolish, William. We'll put her in the cottage and lock it up, until the police arrive.'

'What about Dee? What'll we do about him?'

She thought for a moment. 'I'm not sure. You mustn't let him get his hands on that weapon. Maybe we should throw it in the lake.'

'I'd rather keep it close to me, Gran. You just never know when we'll need it.'

'Very well. Now let's go move that poor girl's body.'

My breath came in short gulps and I began to tremble again. Somehow, this was different. The others were accidents, but this was murder – cold-blooded murder … and the mess. I didn't think my stomach could stand it. Gran led the way and reluctantly, I followed. Trying to delay the event, I stopped her, 'Gran, how did I get in the house?'

'I told you, Dizzy and I carried you.'

God. I swear my heart sounded like native tom-toms. Some holiday this turned out to be. Addy was lying where she had fallen. Gran took her feet and I got the messy end. I placed the shotgun on the bloodstained path and then almost fainted again as I touched her. She was extremely cold and the body was stiff, like a dummy, but it was real. In this terrible and awkward fashion, we carried her to the nearest cottage.

We put her down and I ran back for the gun. Dee was nowhere to be seen. While I was collecting the weapon, Gran had opened the door. We carried the body in and placed her on the bed. Didn't matter about the mess. For ten cents, I'd have burned the whole place down. Gran locked the door as I stood trembling and leaning against the wall on the outside.

'I'll never get over this, Gran. Look at me. I don't think I'll ever sleep again. This is a real living nightmare.'

'Let's go to the kitchen, dear. We have things to discuss.'

I don't know how, but somehow I managed to keep up with her. Gran was a real brick, solid as they come. The shotgun gave me some courage, though it wasn't loaded. It's funny how the world changes after a disaster like that. It seemed that even the birds knew there was something wrong.

The house gave no comfort, either. Gran locked the front door and we walked to the kitchen. I felt like the mouse that was being followed by a hungry cat. Gran seemed confident and had an air of control.

'Put that thing down and sit.'

I put the gun on the table and sat. Gees ... that chair was welcome, my knees were beginning to buckle under me. I have never been so shocked and scared.

'What'll we do, Gran?'

She put her hand on my shoulder and said, 'Take a deep breath, William. First, I feel we must find and apprehend Dizzy. It's most obvious that he murdered that poor girl during the night. At least, it would look that way. There are a couple of things that puzzle me, though, things that do not seem to add up.'

'Like what?'

'The body is too cold; rigor mortis doesn't usually set in that quickly – at least not in this weather. Though I am not an expert in such things.'

'What are you saying, Gran?'

'I don't know, I'm just thinking aloud. It does not add up. I am no Sherlock Holmes, yet I can see that it does not add up. In this case, two and two definitely make five.'

'How do you mean, Gran? I don't understand.'

'Well, think about it, William. Who's idea was it to come here? Who made all the arrangements?'

'So what?'

'Dizzy would not have come if you hadn't asked him. How would he know about Uncle Edgar? Was it his plan to search for hidden treasure on this island?'

'I don't see what you mean, Gran.'

'If Uncle Edgar was in fact murdered, then it has to be part of the same conspiracy. On the other hand, it could be a most unlikely series of coincidences. I honestly thought Edgar was murdered and I felt that Pete could have been. It is obvious that Mr Henderson could have been struck by a piece of wood or something and then drowned. Now, as for Adeline – this is obviously no accident. Even the police would have to admit she was murdered.'

'I wish the police were here now. I don't like any of this. I don't understand your theory, Gran. You're not making any sense to me.'

'It's a puzzle, William. I certainly never expected this outing to turn into such a terrible affair. Perhaps if we corner Dizzy, he will explain why and how this all came about, should he know the answers, that is.'

A cold flush flooded over my entire body as I thought about the implications. I picked up the shotgun and smelled the barrel.

'I'm no expert, Gran, yet even I can smell the gun hasn't been fired. The barrel is as clean as a whistle. That means there is another gun on the island.' Carefully and slowly, I pulled the three cartridges from my pocket and pushed them into the loading slot one by one.

'What are you doing, William?'

'Well, I figure there has to be another gun on Fiend's Rock. When I find who's holding it, I want to be able to say snap. Get my drift, Gran?'

'Yes, William. I don't like guns but, under these circumstances, well, as long as it's you. Whatever you do, don't allow it to fall into anyone else's hands. Now, do you get my drift, young man?'

'Yes, Gran.'

Of course, there remained at least one pressing problem. What happened to Dee? The nightmare was not yet over; no one had showed up to rescue us. I wanted to just hide and cry, but I had to put on a show for Gran. Who would kill Addy? I couldn't believe it was Dee, not by the way he acted, yet they were fighting. My nerves were getting almost as bad as Alic's. I jumped at the least little noise. It was difficult stifling back my natural urges, but Gran's hot tea helped.

'I'm not sure what to do, William. I think we should find and restrain Dizzy. Do you think he's armed?'

I shrugged my shoulders. 'Dunno, Gran. I figure we should stay close to each other; that makes it two to one.'

'Very well, drink your tea and we'll go see if we can find him.'

Another task I was not looking forward to. 'Alright,' I said with resolution. 'Let's go, Gran.' Man, I'd seen more dead than most soldiers. What the hell else was outside?

Gran carefully locked the front door after we exited. 'We'll make a circle of the island, William. Let's start at the pier.'

'Okay, you're the boss.'

I carried the shotgun at the ready. It made me feel like a soldier about to see combat for the first time. Slowly, we approached the boathouse and then walked to the pier. No sign of any boats floating or otherwise. Back round by the cottages, Gran tried the doors – all were still locked. Gingerly, we approached the pump house – still no sign of the enemy.

Slowly, we rounded Beacon Hill and went right up to the south tip of the island. Still no boats and no Dee. As we headed east round the rocky foreshore, the trees obscured the house.

'Let's walk to the cemetery,' I suggested.

'Very well, dear.'

The graves were just as we'd left them. Somehow, they seemed friendlier than the rest of the island. You could see the house from the cemetery through the trees. We walked towards the beach. A body lay deathly still on the sand.

'Dee,' I shouted.

He rolled over and glared at me. 'Piss off, I don't want to even see you,' he yelled.

'Dee, come on. We're going to lock you up to keep you safe.'

He jumped to his feet. 'No you bloody ain't. You murdered Addy. I ain't gonna let you kill me, too.' Like a deer, he leapt onto the rocks and ran across the patio to the north of the house.

'What'll I do, Gran?'

'Don't worry, William, he's obviously quite mad. I think we should barricade ourselves in the house until we are rescued.'

# Chapter 20

## Then There Were Two

With mad Dee running around the grounds, Gran and I locked ourselves in the house for safety. We locked all doors and checked all windows. No way were we going to let that shotgun out of our sight. Insanity seemed to have set in, as Dee must have forgotten he murdered Addy – the idiot blamed me. I sat in the kitchen cuddling the shotgun for comfort.

'What are we gonna do, Gran?'

She exhaled, expressing fatigued annoyance. 'We must wait until we are rescued. Today is Saturday, therefore there is bound to be someone who will notice our predicament.'

'What if Dee tries to get in? What'll we do then?'

'We'll deal with that when and if it should happen. For the present, we are safe in here.'

'I like your idea of arresting him. We could lock him up somewhere.'

'And where would we put him? No, William, I think he's safer out there as long as we're in here.'

Suddenly and with a crash, one of the windows exploded into fragments. Gran and I ducked. The rock bounced off the counter and fell noisily to the floor. Dee was outside and began shouting. 'Come out, you bastards, and face me. I know who did it.'

'Oh, shit, Gran. What'll we do now?'

'First, William, we will refrain from swearing and the use of coarse language.'

'Sorry, Gran.'

'It's a serious situation. Do you think he has a weapon?'

'Don't know.'

'Either way, we will have to go and meet him eventually and preferably before he resorts to burning us out of the house.'

'Oh God! Do we have to, Gran?'

'Yes, I fear so.'

I cocked the shotgun and moved in the general direction of the front door. Already, my knees began to knock. School was never like this. Gran carefully unlocked the main door.

'Do be cautious, William. We don't want to harm the boy if it can be avoided,' she said softly.

'Right.' Gingerly, I led the way into the great outdoors. Dee was nowhere to be seen. 'Come on, Dee. I'm out, show yourself,' I shouted.

His voice came from the trees to the west of the house. 'So you can blow me away with that shotgun, eh? I ain't as mad as that, Bill.'

'You got it all wrong, Dee. I didn't shoot Addy. I thought you did,' I yelled in his direction.

'Me? I don't even have a gun. You're the one with a gun.'

'What'll I do, Gran?'

'You go indoors, I'll talk him round.'

'And leave you to his mercy? Not on your life.'

'Not to worry, William. I'll convince him you will shoot him if he harms me. I think I can manage it. Now you toddle off, but stay within earshot.'

I didn't like it, though I guess there was no alternative. 'Alright, Gran, if I hear you yell, I'll come running.'

'There's a good boy, William. Now, you go indoors and listen, alright?'

Reluctantly, I walked back through the front door and closed it, then gently and silently opened it again. I wanted to hear every little noise, every single word spoken. Holding the gun close and at the ready, I put my ear to the crack in the door.

Gran called to Dee and then walked over towards the trees. I was scared stiff. What if he did have a gun? After about three minutes that seemed like an hour, Gran called to me. 'William, we're coming in, don't shoot.'

I opened the door. 'Okay, Gran, come on in.'

Dee looked wild and dishevelled. His eyes were wide and staring and his clothes were filthy. He snarled at me and said, 'You bastard. You killed her – you killed Addy. Did yah think I wouldn't know, eh?'

I shook my head slowly and stared back. 'You're nuts, Dee. What would I gain? And this gun's never been fired?'

'The gold. She told you where it is, didn't she, eh?'

'Dummy, there is no gold. I didn't hurt her. I was here with Gran in the house all night.'

172

'I was in my room. It had to be you. There are only three of us on the island.'

I had to think for a moment. 'Dee, I wouldn't hurt anybody, least of all a woman. Hell, man, you know me.'

'Then who did, eh? There ain't nobody else.'

A leading question. It wasn't Gran and it sure as hell wasn't me. If it really wasn't Dee, then who? 'Gran, what do you think?'

She looked at me with scalding eyes. 'I think we should all have a nice cup of tea, dear.'

Tea, all she thought about was tea. 'Gran, what'll I do with Dee?'

'He's as innocent as you are, William. Someone is trying to divide us and in that way, conquer us. There has to be someone else on this island.'

'But that means ...'

'Yes, William. It means we are not alone and our unseen enemy has a shotgun. I would strongly suggest that he, or she, is not a ghost.'

I ran back and locked the front door. Fear was rapidly replacing revulsion and sadness. No way was that shotgun going to be out of my hands. 'Alright, let's go in the kitchen and all stay together.'

Dee smiled. 'I'm scared, Bill. I can't figure out what's going on. It just has to be you.'

'Join the club. But Gran'll figure it out. Someone is trying to drive us out one way or another.'

Somehow, I didn't trust Dee. I made sure he stayed well clear of me. I sat in the corner near the counter, with the gun firmly held in one hand. Gran busied herself making tea. I didn't want any. A good slug of hard liqueur would have been more appropriate and certainly more relaxing.

'Do you have the key to my cottage?' Dee asked.

I nodded. 'Yeah, why?'

'I left my Swiss army knife there. I'd like to go get it.'

Sucking my bottom lip for a moment or two, I thought about the implications. 'No. You stay here; I'll go get it if anyone goes.'

Gran pulled a can from the cupboard. 'Biscuit, anyone?'

'No, I don't want anything, Gran. Doesn't this situation worry you at all?'

Dee grabbed a couple and stuffed them in his mouth. He looked pathetic.

'What you want that knife for, Dee?'

'I'd feel safer if I had it. You've got that gun. You know what I mean, eh?'

'No, I don't.'

'I'd feel safer with a weapon of my own. What if he gets you?'

'Who?'

'The guy who killed everyone else.'

I had to think about that one. 'What exactly do you mean, Dee?'

'Gord, you're slow, just as Addy said. She said Edgar was murdered. So was Pete and Henny. I figure the killer heard her telling me, that's why she's bought it, see what I mean, eh?'

'You're as nutty as a fruitcake, Dee. It doesn't make any sense. Why would anyone go to such trouble? If there is someone else on the island, they could have and probably would have killed us by now, and for what reason?'

'Gold, gold. You know, that yellah shit, eh? Use your thinker, Bill. Addy said the killer murdered Edgar by knocking him out and then puttin' a candle in the cabin.'

'How would a candle kill anyone?'

''Cause then the killer opened the valve on a propane cylinder and left it to fill the cabin. Soon as the gas reached the candle flame, boom. No Edgar, see what I mean, eh?'

'I don't believe it.'

'What about Pete, then. Addy said she just turned her back and he was dead. He'd been stabbed with the point of the weather thing. See what I mean, murder number two, eh?'

I shook my head sadly. 'No. I don't believe a word of it. How could someone live on this island and not be detected?'

Gran stepped in. 'Well I think it makes some sense. Someone is out there with express determination to eliminate us all. Someone who knows this island far better than we do.'

'But why, Gran?'

'All I can think of is the gold, just as Adeline said. I remember a story by Agatha Christie. It was about some people marooned on an island and one by one, they died mysterious deaths.'

'Well this isn't a story, Gran.'

'Nonetheless, this scenario is being played out in exacting pulchritude.'

'Wha's that? A dance?' Dee growled.

Gran smiled. 'Silly boy. A story, literary beauty. A play … I believe you youngsters say "scenario".'

'Oh. But who and why?' Dee asked softly as if not wanting to be overheard.

'So what are we going to do?' I asked, looking at Gran and ignoring Dee's question.

'I think I should prepare a meal. You two make friends. We must remain alive and cohesive until the police arrive. I'm sure it won't be long before Inspector Spadafora realizes we've disobeyed his express orders. After all, he did say he wanted us out of town.'

I forbade Dee to leave the house. Both of us remained within arm's reach of Gran. Whoever was out there trying to reduce us to one, or less, was firmly locked out of the house. Or at least we hoped so. Gran's meal was, as only to be expected, perfect. We all sat at the kitchen table and surveyed the ample repast, but none of us actually felt hungry.

The shotgun lay across my knees as I sat at the head of the table. It seemed such a terrible waste not to eat. Slowly, I picked and nibbled. 'Sorry, Gran, I'm just not hungry. I think we should be working to get off this island, instead of sitting around waiting to be knocked off one by one.'

'I cannot swim well enough to make the next island; therefore, I shall have to remain here, William.'

'We could build a raft, like Dee said.'

'I think not. The police will eventually arrive. All will be well.'

I found it very hard to believe that to be true, yet I couldn't think of a reasonable alternative. Gran kept herself busy. Dee and I drifted around the kitchen uneasily, just waiting for the next boot to drop, so to speak. Eventually, the sun began to sink into the horizon and still no boats to the rescue.

'We will all stay in the same room,' Gran said. 'I suggest the family room.'

'Okay, I agree,' I said. 'Let's all go in there. We can watch the grounds from the south windows. So where's this seventh cavalry when you need them?'

I was determined that tonight I would stay awake. Not wanting either Gran or Dee to be out of my sight, I made sure everyone stayed close together. We spent quite a lot of time searching for Gran's mobile phone and found no trace of it. We also spent a great deal of time trying to figure out where the phone line was and why the regular phone wouldn't work. No luck there, either.

Eventually, we settled down to a night watch. Only Gran and I were going to do the watching and I kept the gun. We put the lights out and settled in for an identical tour of duty as the night before. I let Gran sleep first, thinking that maybe I could stay awake until three or even four in the morning.

As difficult as it was, I managed to keep my eyes open. Dee snored like a trooper, but Gran was more petite and although she snored, it was a more gentle sound. I remained awake in the near total darkness. As the two of them slept in peace, my mind was free to wander and wander it did. I reflected on how my life had changed. Riches didn't bring the happiness I thought it would. Unnecessary worries fleeted and collected in one's head, like what if the bad guy shuts down our generator or poisons the water supply, or …

The moon turned the sparse clouds into spirit-like forms and lit the trees in relief; a ghostly scene as the trees gently swayed in the mild breeze. There were no lights on the lake, except for the beacon over on the rocks. The rocks – Jesus! What a fool. I suddenly realized something. There was a Ministry of Transport light operating on the shoal, only 200 metres south-west of Fiend's Island.

Excitement exploded inside me. I wanted to wake everyone up and give them the good news. What dummies we had all been. All ministry lights have a system to report problems. All I had to do was swim 200 metres and smash the lamp. A boat with a technician would arrive very quickly, as the alarm would sound somewhere on the mainland.

At length, I awakened Gran. 'Gran, Gran. It's time for you to watch.'

'Oh, very well, William.'

'Come sunup, Gran, we'll be free of this place.'

'Oh, and why is that?'

'I'm going to swim out to that beacon out there. The ministry will send someone to repair it.'

'But it's not broken.'

'It will be when I swim out there, Gran.'

She giggled, rather like a young girl. 'I knew I didn't have any stupid relatives. I think it's an excellent idea. You get some sleep and conserve your energy, William. In the morning, we'll execute your plan and all will be well.'

I felt excited and pleased. The end of the nightmare was in view. Police or no police, we would get off this stinking rock, never to return. Very quickly, I fell into a deep slumber. My dreams were wild and vivid, filled with danger and excited confusion.

It was still dark when Gran began shaking me vigorously. 'Wake up, William, wake up.'

With bleary eyes and fuzzy headed, I awoke. 'What's up, Gran?' The light in the room was on.

'Oh, dear, oh dear, William. I must confess I fell asleep. Just a catnap, but I still closed my eyes.'

'So?'

'Dizzy has gone.'

Those words were like thunder; I was fully awake and jumped to my feet. In panic, I looked for the gun – it was quite safe.

'I'll go look for him, Gran.'

'Search the house first, William.'

With gun in hand, I ran to the foot of the stairs and yelled, 'Dee, are you up there?' I yelled several times and then ran up the steps. There was no reply. All the rooms were empty. My heart pounded as I thought of the implications. Running downstairs, I rushed to the front door. My worst fears were realized, as I found it to be unlocked.

'Gran, Gran, you alright?' I yelled.

'Yes, William.' She emerged from the kitchen. 'He's not in the house, is he?'

'No, Gran, he's not.'

'I think we should await the dawn, William, before venturing outside.'

I thought about it for several seconds. He could be out there needing my help, unless the spirit of Fiend's Rock had already got him.

'I gotta go, Gran, he might be out there needing my help.'

She smiled and said, 'You're a good boy, William. I'm sorry that this terror has befallen us. If you find him out there, come back here quickly. We have to stay together.'

'You're coming with me, Gran. I can't leave you here alone.'

'Very well. Come along, then. Let's begin this search. I'll get the flashlight from the kitchen drawer.'

Like a tin soldier, I stood there with the gun slung across my arms as Gran walked away. The reality and terror of the situation was beginning to sink in. Funny thing, this time I didn't want to run and hide. I guess you reach a point of inevitability, where you have to stand and fight. There was just me and Gran against whatever or whoever may be out there.

'I'm ready, William.'

I gave her a sort of sickly grin of encouragement. 'Don't worry Gran, we're gonna pull through this, one way or another.'

Like a pair of frightened mice, we crept through the front door and Gran locked up after we'd passed through. The whole island had a macabre and eerie look. A mist seemed to stream around the outside lights. A foghorn sounded way out in the distance, adding a Dickensian touch to an already dire scene of mysticism.

A light on the corner of the cottages glowed with a halo round it. The eerie silence allowed our footsteps to echo. Save for the marine sounds in the distance, there was perfect silence. Even the lake was calm – making no more sound than the water in a bathtub.

'Dee,' I yelled. My voice echoed off the house and the cottages. The trees also sent back a reply, but no human answered. 'Dee, where are you?' I yelled again. Still there was no answer. 'He's either hiding or dead, Gran.'

'Hush, William. Listen for a moment.'

We stood, straining our ears to pick up any sound that may give us a clue. The pounding of my heart in my ears drowned out every sound. I could hear my own blood, like Niagara Falls. Slowly, we crept to the end of the cottages; one had the lights on. My breath came in short, cold gulps. The door to the cottage was open; it was the one allocated to Dee.

Gingerly we approached, dreading what we might find. Dee was there alright, sprawled out on the floor, still and silent. I stood guard, shotgun at the ready, while Gran examined the body.

'He's dead,' she whispered.

'Oh, God! No, Gran.'

'I'm sorry, William. Someone has bashed his brains in with a heavy object.'

# Chapter 21

## The Vial

We found Dee alright, but he was as dead as the proverbial dodo. Gran spent several minutes examining the body, giving the occasional grunt of understanding. My heart felt like lead and my body as conspicuous as a crow in a canary cage.

After a while, Gran said, 'Come in, William, and close the door.'

Man, that was the last thing I wanted to do. Nonetheless, I followed her instructions. The cottage light was on and I could see far more than I really needed. Poor Dee, he was such a nice guy. Why would anyone want to harm him?

Gran growled at me, 'Check the bathroom, boy.'

Quickly, I checked it – nothing. The world seemed to be closing in on me and growing smaller by the minute.

'So what's going on, Gran? Who the hell would do this to us?'

'I would have thought it obvious by now,' she whispered. 'And please modify your language, young man.'

'Obvious? What's obvious, Gran? The only obvious thing is that Dee's dead.'

'We're not alone on this island, unless you think Dizzy bashed his own brains in.'

'Well, no, but –'

'But nothing, William. Our only chance is to play their game, whoever they may be. We must catch them out, by playing to their rules.'

'I haven't any idea what you're talking about, Gran. Everybody's dead, except you and me.'

'Keep your voice down, boy.' She moved closer to me and whispered in my ear, 'I think we're being monitored.'

'Monitored? What? How?'

'Shush. Listen carefully and don't argue with me.'

'Okay, Gran.'

'Someone is slowly whittling down the opposition. I cannot fathom out the reason or the purpose, though it is evident one of us is to be the next victim, there being a definite shortage of alternatives.'

'So what are we going to do, Gran?'

'If our nemesis believes that he or she has convinced us of their intentions ... well, then we can have him or her as the next victim of their own foul deeds.'

'You've lost me, Gran. Could you explain in common English?'

'If it weren't so serious, boy, it would be funny. Now, listen to me carefully. Whoever this person is, he or she has carefully and accurately planned this charade. Like fools, we have fallen into the trap at every turn. I think it's time the mouse turned and bit the cat.'

'I still haven't a clue what you're talking about, Gran.'

'Good, let's hope he or she is as thick as you are. Who have we been blaming all along for these mysterious deaths, William?'

'Addy, I guess?'

'No. Each other. So let us continue the suspicion and allow our clever foe to believe they have us exactly where they want us.'

'But he or she does. Don't they?'

'Not quite, dear William. To convince him or her that their plan is 100 per cent successful, you will have to believe I am the murderer and you'll have to kill me.'

'Not bloody likely, Gran.'

'Listen, foolish boy, I don't think we have much time left. We must play the charade as convincingly as we can.'

'Charade? I still don't understand.'

'Then shut up and listen. Someone is out there waiting till there is just one of us left. I do not know why and I do not know what they will do when one of us two is dead. Though, I think we can give them a very nasty surprise, my boy.'

'Alright, keep talking, Gran. I think I'm beginning to get your drift.'

'I am going to run out of here screaming and I'll run to the house and supposedly lock myself in the bedroom. You must pretend to be very angry and chase me. We wish to convince our nemesis that their plan has worked. You may fire that weapon to attract their attention and then you should chase me, break down the bedroom door and burst in. There, you will fire that weapon once again. I shall scream as convincingly as I can. It will sound as though you have murdered me, which is what our enemy wishes.'

'Then what?'

'Then there is only one, or at least he or she will think there is only one of us left. Then you must go downstairs and slowly walk back here. Remember, you are most sad and afraid; you have just murdered your grandmother. Try to look as though you have.'

'So then what will happen?'

'I am sure you'll find our killer will show him or herself, if only to boast of their great cleverness. We will then have the advantage, for they won't know there are two of us still. I will creep up on him or her and together, we will vanquish them. If all goes well, this nightmare will be over and the doer of foul deeds will be in our hands.'

'Well, Gran, that sounds like a good way to get one of us killed, if not both.'

'Do as I say, William, please. It is our only hope.'

'Alright. Ready when you are.' Instantly, my heart began to pound. I could feel a cold sweat breaking out all over. Acting was never my best forte.

She kissed me lightly on the cheek and then opened the door. With a shriek that almost made my knees buckle, Gran ran from the cottage towards the house. To make her plan look good, I steamed outside and fired the gun but, of course, not at Gran. The bang was enough to awaken the dead. It echoed off the trees and house like a roll of thunder.

Gran kept up her screeching all the way to the front door. She opened it and fled inside. God, I said to myself, I hope this is going to work out the way she thinks it is.

'Alright, you old bat,' I shouted. 'I'm coming for you. No one kills all my pals and gets away with it, not even you.'

I ran to the house and, just like Gran had arranged, ran upstairs. Her bedroom door was closed. Giving the door an almighty kick, which almost broke my ankle, a wave of fear swept over me. Shit, did my ankle ever hurt! The damn door didn't budge. Then I heard a little voice whisper, 'Try the handle, William.'

I tried it and it opened. Gran screamed so loud it made me jump. I pointed the gun at the window and fired. The glass exploded, crashing down to the ground outside with a fearful noise. Gran screamed again and stupidly, I fired the last cartridge in the excitement of the moment. Damn it. I'd used all the ammunition.

'Shit, Gran,' I whispered. 'I've used all the cartridges.'

'Don't worry, William. I'm dead now. Only you and I know the weapon is empty. Now, go outside, there's a good boy. Play the charade to the end.'

181

What with the excitement and fear, my body trembled from head to foot. Gingerly, I descended the stairs, not knowing what to expect. Would they jump out and try to kill me, too? Maybe he or she would confront me as Gran had suggested. With shaking hands, I opened the front door. It was dark and uninviting outside. Taking my courage in both hands, I ventured out into the darkness.

Feeling as obvious as an elephant at a tea party, I inched into the realms of the morning spirit. A slight mist was rising, caused by the heat and the water. Slowly, I advanced towards the cottages, empty gun at the ready.

Suddenly, a soft voice spoke behind me. 'You won't need that gun,' she said in a gentle Australian accent.

I spun round. She was sitting at a picnic table on the patio. The only light was the standard lamp behind her.

'Addy?' I quizzed, unable to believe my eyes and ears.

'Come and sit with me,' she said softly.

'Are you a bloody ghost or what?'

'Come, sit with me.'

A cold flush rushed over my entire body. All I could see was the dark silhouette. As I approached, her features became apparent. It was Addy or a facsimile thereof.

'How?' I gasped.

'Sit, William.'

I moved closer and sat in a position that gave me a better look at her. On the table were two glasses and a bottle of wine. Gracefully, almost mystic-like, she poured two drinks.

'Will you drink to my success?'

I must have looked rather stupid with my mouth hanging open and my eyes wide. 'Addy, I don't understand.'

She looked at me with those big, sparkling eyes. 'Drink up. Here's to success and a load of gold.' She downed the entire glassful.

I stared at her in total disbelief. 'But you're dead. I saw you. How –'

'Drink up and shut up, mate. Now, do I look dead to you?'

I took the glass and sipped the sweet wine, thinking that it may bring some sense of reality back to me.

'I know you were dead, no one could live through that. I saw it. It wasn't make-up.'

'What you saw was my mate, not me. She's bin dead weeks.'

I sucked up the rest of the wine and gasped, 'Weeks? What d'you mean weeks? What mate?'

'She's bin stored in the freezer chest in the boathouse. Lucky Edgar had a nice big one.'

My head was spinning, as the situation seemed totally surreal. 'In the boathouse?' I echoed like a fool.

She poured me some more wine and then placed a very small bottle on the table. 'Drink up, William, this is your last day.'

'Last day?'

'Exactly. Tomorrow, the police will find you dead, maybe.'

'Maybe? I don't have a clue what you're talking about.'

'You always were thick, William. The game's over. I win. Check and mate.'

'Win? Win what?' I sucked up more of the wine. My head seemed to spin as though I was nearing intoxication.

'Did you blow the old biddy away with that gun, Billy boy?'

'Er ... Hey, oh yeah.' I pointed it at her. 'She was ... I thought she killed Dee. But she didn't, did she?' It felt important to keep up the pretence.

Addy shook her head slowly. 'Great screaming dingoes, you dummy. You're the perfect patsy – thick as two broad planks. You poor, dumb sucker.'

'Well ... never mind the platitudes,' I said. 'So I'm a little slow on the uptake. Tell me how clever you are.'

'Firstly, there's no ammunition in that gun. How's that for clever? Like an idiot, you've used it all splattering your poor old granny all over her nice clean bedroom walls. Guess whose fingerprints are on the gun?'

'What?'

'Well, when you commit suicide, who do you think the Old Bill is going to blame?'

'Old Bill? Blame? I've no idea what you're on about, Addy. I'm totally confused. How did you get the body out of the freezer? How did you get it in?'

She laughed a hollow laugh. 'Poor William, you were born confused and you've never improved. I suppose you're too stupid to feel stupid.'

I sort of cringed; nothing she said made any sense to me. 'I still can't figure out why you're not dead.'

'I'll try to bring you up to speed before you die, Billy boy.'

'Die?'

'That wine was poisoned. You didn't think I'd take any chances with a muscleman like you, did you?'

I dropped the glass – it smashed with a clatter on the concrete. 'Poisoned?' My breath began to come in panicked gulps. 'I'm too young to die.'

A sly smile slowly spread across her evil face. 'God, you're stupid. I want you to sign this island over to me, like give it to me as a pressie. Then, and only then will I give you the antidote to the poison.' She held out a small vial, holding it lightly with two fingers. 'Move fast and I'll drop it. Goodbye William. I still get the island, being the only living relative.'

My head began to spin. Death was not on my calendar. 'Give me the antidote and we'll talk.'

'Oh, no. I lead this troop, mate. We'll just talk for a bit and then I'll give you the antidote, alright?'

'I guess so. But why?'

She smiled and leaned back in the chair. 'You still don't understand, do you, William? Thick as the Great Barrier Reef.'

'No. But ... well, I'll listen.'

'Well, you're between a rock and a hard place. When I give you the antidote, they'll arrest you for all the murders, including Uncle Edgar.'

'I didn't do it. I've killed nobody.'

She laughed again. 'No, William, you didn't do it. I did. I killed them all, except one. I'm not even Adeline Reyley.'

'You're not. Well, who are you? What do you want?'

'My real name is Freda Davis.'

'Freda Davis? But I thought you were Addy, you look like Addy.'

'You stupid dingo. Uncle Edgar wrote to Adeline telling her the story of Fiend's Rock. I believed it. She thought it was just a silly story to get her to come all the way out here. I thought it would be fun if I came. So I came here and pretended to be sweet Adeline.'

'I still don't understand; why would Uncle Edgar invite Adeline Reyley to Fiend's Rock?'

'Your Aunt Jane went to Australia, married and had a kid – Adeline. She was your cousin. Aunt Jane and her idiot husband died in a motor car accident, kind of convenient. Addy and I were in the same home for awhile. So when I came here, at last I was free. Edgar was going to leave me all his property. The poor sucker was in love with me. I was good to him. The bastard changed his will, so when I killed him I still didn't have this island. By rights, it's mine, all of it; including the gold.'

'You've gotta be kiddin' me.'

'No, William I'm not kidding. Your stupid cousin turned up in person and spilled the beans to Edgar. She was the bitch that spoiled it all for me.

I didn't know he'd changed his will, so that night I killed him and used that gun on Addy. I figure it improved her looks no end.'

'But the clothes, how could you know what she would be wearing?'

'Stupid, I bought identical clothes for the occasion. I knew the opportunity would arise. When she started to thaw out, she looked real spectacular. The melted ice made loads of good-looking blood.'

I just sat and listened, hardly able to believe what I was hearing. She didn't look like a cool, calculating killer.

'Give me the antidote. Or I'll have to use this gun again.'

'Shut up and sit down, stupid. The gun's empty. You should last about twelve hours before you die. I don't think you have any idea what's happening, do you? I can see the ignorance in your simple face.'

'Yes, I think so. What do you want from me, Addy, or whatever your name is?'

'I already have it. Now it will all come to me, one way or another. Either as the last relative or you giving it to me all signed, sealed and legal-like.'

'Alright, if I give it to you, everything you want, then what? The cops will arrest me and throw me in jail till the bars rust through. Is that what you want?'

She smiled. 'You have no imagination, that's your bloody trouble, mate. The only problem is Gran. You've blasted her all over the bedroom. We can feed the fish with Adeline and Dizzy, but Gran's a bit of a problem.'

I began to feel bad, as I knew the poison had begun to work. I could feel it; my toes were tingling and my stomach was rebelling.

'Please give me the antidote.'

She toyed with the little glass vial, even tossed it in the air and caught it.

'Do you realize, William, your life is in this little bottle. I am the most powerful person on this island.'

'Alright, alright, I'll give you everything you want. Let's go into the house and I'll sign anything for you, but please, please, the antidote.'

'Don't rush me, darling. I'm enjoying this. After all, I have worked real hard for it. That filth Dizzy had his hands all over me. I enjoyed killing him. I never expected it to be so easy. He went to the cottage in the middle of the night. You should have seen his face when he saw me.'

'How, how did you do it?'

'The poor bastard really thought I liked him. He had the audacity to ask me to sleep with him even after the fight we'd had. When he turned up

185

with that stupid grin on his face, I conked the bastard with that lovely heavy ornament. He deserved it.'

'Well, what happened to your boat?'

'I couldn't let you off the island. I'd lose control, wouldn't I? So I used the electric drive. While you were all getting ready, I mounted it and turned it on. It was easy to jump off. I thought you fools would see it. Do you know it was only just round the bend when you came back?'

'I don't believe it, any of it. You have to be making it all up.'

She giggled in a girlish way. 'Willy, dear. May I call you Willy?'

'I guess so.'

'Willy, dear, you could marry me and we'd live here for the rest of our lives.'

'Marry, live here? I, er … Please give me the antidote. I can feel the poison working.'

She placed the vial on the table, standing it on end. Glaring at it, she said, 'William, you must promise me you will love me and cherish me.'

'I do, I will, sure, yes, anything.'

'Then I'll save you from the Old Bill.'

'Who's Old Bill?'

'The cops, stupid. I'll save you. They're so dim, they'll never catch me. Did you know, I murdered my mother and stepfather? Murdered them. Murder, a neat and meaningful word, wouldn't you say?'

Slowly and almost unperceived, I inched forwards. I wanted to grab that vial. She had no idea that Gran's plan had worked. But I could feel my breath coming in ever-shorter gulps. The time must be getting close. That's when things went wrong – or right.

Suddenly, the night silence was invaded by the sound of a powerful marine engine throttling back. Addy looked in the direction of the sound. Someone was standing by the house door. Addy leapt up and knocked the table. The vial rolled across the top and I grabbed unsuccessfully at it. With a heart-rending tinkle, the little vial smashed on the concrete slab floor.

# Chapter 22

## Latitude 45:19

After all the death and destruction, and I may add towards the end of my life, a boat arrived at our island. A strong white light suddenly burst forth, penetrating the darkness like a giant, luminous finger. The powerful motor boat seemed to be circling just off the jetty and sweeping my island with its brilliant light beam as though looking for something.

'Are you alright, William?' Gran shouted from the house doorway.

I was grovelling on the floor as my last hopes of life soaked into the concrete. 'She's poisoned me,' I bleated in a shaky voice. My vision was becoming clouded with tears. I could almost hear St Peter calling.

Gran came over to me. 'What are you doing down there, William?'

'She poisoned me, she poisoned me. The antidote was in that vial. She dropped it when you scared her.'

'Who was she, William?'

'I don't care; my antidote's soaked into the concrete. I'm dying.'

Gran touched the wet spot and sniffed her finger. 'Stand up, you silly boy.' She took the bottle of wine and sniffed it. Putting it down, she grabbed my arm and dragged me to the seat. 'Sit and listen, William.'

'We've got to find out what the antidote was and make some more, like quick, Gran. I've only got a few hours left. I'm doomed.'

'Years, I would say, not hours. And you certainly will be doomed if you don't pull yourself together.'

'What? What d'yah mean?'

'The wine smells good; I tasted a small bit on my fingers. I think you have been duped, William.'

'Duped?'

'Whoever that was, she gave you good wine and the antidote is the poison, you foolish boy. The antidote smells of foul deeds.'

'What?'

'Oh, my goodness. Your antidote smells like strychnine to me and I'm sure the wine is clean. Did she drink any of the wine?'

'Yeah, yeah, she did.'

'Good. Now cheer up. We're rescued. Look.'

The boat with the powerful light had circled the island and was docking at our pier. The searchlight was still on and sweeping the south end of the rock around Beacon Hill. Suddenly, a familiar voice shouted at us.

'You alright, Mrs Hubert?' Inspector Spadafora yelled. He came striding masterfully across the lawn, with a large flashlight in one hand.

'Oh, my goodness,' Gran said. 'Are we ever glad to see you. We've been prisoners here for days.'

The inspector had a big, cheerful smile on his face. 'Well. I'm glad to find you alive. Where's everyone else?'

The tension fled from Gran, leaving her weak and tearful. She sank to the seat by the table and with a quaver in her voice, said, 'The other's are dead, all dead. We've had a fearful and terrible time here. How did you know to come for us?'

'Don't worry, Mrs Hubert. I think I've figured it all out – albeit a little on the late side. The warden of Killbear Provincial Park found a boat late last night. Well, one of her rangers did. Anyhow, she called me from her headquarters and reported the boat as a rather unusual find.'

'So how did you know to come here, inspector?'

He chuckled. 'It was that Aussie girl's boat. Like the *Mary Celeste*, there were no clues as to what happened to the crew. Knowing the potential dangers on this island, I sailed straight over, after inspecting the vessel.'

Gran stood up and gave the inspector a little hug. 'Thank you. We cannot thank you enough. I am sure we can work out a reward for you. I am so pleased and relieved.'

'Give it to the benevolent society, Mrs Hubert. I can't take your money.'

'It was Addy,' I said excitedly. 'She's still around and she poisoned me.'

'Poisoned you?' he quizzed.

'Ignore the boy, inspector. There's nothing wrong with him that a good cup of tea wouldn't fix.'

'Let's walk to the house,' Spadafora suggested with a firm, reassuring voice. 'I'm sure a nice cup of coffee will help us sort all this out in the shortest possible time.'

I was still trembling from the shock of being poisoned … or near-poisoned. The clean, bright light of the house had the effect of chasing some of the evil shadows away. Funny, it was as if I had lived my entire life in that building and could hear the voices of the dead echoing through the ancient residence. It was if they were all congregating to see the outcome. Spadafora's presence was a strong boost to my ego and a powerful reassurance. He looked the part, with his revolver strapped to his side, his radio and all that leather. He looked to be a tall, powerful figure of a man, probably close to retirement.

'We'll talk in the kitchen,' he commanded.

You could see the relief in Gran's face. She was almost her normal, smiling self. In her usual and inimitable way, Gran rounded up the utensils for a tea break – even found some biscuits.

'It'll be ready in a few minutes,' she said, smiling.

'Good. Now let's all relax, sit and you can tell me what has been happening on this island.' Spadafora didn't sit; instead, he put one foot on a chair and stared at me. 'You look like you've been wrestling with the angel of death, lad. Why don't you begin?'

'Yeah, sure. Well, well, you see. It was Addy, well, not Addy, the girl that looked like Addy, I think.'

Spadafora smiled. 'Now calm down, son. Everything's going to be alright. Tell me what has been happening here.'

'Yeah, sure. Everybody's dead, she killed them, she killed them all, except Alic, maybe.'

'Alic?'

'Oh, yeah, Alicia. She's a student. We were at uni together.'

'Oh, Miss Alicia Morris. That's a start. Now, just who exactly is this other woman you are referring to?'

'She's a girl from Australia. She pretended to be Addy; she killed Addy and stored her in that freezer in the boathouse. She murdered Uncle Edgar, 'cause the real Addy told him everything. Spilled the beans on whatever her name was and everything.'

'So where is she now?'

'When you turned up, she ran off. Has to be on the island somewhere, though.'

The inspector smiled. 'Ran off, on this huge continent. Just where do you think she could have run off to?'

'I don't know.'

He unclipped his mike from his lapel and spoke to it. 'Spadafora to Brown. Secure the island; keep a lookout for a blond female in her twenties.' He looked at me and said, 'Is she armed?'

'No, I don't think so.'

He whispered into the mike again. 'Treat her as armed and dangerous.' Again, he addressed me. 'Is there any way off of this island?'

'Not that I know of or we'd have done it. But Addy's a good swimmer.'

'I suspected her in Edgar Reyner's death, but it was a very clean and evidence-free job. Do you know how she managed it?'

'Easy,' I said. 'She bashed him with something and then took the boat out, set the auto pilot, lit a candle and opened the valve on a gas cylinder.'

'How did she escape?'

'She's a hell of a good swimmer. I guess she must have swum home. The boat could have gone on for ages before it blew up.'

'And you say she's hiding somewhere on this island?'

'Yeah, you'd better not leave your boat unattended. I think you should call for reinforcements. We've got dead bodies all over the place. Knee-deep in them.'

Spadafora smiled and rubbed his chin thoughtfully with one hand. 'So, how did her boat get to Killbear Park?'

'She set it adrift to maroon us.'

'And your boat? Where is your boat?'

'Don't know. I think Alic took it in a fit of anger. I figure you should check to see if she got home okay.'

He nodded and said, 'So you two are the lone survivors?'

'Yeah.'

'And no Fiend's gold?'

'Yeah, that's right. Addy, well … not Addy, the girl who pretended to be her, she said that Edgar had found it and she killed him before he told her where it was.'

'Doesn't sound very intelligent. I want you two to remain in the house. I'll take charge of that shotgun if you don't mind. Consider yourselves under house arrest until further notice.'

'Well … really,' Gran gasped and stood up. 'I'll have you know this is our island and I would thank you to treat it likewise.'

'Sorry, Mrs Hubert. Just play along with me for awhile. We'll soon clear this thing up, professionally. I'll send a constable to accompany you. Can I trust the pair of you?'

I nodded in the affirmative.

Gran sat down again and said, 'Very well, but the chief constable will hear of your conduct, inspector. I for one am not impressed.'

He took his mike and mumbled a few words into it as he headed for the exit. The sun was just lifting its head above the mainland and the sky

190

was streaked with yellow and gold, reminding me of the hidden treasure. No sooner had Spadafora walked out of the door than another cop walked in. He was uniformed and carrying a gun in his holster.

'Would you like some coffee or tea, officer?' Gran asked.

'Thank you, ma'am.'

About twenty boring minutes later, we heard the thrashing sound of a helicopter. It flew over the house and landed in the lake near the pier. I ran to the family-room window to get a better view of what was happening – couldn't see anything. Running back to the kitchen, I asked the cop if I could go upstairs.

'Certainly, sir. But please do not leave the building.'

In a flash, I ran up the stairs and into the south-west bedroom. From that vantage point, I could see the helicopter. They had shut down the engine and two people were coming ashore in a rubber boat. It was a beautiful, clear morning and the lake was as calm as a millpond. The sun had chased all the fog away and the police had chased all the ghosts away.

Bored with the lack of activity, I walked to my room. My sickly feeling of being poisoned had passed. I guess the coffee had drowned it. Very strange, though; someone had been searching through my things. Some of the bureau drawers had been pulled out and the contents were scattered on the floor. My first thought was that it could have been Dee and then I wasn't sure. What had he or she been looking for? And had they found it? The mess must have been made recently, probably last night. Slowly, I began replacing the things – most of them weren't even mine. Then it dawned on me; whoever it was had been looking for something of Edgar's. This had been Edgar's room. The only person that wanted something from my uncle was Addy or whatever her real name is. As the reality of the intrusion began to sink in, I found myself joining in the search. Of course, Edgar knew where the gold was. Addy said she'd seen the chart and graphs. Why would Uncle Edgar use graphs; graphs of what? That must be the clue. All I had to do was find the charts or graphs and see what they were of – the lake, maybe.

I chewed my right thumbnail as I pondered over the puzzle. If I were Uncle Edgar, where would I hide charts? Not in the bureau drawer, that's for sure, so where? I continued my fruitless search for some time and then, in disgust, I walked back downstairs to Gran. She was working in the kitchen.

'I've solved it, Gran,' I said as an opener.

She looked up from her labours at the sink. 'Excellent, William. What have you solved?'

191

'Well, all we have to do is find Uncle Edgar's charts and that's where the gold will be marked. He could even have told Addy and she didn't understand.'

'Charts. What sort of charts, William?'

'I don't know. That's part of the puzzle. Probably sea charts or weather graphs, or something to do with the lake. I don't know.'

'Did you look in the safe?'

'Safe, what safe, Gran?'

She smiled and placed her arms akimbo. With a grin like a Cheshire cat, she said, 'You've spent too much time outside. The safe is in the sitting room, behind the painting of the praying female.'

I dashed off to the sitting room. Looking around, I saw three paintings: one of a sailing shipwreck and one of some old woman sitting in a chair in front of a barn. The third was of a young woman praying at an altar. Carefully, I looked behind the pictures. The one with the woman praying was hiding my quest.

A neat-looking wall safe, but who has the key? I ran back to Gran. 'Gran, I didn't see any nudes, though I did find the safe. We'll have to get a locksmith to open it for us.'

'A locksmith, William?'

'Yeah.'

'Then why not use this key.' She opened the counter drawer and pulled out a very large, old-fashioned-looking key. 'I think you'll find that this one will work.'

I took the key and ran back to the sitting room. No sweat. The key fitted and the heavy door swung open. Just as predicted, there were charts in there. My heart pounded with the excitement; all that screwing around and the information was right under our noses.

Excitedly, I took the charts to the table and unrolled them. Didn't make much sense, though. They were just regular nautical charts of the area; one had Fiend's Rock on it and it was marked with a large red tick. I felt like tearing the stupid papers up. It meant nothing to me. Maybe Gran could make sense of them.

Disgruntled, I rolled them up and walked back to the kitchen. 'I got 'em, Gran, and they make no sense at all. I guess I may have been wrong.'

She took them and rolled them out on the dining table. One by one, she examined them and read the cryptic marks in the border area. 'I do believe these are not the ones you're looking for, William.'

'Why?'

'They refer to Fiend's Rock by geographical position, just as a surveyor would. Though as you so badly put it, it makes no sense at all. We already know where the island is. I'm no navigator but, you see, it says 45:19:23.5. That's not a date; it has to be the latitude. Yes, you see, there's the longitude. That's most peculiar. Why would he write it on the map? The edge reference grid shows where it is anyway.'

'Maybe he had a GPS.'

'And what would that be, William?'

For once, I knew something she didn't. Now that filled me with pride. 'Well, they have things called GPS's; Global Positioning Systems. It works from satellites – gives you a position as close as a metre or two anywhere on earth.'

'Does it now? Then, perhaps we have found the solution to this dilemma. Where can we obtain one of these instruments?'

'Well, there was one on our boat, but who knows where that is.'

Gran sat thoughtfully and stared at the chart. I could almost hear her brain ticking over. She was about to come up with a plan, I just knew it.

'Not to worry, William. The solution is at hand. Please put these charts back in the safe and lock it.'

Having nothing better to do, I did as she asked. There was nothing else in the safe, just the charts. Spadafora eventually came back. He walked into the kitchen and sat noisily on a chair, exhaling with a sigh of boredom or fatigue. 'Well,' he said. 'Other than a dead girl and a dead boy, we've found nothing. I think we'll have to start with your statements. Would you like to tell me here or would you like to go to the detachment for a full disclosure?'

'Should we decide here,' Gran said, smiling. 'Will you be staying with us?'

'Until you've given your statements, yes.'

'Then are you leaving this island?'

He shook his head. 'No, this island will be Yellow Petered.'

I looked at him and frowned. 'That's the second time I've heard that expression. What's it mean?'

'The Yellow Peter is the flag of quarantine. No one on and no one off.'

'Oh.'

'Inspector,' Gran said slowly. 'Does your helicopter have a GPS?'

'That's a very strange question, Mrs Hubert. Why would you want to know that?'

'I have a theory, that's all. Well does it?'

193

'I've no idea. Shall we proceed with the statements?'

'Certainly, inspector. Would you be so kind as to ask your pilot if he has a GPS?'

'If it makes you happy, Mrs Hubert, I'll call him.' He snapped the mike from his collar. 'X-ray nine, six. Are you there?'

'X-ray nine, six. Sure … is that you, Jim?'

'Yeah. A witness here wonders if you carry a GPS.'

'Sure, what does he want to know?'

'It's a she. I'll call you back.'

# Chapter 23

## Well, Well, Well!

Thank goodness Inspector Spadafora was unhappy with our stories; that's one reason he had returned to our island. There was no evidence whatsoever to support our innocence, yet he believed in us. To all intents and purposes, we could have killed Addy and Dee, or everyone else for that matter. Having no alibi could easily throw suspicion on us for the murders of all the others; though, for the moment, murder had not been officially established in most of the dead. They were looking for Alicia who, according to us, had stolen my boat and sailed off into the blue.

The entire island had been searched from north to south and from east to west and Addy, or whatever her real name was, could not be found. Gran didn't appear to be alarmed at the possibility of being arrested. She carefully and loyally served the police with tea or coffee as if she were running a police cafeteria.

Gran placed the teapot down carefully and looked at Spadafora. 'Well, inspector, are you going to arrest us?'

'I'm sorry, Mrs Hubert, the way things look I have no alternative.'

'Good, does that mean we will leave this dreadful place under your protection?'

'Certainly. I'll have to take you to the detachment.'

Gran smiled and sat down. 'I haven't lived this long, inspector, without learning a thing or two about human nature.'

'Meaning?'

'I believe William. If he said he was poisoned by some girl posing as Adeline Reyley then he was. The question that I ask is where is this girl now? Am I right?'

'Sure, go on.'

'I feel this whole terrible saga is based on the belief that Fiend left his gold for some entrepreneur to find. Our impostor is the brains behind this entire sad affair. The reason we cannot fathom the answer is simply because we're not paranoid. Adeline is obviously insane and her reasons are beyond our understanding. She has murdered and plundered, with the sole intention of becoming the legal owner of this island, merely to collect the legendary gold.'

Spadafora sighed very loudly and said, 'Sure, Mrs Hubert, and where is this unknown girl? To me, she's as real as Fiend's ghost. Produce her and your story is proven. Without her, I have no alternative but to lay the blame squarely on your shoulders. Do I make myself clear?'

Gran was still smiling. She knew something that I hadn't figured. I saw the girl run to the south of the island and there, she vanished. She could have swum away, maybe to the next island. Though, I didn't really believe that, because the helicopter would probably have seen her in the water.

'I don't know,' Gran,' I chipped in. 'I saw her and then she vanished. Maybe she's the ghost of Jeremiah Fiend.'

Gran laughed. 'She's here, as she has been all along. Inspector, you found her boat, deserted.'

'Yes, we also found her body over there in one of your cottages. As far as I can ascertain, the girl is dead.'

'Would you do me a favour before we surrender to your arrest?'

The inspector pouted his lips and thought for a few seconds. 'Depends on what you want.'

'Is that helicopter of yours returning to the mainland?'

'Yeah.'

'Will you be on it?'

'No, only the team that came in it.'

'Good. Please call your officers and ask them to hover over this exact spot, according to your GPS thing.' She handed him a piece of paper.

The inspector's eyes sparkled as if someone had cracked a joke. He looked at the paper and then his eyes lifted to Gran's. 'So what's this mean, Mrs Hubert?'

'I do believe it's the exact geographical location of very legendary Fiend's gold.'

Spadafora slipped the piece of paper into his breast pocket. 'And what if it is?' he said with a smirk.

Gran walked closer to him and whispered something into his ear. Whatever she said surprised him. You could tell by the expression on his face.

'Alright,' he said and marched out of the room.

'What did you say to him, Gran?'

She smiled and winked. 'Well, William, I think I have solved two mysteries in one shot.'

'How and what?'

'Hush your tongue, boy. Wait and see what Mr Spadafora decides to do. Everything revolves around him.'

I guess it was about ten minutes before the inspector came back.

'I would like you all outside,' he said, motioning his arms as if sweeping us into the great outdoors.

Having nothing better to do and willing to learn the reasons, I followed everyone out of the house. After a few moments, the helicopter took off from where it had been anchored at the end of the pier. In moments, it flew over the island near us and then headed south. The inspector spoke into his microphone. He was using the privacy earplug, to prevent us from hearing the other side of the conversation.

The helicopter stopped and hovered over Beacon Hill. The machine just stood there only a few metres above the trees. Spadafora spoke to the pilot. The conversation lasted several seconds. I have no idea what they said. Suddenly, the machine veered off and returned to the water. With all the noise gone, we could talk again.

'So what happened?' I asked. 'What was all that about?'

Inspector Spadafora looked at Gran. 'You're a genius, Mrs Hubert. That position was exactly over the beacon.'

'I thought so,' she said. 'The gold was buried "well". I wondered if the beacon could have at one time been the original well. Just as you said, William, it could only be buried in the primeval rock. Otherwise, it would have been found before they brought the soil here.'

'That doesn't make sense at all, Gran. The well is the obvious place, I mean ...' I paused to allow my brain to catch up with my mouth. The metal detector gave a huge reading at Beacon Hill, but we took that to be normal.

Without further ado, we all began wandering towards the beacon. It was constructed as a hillock of rocks, with earth poured over it. There was an old iron thing to hold the actual light – I suppose it was a sort of a fire basket – and a concrete slab path encircled the small hill. Well, maybe not concrete, maybe carved, natural rock slabs.

'I don't see anything, Mrs Hubert,' the inspector said. 'It's just the beacon.'

Slowly, the three of us walked round the path, while the other cops stood watching. All the slabs looked the same; none had been moved in centuries.

'What are we looking for?' I asked.

'Your girlfriend,' Spadafora said with a grin.

When I thought about it I realized there could be something in what he said. I couldn't see how anyone would be hiding, though the gold sure as hell could be there. Dee had been digging in the wrong place. On the other hand, if Addy had seen the charts, why didn't she know where the treasure was hidden?

'We'll dig it up,' I suggested.

Spadafora nodded his head towards the house and said in an overly loud voice, 'There's nothing here. We may as well take these people to the detachment and make the charges.'

I was shocked at his sudden change of attitude. 'Wait a minute,' I protested.

'Sorry, Mr Reyner. That way, please.'

We all wandered towards the house. On reaching the first cottage, Inspector Spadafora turned to Gran. 'Sorry about that, Mrs Hubert. I was just playing along with your theory.'

Spadafora snapped the button on his mike and said something into it. Moments later, the helicopter started its engine. He said something to the other cops. All but two went to the boat and cast off. The powerful engines burst into life. In moments, she was under way, leaving only five of us on the island.

I looked at the inspector, confused. 'I don't understand,' I said. 'Shouldn't we be on that boat?'

Spadafora smiled. 'You catch whales with a harpoon and small fry with bait.'

'Bait?'

'Do you have the key to this cottage, Mrs Hubert?'

Gran jingled in her bag for a few seconds and produced the keys. She handed them to the inspector. Without speaking, he selected a key and tossed it to one of the other cops and then nodded his head towards the bungalow. Then he opened the one nearest to us.

'Inside, please,' he said softly.

Gran, Spadafora and I entered the end cottage. It was the one that had been Dee's. The Inspector closed the door.

'I don't think we'll have long to wait.'

'Wait. What for?' I asked in all innocence.

He looked at me with an expression of admonishment. 'Now, we'll all be nice and quiet. Don't want to scare the quarry away, now do we?' He took the only chair and placed it near the window. Then he sat near the venetian blinds, so he could see out. Making himself comfortable in the chair, he sat looking south.

'What are we waiting for?' I asked.

'Your Gran believes that the little Australian miss is hiding on this island. That's how she's been able to control the situation. You see, she's been here all the time.'

'Oh. Well ... why would anyone want to burn her house down?'

'She did that herself,' Spadafora said. 'There could have been incriminating evidence in there. As you two had let yourselves in, she decided to leave no trace.'

Gran said, 'You see, William, there really were two of them, just as the old gentleman had said. One was your cousin, that's the poor girl lying dead in the other cottage.'

'I had the bodies removed, Mrs Hubert.'

'So what happened to Alic?' I asked.

'The Hamilton police haven't found her and your van is still at the dock in Parry Sound,' Spadafora said, keeping his voice deliberately low and his eyes looking south.

The implications were bad. 'So what do you think happened to her?'

'She's still here,' he said in a low growl.

I could feel the tears begin to well up as I thought of poor Alic. She was such a nice girl. 'So what happened to my boat?'

The inspector turned to look at me. 'You really didn't know?'

'No, I don't know. What happened to it then?'

'The helicopter saw a boat on the bottom, just off your west shore. It's sitting in 7 or 8 metres of water about 60 metres out.'

'Sunk?' I gasped.

'Sunk.'

'Holy shit ... Sorry, Gran. Do you think Addy sank it, then?'

Spadafora said, 'Shh. I think we've got action.' Slowly, he rose to his feet and pulled his microphone close to his mouth. 'We've got contact,' he said softly.

In a sudden movement, he snatched the door open and stepped outside. I didn't see what happened after that, but I did hear him shout in a commanding voice, 'Come on, miss. The game is over, you lose.' A moment later, he stepped back into the cottage. 'She's gone to ground again.'

'What?'

'There's no sweat, now we know for sure where she is.' He pulled a folded photocopy from his right breast pocket. 'Take a look at this,' he handed it to me.

Eagerly, I opened it. It was a copy of an engineering work order. 'So?' I said sarcastically.

'Read it.'

I read it. It was just the costing for digging a new well. Its position was given as 60 feet north of the old well, that's about 20 metres. I read it carefully again. It still made no sense. Everyone knows where the well is. 'So, I still don't see any significance,' I said, handing it to Gran.

Gran giggled with delight as she perused the document. 'William, use your brain. What's 60 feet south of the well? Say 18 metres south.'

I shrugged. 'Dunno.'

'Think, boy.'

'The only thing out there is Beacon Hill.'

She smiled. 'Got it in one.'

'Beacon Hill. You mean that's the old well?'

'Exactly, that's where the GPS thing indicated. That's the hiding place of both the ghost and the gold.'

'Holy sh ... Good gracious, Gran. That's the place where the metal detector first indicated a good reading.'

'Come on,' Spadafora said. 'She's gone back underground. Somehow, we'll have to ferret her out.'

We all walked out of the cottage and ambled towards the beacon. Of course, Addy was nowhere to be seen.

'So where did she go?'

'She ran round the back of the hillock. I would guess the entrance is on that side.'

'I don't believe it,' I protested. 'Addy doesn't know where the gold is; that's why she's been knocking everyone off. She figures owning the island will give her the time she needs to find it. I reckon you're wrong.'

We rounded the hill. Addy had vanished into thin air. The rocks ran right down to the water, making no room for a beach. Spadafora walked out onto the rocks to ensure she wasn't hiding there.

'There has to be a way into the well,' he said, walking back to the beacon.

An idea suddenly struck me. Like a man possessed, I ran to the cemetery and grabbed the shovel Dee had been using. Running back to the beacon, I said, 'I'll dig the whole bloody thing up.'

Spadafora smiled and took a step backwards. 'Not the whole thing, just the slabs. I think one must be the door. Look carefully, there must be a clue.'

There were twenty blocks or slabs, each about a metre by a metre and a half, arranged in a circle. With determination and vigour, I attacked the first one. Driving the shovel under it, I levered upwards until it lifted high enough to see under it. Just bugs and stuff, so I moved to the next one and after three swipes, managed to lever it up. More worms and stuff. By the time I reached the eighth stone, I was approaching exhaustion. Man, those rocks were heavy. After a short rest, I attacked the ninth rock. It was a tough one and flatly refused to move. Digging the junk out from underneath it, I realized that this rock was different. It was sitting on another rock, making it impossible to dig it out.

After a few moments, I managed to drive the shovel in the crack separating the stones. Suddenly, the top flag yielded to my efforts and began to rise. With a resounding bang, some of the rock exploded. In shock, I fell backwards, dust and debris falling all around.

'What happened?' I yelled.

'Stand back,' Spadafora said. 'That was a shot from a gun.' He unbuckled his pistol and so did one of the other cops. 'Alright, you two go back to the house,' he said, pointing to Gran and me.

'No way, man. I'm here and I stay here. I'll lift the rock ... you talk to her.'

'No.' He beckoned one of the other cops over. 'You take the shovel, I'll talk.'

The cop took the shovel, but he couldn't get the rock to lift.

'Let me do it,' I said, snatching the tool from him; after all, I was bigger than him.

'Alright,' Spadafora agreed. 'Keep low and keep out of the line of fire.'

'Right.' I forced the spade in as I did before and, wriggling it, I then managed to force it a good way into the crack. Then, lying on the ground, I pulled down on the handle slowly. The flagstone creaked as it lifted up.

'It's over, miss,' Spadafora called. 'We're all armed. Give yourself up and call it a day. There's no escape. We won't harm you. Please come out with your hands where I can see them.'

Suddenly, the stone lifted itself, till it stood almost vertical. I dropped the spade, leapt up and ran from the site. I didn't want to confront a pissed-off gun-toting broad from down under. She'd blow me away with the same ease other people would blow their nose.

'You want me ... come and get me,' she yelled.

Spadafora slowly approached the hole in the ground. Suddenly, there was a very loud bang and he dropped to the ground.

# *Chapter 24*

## *Blood and Bullets*

Somehow or other, Addy had found a secret entrance to the old well. Man, oh, man. A bang rang out and a cop fell to the ground, that's enough to scare anybody. Hell, I didn't want or need any more dead people on my island. I don't know what possessed me, but like a madman, I jumped up and ran to the lifted slab.

'Addy,' I yelled. 'It's me, Bill, don't shoot.' To everyone's surprise, I reached the orifice alive.

Spadafora growled at me. 'Come away, you fool, she's dangerous.'

Looking into the interior of the hill through the opened rock, electric illumination allowed me to see a desk and a chair. I couldn't see Addy anywhere.

'Addy, I'm coming down, don't shoot. It's Bill.'

'Keep that bleedin' copper out,' she said softly.

There was a rusty iron ladder that led vertically down to the chamber below. Gran's mobile was on the desk, being used as a paperweight. My breath came in short gulps – probably the fear. She could, and most likely would, kill me. Looking round, I saw her in a dark corner, sitting on her haunches with a very large pistol in her hands.

'What d'yah want, Canuck?' she growled softly.

'Addy,' I said, trying hard to sound friendly. 'Addy. We all love you. Please come out like a nice girl.'

She squared off, pointing that cannon directly at my head. 'You're an arsehole,' she growled. 'Make one move towards me and you'll be a dead arsehole.'

The black pitch-painted walls sucked up all the light, giving the den a surreal ambience. You could see that it had been made of crude bricks and then it had been painted with a really thick black goo. The floor was made stone and in the centre lay the well; just another large hole that stretched down to infinity. I gingerly stepped off the ladder.

'Come on, Addy, let's be friends. You don't want to shoot me, now do you?'

'I hate you, you bastard. You've ruined everything.'

'No, Addy. I've deciphered Edgar's codes. I know where the gold is. We could share it like you said. We'd be super rich.' The room echoed like an old tin can, making my words sound hollow and meaningless. I could see she had been crying. Her face was all tear-stained and her eyes were red and wild-looking.

'Do you love me, William?'

'Yes, I do love you. Come on, Addy, hand over that gun.'

'Liar, liar. I hate you.'

With a deafening explosion and a blinding flash, the gun went off. I felt the shock wave. It almost knocked me off my feet. The bullet disappeared into the wall with a thud. I think my heart must have stopped and my knees went all wobbly from shock and fear. I wasn't sure whether she'd actually shot me or not. My knees crumpled under my weight, no longer able to support me.

'Addy,' I whined, slithering to the stone floor.

'I did love you, William. You were the only one for me.'

'Addy, please don't shoot.'

She began to cry again. The tears swept down her face like a monsoon as she choked and gagged on her own passion. Suddenly and in some terrible desperation, she pointed the pistol at herself. I realized her intentions. Heaven knows where the strength came from, but somehow I leapt up and made a dash for her. The gun went off. All hell broke loose for a second and total confusion reigned. My thoughts were scrambled and my emotions rent asunder, to say nothing of the pain and shock.

Not knowing exactly what happened, we both ended up on the floor. I was on top of her. You wouldn't believe the incredible pain in my head and shoulder. Somehow, the world seemed to be getting farther away, reality slowly dissolving into a dreamlike oblivion.

I could hear her sobbing, more as an echo in my head than reality. My eyes wouldn't focus; it was the worst nightmare you could imagine. Nothing in the world had remained real.

When I finally managed to open my eyes again, the entire world had changed from black to white. I looked around, trying to assimilate my surroundings, when all of a sudden it came rushing back to me. This was a hospital. There were stupid doodahs making pinging sounds and I had wires attached to me. My throat felt like the entrance to a coal mine. The nurse heard the change in the monitoring devices and came running.

'Hello, Mr Reyner. And how are we this morning?'

'Morning?' I croaked. 'I'm terribly thirsty.'

With a sweet smile, she helped me sip some moisture from a funny-shaped cup that had a lid on it. 'Now you've regained consciousness, you'll soon be out of here, Mr Reyner.'

'Where's my Gran? I want to speak to my Gran.' My throat felt much better, but still had that sandpaper edge.

The nurse walked to the foot of the bed and cranked it up a little. 'Mrs Hubert has been by your side all night. She's just popped out to the Ladies to powder her nose.'

As the nurse spoke the words, Gran walked into the room. I tried hard to raise myself to greet her, but nothing seemed to work properly.

'Now you hold hard there, William,' she said and walked to my side.

'What happened, Gran? What's going on?'

'Now you relax, William. It's all over; everything has worked out for the better.'

'What happened? Where's Addy? How'd I get here?'

'I told you to relax, William. You'll get me thrown out of here if you don't quieten down. We have the rest of your life to relate the happenings at Fiend's Rock.'

'I want to know now, Gran.'

She stroked my forehead. I could see the relaxed satisfaction in her eyes. 'Very well, William. I'll tell you all about it.'

'Good. I can't remember a thing.'

The nurse checked the instruments and smiled. 'He'll be alright, try not to tire him. He's out of danger completely.'

'Great. Now tell me, Gran, before I explode.'

'Well, when Freda Davis fired at the inspector –'

'Who's Freda Davis?'

'Freda is the girl who pretended to be Addy. She impersonated your cousin, to wheedle her way into your uncle's life. All she was after was the Fiend's gold.'

'Okay, I understand, go on.'

'She fired at the inspector, but the bullet hit the stonework and exploded. Fragments of it and some pieces of rock struck him in the face. He has had an operation on his eye, last night.'

'Is he okay?'

'Oh yes. He was out of the fight, because he couldn't see. We were all shocked when you threw yourself into the breach, so to speak.'

'I did?'

'Don't you remember? You went down the pit to confront the girl. Very silly thing to do, dear.'

'No. Yes, yes, I do remember. But I can't remember what happened.'

'No, you wouldn't remember, William. That beastly girl shot you.'

Funny how the mind works. Slowly, the memory of what happened crept back into my consciousness. I remembered she was trying to commit suicide. She was going to blow her own head off. That's when I jumped her.

'So what happened to Addy or whatever her name is?'

'Freda. Well, when we heard the second shot, Constable Nolan crept to the opening and peered in. He couldn't see either of you. Bravely, he entered and descended the iron ladder.'

'And then what happened?'

'Do have patience, William. Well, he found you sprawled out on the floor, lying on top of that girl. Both of you were unconscious and both of you were covered in blood. He called for help and another policeman went down the hole.'

'So what happened to Ad ... er, Freda?'

Gran sighed a deep sigh. 'I'm coming to that. Do have patience, boy. Well, they found that you were still alive, with a deep wound to the side of your head. It's a bit of a mystery as to exactly what happened. She had severe damage to her chest and throat; burns and blast damage. You seemed to have received the bullet from below. It scraped along your wooden head and left the area. All you received was a nasty bang on the cranium and a cut, where the missile scraped the side of your bony cranium.'

'But what about Freda? Is she dead?'

'No, she's as mad as a hatter, dear. Doesn't even know where she is or what has happened. She thinks she's a child somewhere in New Zealand. They have taken her to Penatanguishine. There's a mental hospital there.'

'What about the gold? Was it in the Beacon Hill well?'

'With an injured policeman and two unconscious people, we were not about to start a treasure hunt, my dear boy.'

'So you haven't found the gold?'

She sighed heavily to show her contempt for the question and then said, 'The helicopter came back and took all the injured to the mainland. After some treatment, Freda was shipped to Penatang. You and Inspector Spadafora are off the danger list and I haven't been back to the rock since.'

'So what are we going to do, Gran?'

'Well, my boy. As soon as you are fit to travel and the police return control of Fiend's Rock to us, we'll hire a boat and go collect our belongings. Then we shall divest ourselves of that dreadful place and go live a quiet and peaceful life in Dundas.'

'Sounds good to me, Gran. When do I get out of here?'

She leaned over and kissed me on the forehead. 'I love you, you foolish boy. I have to go tidy myself up a little. Now I know you're alright, I shall go rest and come back later. I have a room in a local hotel here.'

'Where's here, Gran?'

'Parry Sound, dear.'

She blew me a kiss and then walked out of the room. Man, there was still so much I didn't know and I wanted to get the hell out of this place as soon as possible or even sooner. It wasn't until Gran left that I began to feel the pain, all down one side of my face. The nurse noticed my predicament and gave me something to make me feel better.

When I woke up again it was lunchtime. I hate hospitals. Oh, I know they do a fine job and all but, well, I hate them. Fortunately these days, if you can walk, they'll throw you out - I was freed the very next day. They're worse than hotels for timing. It was exactly noon when they finally released me. Gran was a real brick and had everything organized.

I don't know if it was just the effect of leaving hospital or real trepidation, but when we walked down to the dock to get the boat that Gran had hired, I began to tremble. Somehow, flashes of Fiend's Rock burst through to my consciousness, like snapshots of a crime scene or pictures of hell.

'Are you alright, William?'

'Yeah, sure, Gran.'

'We don't have to go today if you're feeling a little weak. There's plenty of time.'

'No, no, it's alright, Gran. We've got to get this over with.'

Gran had hired a boat from Smithers; it had his name on it. Switching on the engine and pressing the starter, I somehow felt older. The child in me had suddenly become a man. The roar of the engine brought back happier thoughts, like when Henny fell in the water. Tears crept into the corners of my eyes. The lad that worked for Smithers turned up and cast off for me. Engaging the prop and after a quick throttling up, we were on our way again, back to hell's island. Now I know how Douglas MacArthur felt when he finally returned to the Philippines. Nothing had really changed – it was the same water, same islands and even the same stinking-hot weather, yet it felt like an entirely new adventure and a different world.

The rock looked totally pathetic and deserted. I bumped the boat gently against the pier, throttled down and jumped out to tie off. When I boarded the boat and shut down the engine, the silence became deafening. The wind and the gentle surf seemed to be hiding the voices of the gang as they played somewhere on the island. Gran noticed me standing and listening.

'There's no one here except us,' she said softly.

'I know, Gran, I just can't get those memories out of my head. This place has more ghosts than enough.'

Everything looked neat and tidy; all doors were shut and even the blood on the stones had been washed away.

'Where's our boat, Gran?'

'Mr Smithers has employed a salvage expert. Sometime next week, they're going to raise it. Smithers says it's junk, quite probably.'

'I don't want it back. We'll buy … No; we'll leave here for good. Did they ever find out what happened to Alic?'

Gran cast her eyes down. 'I'm sorry, dear. I really did not want to bring the subject up.'

'Well?'

'She's dead, I'm afraid.'

'I figured so. Was she on the boat when it sank, was she …?'

'No, the police investigators found her in the boathouse, dear.'

'In the boathouse?' I said with surprise.

'Yes, dear, she was … well, she'd been put in the freezer chest.'

Although I felt like crying, nothing happened. I was all cried out and had nothing left to weep with.

'I don't think we'll stay here, Gran. Let's get our stuff and get the hell out of here ASAP.'

She nodded her approval. 'So you've given up on the gold, then?'

I shrugged. 'Dunno, Gran. I'm not sure that there ever was any. What d'you think?'

She shook her head. 'Would you like something to eat before we leave? I do believe we are still well stocked.'

I had to think about it. Hunger was not top of my priority list, but there was no longer any danger now that mad Freda was safely locked away in the nuthouse.

'Just a snack, Gran.'

'Alright, pack your things; we'll leave in say … how about an hour?'

'Sure.'

Gran walked away in the direction of the house. I think she just liked preparing food – it probably soothed her. I couldn't enter any of the bungalows, as they reminded me of death row. Slowly, unconsciously, I walked towards Beacon Hill, where I'd had my encounter with the angel of death. It was as if an unseen force had drawn me there. For once, Jeremiah Fiend was beckoning me in a friendly way.

It must have been the bullet that rattled my brains, because I seemed to be hearing the events of that terrible day: the bullet exploding on the rock and in my mind's eye, I could see Spadafora fall with his hands to his face. The sheer horror and adrenalin of the moment returned like a bolt from the blue.

'It be yourn, boy,' a ghostly, hollow voice in my head whispered.

You just wouldn't believe how my body shook as I approached that lifting stone. The shovel was still there. In a trice, I forced it under the rock and opened it. The interior lay in total darkness. 'The gold's there,' I said aloud and then turned and ran towards the house. I could hear Jeremiah Fiend calling me. 'It be yourn, boy.' I had to be dreaming.

Looking very alarmed, Gran met me at the front door. 'What's wrong, William?'

'Nothing, Gran, nothing. It's just ghosts of old. I need a flashlight.'

She put her arms around me and gave me a hug. 'Don't tax yourself, William. This terrible place will soon be a shadow in our past.'

'I need a flashlight, Gran.'

'In the kitchen cabinet, under the left sink.'

Old man Fiend guided me. For the first time in my life, I walked to the exact cupboard and collected the light, just as if I knew it was there. I felt a sudden urgency, as if the old man was pushing me to hurry. I ran out of the house and down the path, past the cottages and so to the beacon. I flicked the flashlight on and entered the chamber.

Man, it was spooky down there. I quickly found the light switch and turned it on. Again, I saw a mental image of Addy, or whatever her name was, standing there and pointing that cannon thing at me. She hadn't meant to hit me, but at that range a monkey couldn't miss. Funny thing, the bullet didn't ricochet. It should either have bounced off or shattered.

My flashlight was still on. I scanned the wall, looking for evidence of the bullet. Where could it have gone? The thought struck me that perhaps it was a blank. That would explain how she missed me at such short range. Sense and reason slowly began to appeal to my intellect. I had to get out of that pit; there was nothing, no gold. But old Jeremiah hadn't finished with me.

Preparing to leave, I saw a twinkle illuminated by the flashlight beam. It attracted my attention. Walking over, I discovered what had happened to the bullet she'd fired in my direction. For reasons at that time I couldn't imagine, it had buried itself in the wall. The black pitch-like stuff on the wall had been parted by the impact when the bullet flattened itself. It was now the size of a quarter, sitting on the wall like a button.

What a souvenir. With deft skill, I picked the flattened bullet out of the pitch and popped it in my pocket.

Gran already had the food on the table. I felt elated, like it was Christmas morning. For once, things had gone my way. Somehow, I bubbled inside and couldn't stop smiling.

'So, you found the gold, then?' she said.

You can't keep anything from, Gran. 'How did you know?'

She smiled. 'It's written all over your silly face, boy.'

# Chapter 25

## As Yellow as it Gets

You just wouldn't believe how clever old Jeremiah Fiend had been. He had fooled them all for nearly 200 years. We gave the gold back to the USA. It was American property, which had been stolen. Would you believe – they gave us ten per cent of its value in modern currency. There was 22,507 pounds of the stuff – that's just over 10,000 kilograms. The archaeologists carefully dug it all out, so as to preserve the history and learn of the story of Fiend's Gold. You've never seen such security, though.

The Canadian Government and the Yankee Government supplied the guards and the armoured transport. You'd never figure out how old Jeremiah had hid the gold. Well, when the old man and his boys stole it from the ship and murdered the crew, they knew their lives would be in danger with that kind of treasure on their hands. The plan was simple.

Just before the Yankee clipper ran aground, the Fiends had blasted a nice deep hole in the south of the island to make a new well. Why would anyone want a well, when the island sits in a lake of fresh water? Temperature and purity is the answer. A nice deep hole would allow the water to filter through the rock. It would come out pure, clean, fresh-tasting and at fifty-two degrees F. All year round, even if the lake was frozen.

The old man went ashore and bought loads of pitch or bitumen, while the boys melted the gold and cast it into sand moulds, making bricks from all those coins. When he returned, they melted the pitch and dipped each brick in it. Now, they had 10 tons of handmade pitch-black gold bricks to build the inner wall of the Beacon Hill.

Addy's bullet sank into the gold that no one could previously see or find. When I extracted it, the golden delight was discovered. She had killed all those people and all this time had hidden herself right in the middle of the treasure and yet she still never found it.

In the few short days that we were at Fiend's Rock, I had aged twenty years. Frivolity and booze seemed to be such a childish and boring pastime, I had grown past it. Gran seemed such a sweet and beautiful elderly lady. My love and respect for her could only become stronger. There was one thing changed that none of us had noticed at first – that being that I had developed an uncanny knack of finding gold. Gran said it was the gold that found me.

**More Bill Reyner adventures
coming soon to a bookshop near you.**

## Mania

Cannibalism and carnage seem to be the order of the day. Joining a secret and unholy sect Bill finds that he just might have feasted on the flesh of his latest girl friend. How can he escape the clutches of these demonic characters?

## Edinburgh Cuckoos.

Look out rich people of the world, the cuckoos may already be in your nest.

## Damp Graves

For details and insight visit
www.wentworth-m-johnson.com

Printed in the United Kingdom by
Lightning Source UK Ltd., Milton Keynes
139442UK00001B/89/P

9 780956 103291